Martha Jean Kincaid, the oldest daughter of a poor southern family, struggles to take the place of the mother who ran away and to protect her brothers and sisters from an abusive, alcoholic father. Her strength comes from her own resilient defiance and from her Grandmother Kincaid who has magical powers with animals and who "sings the sun up" every morning. After her father also abandons them, Kincaid has a chance to live a normal life when she is adopted by a loving couple and moves to California.

In this new world, she matures and finds pleasure in swimming, boats and the ocean. In college, Kincaid falls in love with her scuba diving teacher, Chris Palmer, and also Karen, her best friend. Yet in all her relationships—with her adoptive parents, her friends and her lovers—she maintains a well-insulated distance.

She begins to learn about sensuality and trust when she visits captive dolphins at a nearby sea aquarium. It is here that she has an incredible experience in mentally melding with the dolphins.

When a family tragedy forces her to return to the south, Kincaid is also forced to face the childhood she has tried to put behind her. As she begins to integrate her life, past and present, she discovers a precious legacy from Grandmother Kincaid that changes her forever.

Singin' the Sun Up

a novel by Ocala Wings

Published by
Mother Courage Press
1533 Illinois Street
Racine, WI 53405

Cover art by Sudi Rakusin © 1991

Library of Congress catalog card number 90-63947
ISBN 0-941300-20-X

Mother Courage Press
1533 Illinois Street
Racine, WI 53405

In honor of my mother, Wanda Sue Hudson.

In memory of my grandmother, Hazel Lucille Sutton, my grandmother, Telitha Mae Rea, my great-grandmother, Bessie Anderson, and my great-grandmother, Elsie Elizabeth Sides.

And for my partner in life, Rita Wings, now as always, my deepest love.

This book is lovingly dedicated to displaced Southerners wherever they are living. Not only can we go home again, but we must. Home really is where our hearts are, and for us, our hearts are the road home.

Chapter One

"Martha Kincaid?"

The new teacher's Northern accent made her words sound sharp, hard, strange to ears used to softer edges.

"Yes'm, I'm here." The girl hesitated, then finished in a rush, "But my name is Kincaid."

Someone snickered in the back row.

The teacher looked at the girl directly now for the first time and took in the ripped, faded jeans, the white cotton shirt with ironed-in wrinkles, the unevenly cut, shorter-than-average hair. Judgments were made. With absolute self-assurance the teacher turned back to her papers.

"That is your last name, Martha, and I call all my students by their first names."

The girl took on a look her mother used to call "diggin'-in-her-heels."

"But my name really is Kincaid, ma'am. It's what I'm called."

"Who calls you by your last name, Martha?" The teacher sounded annoyed.

"Ever'body."

"Your mother calls you by your last name?" The challenge and disbelief evident in the teacher's voice silenced the sixth grade class.

The girl's eyes dropped. "Got no mother."

"What? Speak up, Martha. Does your mother call you by your last name?"

Not a paper moved. Not a shoe scraped.

"I said, I got no mother."

"Oh? Is that so? What happened, dear?"

It was the girl's turn at disbelief. Didn't they teach manners where this teacher came from?

"Uh, she died."

"I'm very sorry to hear that." She didn't sound sorry. Again she looked at the clothes, wrinkles, hair; her judgments were validated

1

and updated. "Your name is still Martha in my class. And girls, Martha, are expected to wear dresses to school, no exceptions." She turned back to her papers.

Another snicker from the back. "She's lyin' through her teeth. Ever'body knows her mama run off."

Not a child breathed.

"Did you just lie to me, Martha?" The teacher didn't quite eliminate all the triumph from her voice.

The girl returned her stare evenly.

"Answer me!"

"Yes, ma'am." She held her head defiantly.

"You will stay after school today, Martha." Her authority now firmly established, the teacher continued the roll.

At 4:30 the girl walked out of the classroom with her head still held high. No one was left on the school grounds to taunt her. Even the janitor had gone home.

"Damn!" How was she going to explain this to her father? "Damn!" She turned back toward the door.

"My name is Kincaid!" she shouted into the eerie silence. "My name is Kincaid!" She turned on her heel and ran as fast as she could.

Her father waited on the porch, chair tipped back casually, switch in hand. "You're late, Kincaid."

She tried to keep her eyes off the switch. "The new teacher asked me to show her aroun'. I think she likes me."

Her father looked steadily at her and dropped the old wooden chair to the floor with a sharp crack. The switch moved slightly. "You're lyin'. Kept you after, didn't she? You been actin' up, an' on the first day."

"No, Daddy. She really just wanted me to show her aroun'. On account of she's new."

Keeping his eyes on her face, he laid the switch down slowly on the porch rail. "Get inside an' get supper started. I'm goin' out." He stood up and left without looking back.

"Oh, shit!" Kincaid hated when he went out like this. He'd come home late, and drunk, or near enough. It was always worse when he drank.

After she'd bathed the three little ones and put them to bed, Kincaid went out to the porch swing to savor the warmth of the Indian-summer night. The stars, like sparklers against the velvet sky, took her millions of miles from reality. A lone firefly flashed. She sighed.

Fourteen-year-old Bobby and ten-year-old Carol Ann finished their checker game and came out to join her, the screen door banging behind them.

"Don't slam the door," Kincaid said automatically.

"Heard you had some trouble at your school today," Bobby said.

Kincaid shrugged.

"What happened?"

"I had to write 'I will not tell a lie' two hundred times." A slow smile crept over her face. "When I was done, I made like I was cryin' an' spit a big wet spot on my paper an' then I put it right on a fancy pink hanky she keeps on her desk. Made that pretty hanky all wet with my spit."

Bobby snorted.

Carol Ann said, "She was wrong to shame you that way in front of the class."

Kincaid looked at her. "I'll bet the whole damn school knows ever'thing, don't they?"

"Most think she was wrong to shame you."

Kincaid stared darkly at the holes in the toes of her shoes.

"Damn!"

~~~~~~~~

Her father's stumbling woke her. She heard him cursing in the darkness downstairs, heard him stagger upstairs, heard him quietly open the door. She tried not to hear her sister's soft protests from across the room, tried not to hear when they stopped. She tried not to hear her father's heavy breathing. She tried not to hear, but she couldn't go back to sleep. She lay rigidly on her own bed, staring at shadows on the ceiling until he left.

~~~~~~~~

She shot a spit wad at the clock. Splat! Missed. Freddy shot one at her. She fired one back. Scotty got Tom and Lisa with a rebound wad. One more shot at the clock—ready . . . aim . . . fire. Three things

3

happened simultaneously: the bell rang, Kincaid lost her concentration, and the teacher walked in. The wad was low and fell short of its mark to land with a very wet splat on the wall just inches to the right of Mrs. Meyers.

"Oh, shit!" No way could she explain this one.

The teacher stood quite still, her face flushed. With slow deliberation she walked through the silence to her desk and sat down, her face expressionless except for the color. She wrote something on her note pad. Folding the paper neatly in half, she stood and walked back to Kincaid's desk.

"Take this to Miss Walker's office. Now." She turned and walked back to her desk, her heels clicking.

Expelled! Kincaid felt sick. Where could she go, what would she do for three whole days? She couldn't go home, her father would be there. Maybe her grandma's . . . but no, she didn't want her grandma to know.

She wandered around the park for awhile, kicking leaves and climbing trees. Instead of comforting her, the bare brown vastness, empty of people and people sounds, made her feel even smaller and more lonely. She wandered down the familiar streets nearer home and found an old white-haired woman bent over a flower bed.

"Hey, Mrs. Harper! Whatcha plantin'?"

"Irises. I just think they are so pretty, don't you?"

"Yes'm. I like the purple ones best. The light purple ones."

"Why, I got some of them right here. An' some blue. I like blue, don't you?"

"Yes'm. Mrs. Harper? Would you like some help?"

"That would be sweet, dear. It's right chilly out today, makes my old joints ache so. But I just remind 'em how pretty these flowers will be come spring . . . Here, I think a row of these put right over there would be nice, don't you? Yes, there. Now, why aren't you in school today, Kincaid?"

"They called a teacher's meetin' 'bout somethin' an' let us all go early."

"Just all of a sudden like that?"

"Yes'm."

4

The old woman glanced sideways at her. "Why, where are all the other children gone to, I wonder? I ain't seen nary a one—'ceptin' you, Kincaid."

"Uh, uh . . ." Kincaid moistened her lips and swallowed hard.

"Never you mind," she patted Kincaid's knee. "I was a young'un once myself, an' I recollect a few days I played hookey from school. 'Course, I usually waited for spring . . . ." The old woman's face crinkled as she chuckled to herself.

Kincaid silently reached for more bulbs.

Sunlight slanted low, barely topping the trees when the sounds of children's laughter broke through Kincaid's determined concentration. School was out. She stood and wiped her hands against her jeans, reluctantly retrieving her books.

"Bye, Mrs. Harper," she waved.

The old woman smiled and nodded.

Her father stopped her as she came through the door. He held the switch again.

"Kincaid."

"Hey, Daddy."

"I got a call from your school." The switch tapped against his leg. "Get in trouble at school, shame your family, stay out doin' who knows what all day, an' now, you don't even have the decency to look ashamed of yourself. I'm gonna wear this here switch out on you, girl."

"I can explain, Daddy. It was an accident."

"It is clear you need to learn some manners, girl. Come here."

"Daddy . . ."

"Come here."

"But please . . ."

"Come here!"

~~~~~~~

"I brought some salve for you, Kincaid." Carol Ann tiptoed in so as not to wake the youngest one who shared their room.

"You be careful Daddy don't catch you."

"Don't you worry 'bout that, I can take care of myself."

"Oh, shit! That stings!"

5

"Not as much as that peach switch, I reckon. Hold still."

As her sister worked the salve into her bruised and raw skin, Kincaid felt more and more low down. After all, she practically never took a whipping, but when she did, here was Carol Ann right ready to take care of her, while she'd done nothing to help Carol Ann out of a situation far worse, to Kincaid's mind, than an occasional beating.

"Carol Ann, I know what's goin' on," she blurted.

"Whatever are you talkin' 'bout?"

From Carol Ann's tone, she realized she'd made a mistake.

"Uh, uh, I know you're tryin' to butter me up so I'll do your dishes tonight."

"Why, I'm doin' no such thing! Can't anybody ever do anythin' around here just to be nice? I declare!"

"I guess so. I didn't really mean that, Carol Ann. I'm sorry."

For so many things.

~~~~~~~~

"I don't like you hangin' aroun' him, Bobby!" Kincaid stood with her hands on her hips. "An' I don't like him hangin' aroun' here, either! He's no-good trash!"

Her brother whirled to face her. "You are not my mother an' it's none of your business who I hang out with! An' you better never call my friends trash again, you hear me?"

"He is trash an' you know it! He steals, he lies, an' he drinks hard whiskey! I don't like him aroun' the children, especially Carol Ann!"

"What business is it of yours what he does? He don't need your permission to live. An' besides, I already told him to stay away from Carol Ann."

"Just what do you think Mama would say 'bout y'all bein' so buddy-buddy?"

"Mama? Mama! What the hell do you think she'd say? You think she'd care what I do?" He snorted. "If she cared so goddamn much, she'd be here now, wouldn't she?" He turned away. "Don't you give me no more shit, Kincaid. Just leave me alone."

~~~~~~~~

6

Grandma Kincaid hugged her.

"Well, Kincaid, I ain't seen you in a month of Sundays. Where you been hidin', child?"

"I been real busy with school work, Grandma." She knelt down to pet Toby, the old orange tom that purred in her grandmother's lap.

"Uh huh. Your daddy's still actin' a fool, ain't he? Says I fill your head with nonsense, I'll warrant."

Kincaid nodded miserably.

She patted Kincaid's hand. "Well, never you mind what he says. Don't much matter what he thinks of me, any old way. How'd you get loose today?"

"He went squirrel huntin' with Uncle Carter an' Uncle Frank. I reckon he won't be back 'til tomorrow late." She looked out the window at the bushy, brown squirrel happily cracking sunflower seeds from the gourd feeder nailed to the porch rail.

Her grandmother followed her gaze. "I do love t' have the wild ones near. They touch the spirit so."

"Killin' wild things is wrong, isn't it, Grandma?"

"Well, when there's need, there're ways to ease the killin'. Used to be, folks needed to hunt wild ones to feed their families. Nowadays . . ." she shook her head. "Yes, child, it's wrong to kill unless there's need."

"You don't eat squirrels, do you, Grandma?"

"No, child, I don't. Nor rabbit, nor deer, nor 'coon, nor 'possum. Nor any wild one. There's no need for it, I get my food from the store."

"Daddy does. An' he makes us eat 'em, too. Why does he like huntin' so much, Grandma? If it's wrong, why do folks do it?"

The old woman suddenly looked tired. She stroked the cat. "Who's mindin' the little ones today?"

"Carol Ann. Bobby's off somewhere." She sank down beside her grandmother's chair and Toby jumped into her lap. "Oh, Grandma, I wish things was different. I wish I was somebody else. I wish I was Kathy Anderson on 'Father Knows Best.'"

"You do, do you? Well, you're wishin' at a good time—sunset is a mighty powerful wishin' time."

"It is?"

The old woman nodded. "Yes, ma'am. Sunrise an' sunset you best be real careful what you wish for. Strange an' powerful things can happen if'n you go 'bout wishin' just right."

"Are you talkin' 'bout magic, Grandma?"

"Well, I don't rightly know as I'd call it magic, but this old world sure has her own ways of doin' things. An' she's right willin' to share with us if'n we're willin' to learn.

"I know what let's do, Kincaid. Let's walk over an' get them children an' come back here an' make us a grand supper! That is, if'n you're done with your wishin'."

Kincaid grinned and took her grandmother's hand.

~~~~~~~~

"Say, what y'all starin' at?" Kincaid elbowed her way into the crowd on her back porch.

"Travis Tucker's dog caught a rabbit!"

"Is it hurt? Let me see . . ." She pushed into the center of the tight circle. "Oh, it's so scared . . . let me hold it!"

"Kincaid, get outta here! It's Travis' rabbit." Bobby pushed her hand away.

"I just wanta see it a minute. It's scared an' I wanta talk to it. Travis, can I hold your rabbit for a minute?"

The skinny blonde boy shrugged. "Makes me no never mind."

She cradled the soft bundle against her, stroking it gently between its long ears. Cooing and crooning, she rubbed slowly and tenderly until the rabbit visibly relaxed.

"He's beautiful, Travis. Whatcha gonna do with him?"

"I'm keepin' him. My daddy is gonna help me build a cage."

"I think you oughta let him go, Travis. Wild things oughta be free, an' he wants to go home."

The boy shook his head. "I even thought up a name for him. I'm gonna call him Thumper."

"Like as not, he'll be called supper 'fore too long," Travis' older brother laughed.

Travis turned like a shot. "He will not! Don't you dare say that! His name is Thumper an' he's mine!" He reached out and grabbed the rabbit from Kincaid. "He's mine!" He jumped off the porch and ran wildly down the street, clutching the rabbit closely.

Bobby shook his head in disgust. "Dumb kid! His daddy bein' the best trapper in the county an' he thinks he's gonna get to keep that rabbit for a pet!"

Everyone laughed. Everyone except Kincaid.

~~~~~~~~

Coming up the walk, arms aching from the weight of so many library books, Kincaid heard the yelling even before she got to the porch. Praying her father wasn't looking out the front window, she dashed around the side of the house. Stashing the books under the open back porch steps, she ran to the far corner of the yard, to her tree. The sound of hard leather striking soft skin was audible even in the topmost reaches of the pine where she finally settled, hugging the trunk with her knees. Her body jerked with every slap and she cringed each time Jimmy cried out.

It had to be Jimmy because Bobby never made a sound and Billy Ray was still at Mammaw's.

She leaned against the cool, rough bark and concentrated on the wind singing through the branches all around her. Humming, her voice blended with the wind and she lost herself in the effort of keeping pace with pitch and tone and intensity.

Sometime later she drew a deep breath and opened her eyes. The sun, now barely visible on the horizon, told her it was way past time to start supper. She shivered.

The sudden creak of the back screen was startling.

"Kincaid! Kincaid! You get your butt in here an' get supper goin'! Kincaid! You ain't foolin' me none, I know you're out there somewhere. Kincaid? You hear me? You get in here, now!"

She licked her lips and squeezed closer into the tree. In the silence, she could hear his angry breathing.

"Shit! Goddamn you all to hell!"

The back door slammed. The truck door slammed. The truck engine roared. The tires squealed against the pavement.

Stiffly, she climbed down, and quietly, she opened the kitchen door. Supper on the stove, she decided to make a batch of cookies. With raisins. Jimmy liked raisins.

~~~~~~~~

Something woke her. It was still dark and Kincaid experienced a moment of confusion until she remembered her daddy had gone off hunting again and she was spending the night at Grandma Kincaid's house. Moving quietly, so as not to wake the others, she tiptoed downstairs to get a drink. The plastic glass slipped through her fingers and hit the counter with a clatter when, glancing out the kitchen window, she saw her grandmother standing out in the middle of the garden, arms upraised, silhouetted against the dawn-streaked sky. She went to the door and opened it just a crack. The cool morning air seemed inviting. Still in her nightgown, she slipped out to the dew-slick porch.

She could hear her grandmother singing. Not words rightly, but notes. They seemed to penetrate the darkness, to call forth the warmth and light of the rising sun. Kincaid stood, transfixed, as her grandmother sang on and on and night turned to day. Finally, the song ended. Her grandmother's arms came down and she turned around, a smile lighting her eyes when she saw Kincaid. Kincaid waited as the old woman slowly made her way back, climbed the steps, and settled herself comfortably on the old porch swing. She waited expectantly.

Her grandmother took a deep breath and sighed. "I been singin' the sun up ever' mornin' for sixty-seven years. There's mighty strong power in it, Kincaid. First off, it's a thanksgivin' for all the suns that have risen in my life, for all the nights I've had that've become days. An' it's a blessin' for the day to come, an offerin'."

"What do you offer, Grandma?"

"Myself, child. My heart, my mind, my work. An' ever' day for sixty-seven years I have been blessed with another day to live."

"All this time, an' I never knew . . . How come you never told me?"

"I knew you'd be called when you was ready."

"I was called, Grandma! Somethin' woke me up an' when I saw you outside, it was like bein' pulled almost . . ."

10

The old woman nodded. "That's how it works—when you let yourself feel the power. It's your heart's song." She reached out and stroked Kincaid's cheek. "You're a spark from an old fire, child . . ." Her face took on a listening look. "Well, I hear some stirrin' in there, I bet Pattycake is up. That's a sure sign it's time for breakfast." She struggled up out of the swing and went to the door. "How 'bout some pancakes this mornin'?" She motioned Kincaid in ahead of her.

Kincaid knew better than to ask any more questions. The conversation was over. For now.

~~~~~~~~

She dressed quietly. Avoiding the third step, she crept downstairs and out the kitchen door into the early morning darkness. A frosty mist hung low, covering the ground. Her feet crunched frozen grass. At the far edge of the yard near her tree, where the bushes tangled wildly, she stopped and faced east. She raised her arms. Breathing deeply, she began to sing . . . sounds that welled-up from somewhere far inside her, sounds that filled her with light and warmth and power, power that seemed to come from not only the notes she sang but also from the sun itself as it peeked over the horizon, from the stars as they faded, from the plants and trees, from the very air around her. She was singing the sun up!

"Kincaid, what the hell you doin'?" Her father, half-dressed, peered out at her from the back porch.

She dropped her arms. "Nothin', Daddy."

"Nobody gets up 'fore daybreak an' goes outside in this goddamn cold to do nothin'. What are you doin' out here? Answer me!"

She shivered. "Uh, I uh, wanted to see the sun come up, Daddy."

"That old fool's been fillin' you full of that crap again."

"She ain't no fool," Kincaid muttered.

"What?" he roared. "What did you say?"

"Nothin'."

"That's what I thought." He opened the screen door and pointed inside. "You get your butt in here an' fix breakfast. I want bacon an' eggs, an' toast an' coffee mighty damn quick!" He grabbed her arm as she went by. "An' you better never let me catch you sneakin' aroun' this time of the mornin' again, you hear me?"

11

"I hear you."

"What?"

"I said, yes, Daddy."

He waited until the bacon was sizzling before he left her alone.

She waited until he was all the way upstairs before she slammed the refrigerator door.

"She ain't no fool!"

~~~~~~~~

Holidays like Thanksgiving and Christmas were spent at Mammaw's, their maternal grandmother, without their father. Holidays were grand affairs with all the aunts and uncles to say "my-how-you've-grown" and all the cousins to play with—and all the food . . . always more than enough to feed each and every one with plenty left over for just one more taste of favorites. Since Kincaid did the cooking at home, she and the children ate simply most of the time, but holidays were a time to excel. What was served was a source of family pride. The menu never varied: turkey and ham and chicken-fried steak, creamed potatoes, corn and beans and peas, cole slaw, sliced tomatoes, cornbread and rolls and homemade bread, pies and cakes galore. At Christmas there was eggnog, and always there was coffee for the grown-ups and milk and iced coffee (more milk and ice than coffee) for the children. No one ever got tired of it, and no one ever went home hungry.

After the main meal, when everyone sat down together, the adults gathered in groups to talk and the children were free to seek their own entertainment. Twilight games of tag, hide-and-go-seek, and follow-the-leader lasted until it was too dark to see, regardless of the season. Kincaid usually sought out her cousin Charlene, who was as close as anyone to being her best friend.

"Hey, Charlene, wanna go for a walk?"

"Hey, Kincaid. Sure, I'll go for a walk. But don't call me Charlene. I've changed my name to Charley."

"What for?"

"It's so exotic an' mysterious for a woman, don't you think? Charley . . ." she breathed out the word slowly.

Kincaid shrugged. "I liked 'Charlene' just fine."

12

They walked out in the woods behind the house, their feet crunching leaves, their breath visible before them in the crisp November air.

"Why, lookit here," Kincaid laughed. "'Member this?"

"'Member what?" Charley grumped. "I can't see a dern thing no more light than it is. What're you pointin' at?"

"You 'member when we played 'Stallions?' All the young'uns were the rancher's mares an' you an' I were wild stallions an' would fight for who would steal the herd? This here was the corral where the mares waited while we fought an' decided who won."

"Oh, yeah, I remember. That was a long time ago, just kid stuff."

"It was just last year."

"Really? Seems like a long time ago."

Kincaid remembered it as if it were yesterday. The part she had liked best was the pretend fights, the whinnying, pawing the air, and finally falling on each other, wrestling in the musty old leaves. She liked the feeling of never knowing for sure which of them would claim final victory, each being just as strong, just as aggressive as the other. She loved seeing Charlene's hair long and flowing over the leaves, the grass, over her as they wrestled. Sometimes it had almost felt real.

Charley turned away. "Kincaid, you got a boyfriend?"

"Huh? No, 'course not. What would I want a boyfriend for?"

"That's what we gotta do, Kincaid—we gotta get you a boyfriend." Charley sounded very sure.

"What's come over you, anyway? Why are you so all-fired interested in boys all of a sudden?"

"Well, I'm growin' up, Kincaid. I'm almost thirteen, same as you," she reminded, "an' it's high time we gave up bein' tomboys an' started bein' young ladies."

"Oh, yeah? Says who?"

"My mama, for one. An' it's true. No boys are ever interested in tomboys."

"What do I care what they're interested in? They can go eat bananas for all I care."

"Oh, Kincaid, don't be silly. A girl's gotta have a boyfriend, an' you can't wait too long, 'cause then all the good ones will be taken."

Kincaid snorted. "Sounds like you're talkin' 'bout watermelons, not people. Anyway, I don't need a boyfriend."

"'Course you need a boyfriend, stupid. Who you gonna grow up an' marry?"

"Ain't plannin' on gettin' married. What would I go an' do a fool thing like that for?"

"Oh, Kincaid, you are bein' so dumb! 'Course you'll get married! An' you'll have lots of babies—'cause that's just how it works. You're all the time thinkin' you're so different from ever'body else! But you're not! You'll see!"

"I told you, I ain't gettin' married, dammit! I'm goin' to college an' I'm gonna do somethin' important an' become rich an' famous."

"Like what, smarty-pants? Whatcha gonna do that's so important?"

"Well, I don't know yet! Find the cure for cancer or somethin'! Hell, I'm only in sixth grade, I don't have to know right this minute, do I? What's goin' on with you, anyway? I came out here 'cause I usually have fun with you, but this is not fun, Charlene! I'm gonna go see if there's any of Mammaw's apple pie left." Kincaid turned and stomped off.

Charley followed. "You don't have to get so all-fired het-up. I was just tryin' to talk with you woman-to-woman like. It ain't like you got a mama to talk to, an' everyone in the family can see as how you need one."

Kincaid stopped short. Too late Charley realized her mistake.

"Well, now, I mean . . . Dammit, Kincaid, you know how this family talks. No need to get your back up."

Kincaid continued walking.

"Well, we are growin' up, Kincaid, whether you like it or not."

Kincaid let the screen door slam. "Not all in one night, I ain't."

~~~~~~~~

Up in her room reading, Kincaid ignored the yelling pretty well until Billy Ray screamed. The front door slammed as she ran downstairs to find the five-year-old sprawled on the floor, holding his face.

"Billy Ray! What happened?"

He swallowed hard and stopped crying. "I fell down."

She pried his little fingers away from the spreading bruise and saw blood oozing from a jagged split along his cheekbone.

"You musta fallen down pretty hard."

"Pretty hard," he echoed.

She helped him up and turned to Jimmy, who slouched on the sofa.

"How'd this happen?"

Jimmy just stared at her.

They all jumped at the sudden revving of their daddy's truck as it roared down the driveway, gravel peppering the side of the house.

"How d'you think?" Jimmy got up and walked out of the room.

"How d'you think?" Billy Ray repeated.

She took a deep breath and released it slowly. "Billy Ray, let's go on into the kitchen an' get some ice for that bruise."

"I'm bleedin'."

"Well, you can have a Band-aid an' I'll even give it a magic kiss, if you want."

"A magic kiss..." Billy Ray wiped his face dry with a grimy hand and toddled after her.

~~~~~~~~

Kincaid cautiously took the note, unfolded it carefully to see a very unflattering drawing of the teacher. A giggle escaped her. She looked around to try to determine ownership of the note but no one seemed eager to claim the honor. She turned back to find the teacher beside her, hand extended.

"The note, Martha."

Slowly, a sinking feeling in her stomach, she complied.

The dismissal bell rang but Kincaid knew better than to leave. After everyone had gone the teacher called Kincaid to her desk.

"Well, the school term is just about half over and I have decided that it is time to make my position clear in this little war we seem to be engaged in. You are undoubtedly one of the most rotten brats I have ever had the misfortune to have in a class. At Saint Joseph's, where I taught last year, you would have been dealt with much more severely, I assure you. Here, however, standards seem to be a great deal lower, but then, considering what part of the country we're in, they would need to be, wouldn't they? My standards, on the other hand, are what you should be concerned with.

"Your grades are as poor as your attitude. And of course, you are failing in citizenship. My point is this: I plan on allowing you the pleasure of my company not only this year, but next year as well. And I promise you, it won't be any easier the second time around. Have you anything to say, Martha?"

Kincaid looked at her levelly. "Just one thing, Ma'am. Your bra strap is showin'."

~~~~~~~~

"Kincaid!"

"Go 'way, Carol Ann! It ain't time to get up yet." She burrowed deeper into her warm covers. "It's still dark outside. Go to bed."

"Kincaid, it's snowin'! I got up to go pee an' looked out the window an' it's all white outside! Kincaid, let's go out—for just a minute—'fore it gets all tracked up . . . please?"

"You know we ain't supposed to go out this time of the mornin'."

"But, Kincaid, it's the first snow! Pretty please? With sugar on it?"

Carol Ann's excitement was contagious. "Okay, but just this once an' just for a little while."

They stopped at the boys' room.

"Bobby!"

"Go back to bed, Kincaid, it ain't time to get up yet."

"Bobby, it's snowin'! I'm takin' Carol Ann outside for a few minutes to play in it."

"Wait for me downstairs. I'll come with you."

"Mind the third step when you come down."

"Kincaid, just go on downstairs."

The kitchen door creaked as they opened it, just like a scary movie.

"Don't shut it tight so's it locks on us."

"Gee, Kincaid, I never would have thought of that," Bobby said sarcastically.

"Stop bein' so mean, Bobby." Kincaid sounded hurt.

"You stop bein' so bossy, Kincaid."

16

"Come on, you guys," Carol Ann pleaded, "can't we just have fun for a little while without fightin'?"

They stopped glaring at each other and stepped off the porch into another world. Their everyday, ordinary backyard had been transformed in the night. Now, bright city lights that reflected back from a thick blanket of clouds also sparkled off a fresh, unblemished expanse of bluish white. The magic was so strong they didn't even feel the bite of the wind.

"Wow!"

"It's so soft! It feels like a million tiny feathers!"

"A million tiny cold feathers!"

"Oh, hush . . . "

They walked around the side of the house where the wind had piled the snow even deeper.

"Will ya look at that . . . " Bobby held out his arm to stop them.

There, in the side yard, their daddy was making a snowman. In the dark. By himself.

"Well, don't just stand there," he called softly. "I could use some help—this snow don't pack together so good."

They looked at each other and back at their daddy. Then they all ran to help. Silently, because it was that kind of night, they rolled and pushed and patted until the body was all shaped. Then, Bobby went to find some rocks for eyes and the mouth. Kincaid went back inside for a carrot nose. Their daddy got branches for arms. Carol Ann disappeared for a moment and reappeared with an old grey felt hat. Daddy cocked an eyebrow at Carol Ann—they all held their breath—then he smiled and even lifted her up so she could put it on the snowman herself.

They stood back to survey their creation. They beamed at the snowman, and at each other, not even caring that they were soaked to the skin and cold.

Finally, still silent, they turned and went back to the house together.

~~~~~~~~

Kincaid woke to the sound of angry voices downstairs—men's voices, her father's voice, shouting, yelling. The front door slammed, a car raced down the driveway, spurting gravel. There was a long silence, then strange sounds she couldn't rightly identify. She pulled on her bathrobe and crept quietly down the stairs.

"Daddy? Daddy, that you?"

She peeked around the door and saw her father bent over on the couch, head in his hands. He was crying! At first, she stood watching in disbelief, but then as his sobs grew louder, she went and sat beside him. She put her arms around him, patted his shoulder, trying to comfort him just as she would any of the children.

Finally, his sobbing slowed and he turned to look at her, taking her hand and stroking it.

"My little girl! My little baby almost all grown, my little sugar." He shook his head. "Your daddy's in trouble now, sweetheart, in deep trouble for sure . . . Oh, sugar, what's gonna happen now? Trouble. So much trouble . . . "

Every time he said "baby" or "sugar" she felt nauseous. Maybe it was the alcohol stench as he pushed his red, swollen face too close to hers, or maybe the sickeningly sweet way he said it, but whatever the reason, it felt really creepy. She tried to move away but he held her hand tightly.

"You love me, don't you, sugar? You still love me? I'm still your daddy. I'm still your daddy . . . "

She swallowed hard. "'Course, you're my daddy. An' I love you." But even as she said it, she knew it was a lie. Whatever she felt for him, and her jumbled emotions were anything but clear, she knew for certain love was not part of it.

He grinned foolishly. "That's good, baby, that's good . . . " Then his face crumpled again. "But I'm in trouble now, trouble . . . "

She helped him to his feet and struggled with him up the stairs. He fell across his bed, arms dangling, still crying.

~~~~~~~~

"Why, howdy, Travis! How's your rabbit doin'?"

"That's what I come to see you 'bout." He unzipped his heavy winter coat and pulled out a furry ball. He handed it to Kincaid.

"Howdy, Thumper, nice to see ya. He looks real good, Travis. You been takin' real good care of him."

18

"Yeah. Kincaid, my daddy's traps all come up clean as a whistle again. He's real het-up. Says he's gonna lay for whoever is springin' 'em an' tan their hide but good. But the bad part is, lately he's been watchin' real close ever' time I take Thumper outta the cage. I can tell what he's thinkin'. Kincaid, you gotta help me—we can't let that happen to Thumper. I wanta let him go now. Trouble is, I don't know where that dang dog found him. You know 'bout animals, I thought you could tell me. Where should I take him, Kincaid?"

"You should take him right back home, Travis," Bobby said from the doorway. "Your daddy is gonna skin you alive he finds out you let that rabbit go. You go on back home, now, an' take that rabbit to your daddy."

"No! Nobody is gonna eat my rabbit!"

"Travis, your daddy is a trapper, you eat rabbit all the time!"

"Not Thumper!"

"Don't be so stupid . . . "

"Bobby, get outta here an' leave us alone! This ain't none of your concern!" She took the boy's hand. "C'mon Travis, I got an idea."

"You're crazy, Kincaid, you know that? You an' your talkin' to animals bullshit! You're crazy. An' you are gonna get that boy in big trouble!"

"Go flush yourself." Kincaid closed the door firmly.

Once outside she stopped and said seriously, "Trouble is, Travis, we can't just let him go. It's winter an' he ain't had time to build himself a nest or nothin'. He'd die if'n we let him go now."

The boy's face went all hard and he reached for the rabbit.

"Now, hold on a minute, Travis, don't get yourself all worked up. I got an idea. We'll take him to my Grandma's. We can visit him and take care of him over there an' come spring, we'll take him out to the woods. How 'bout that?"

The boy looked skeptical.

"Do you have a better idea?"

He shook his head slowly.

She handed Thumper back to him. "Well then, c'mon. It ain't too far."

~~~~~~~~~

Her father opened the door. He went over to Carol Ann's bed. Kincaid felt anger rise in her throat and come out as a low growl. A growl—icy fury, a she-wolf with bared teeth, cold and deadly. What her daddy was doing was wrong, it was very wrong. And he'd stop doing it soon enough if she were a real wolf. She'd make him stop. A wolf could do that, wolves were smart and cunning. If she were a real wolf . . . the image became clearer, sharper. She was a wolf. And suddenly, she saw a way out, a simple, easy, perfect way out. She could be cunning, too.

The next night, as Kincaid dried the last of the supper dishes, her father sauntered into the kitchen.

"You save me enough supper, girl?"

"It's on the stove, warmin'."

She waited until he sat down to eat.

"The school nurse called me in again, Daddy." When he said nothing she continued. "Yeah, she's been askin' a mess of questions lately."

"Like what?" He sounded casual, but she knew she had his interest now.

"Oh, like who takes care of the littlest ones, who makes supper, an' such." She knew enough to seem casual, too.

"That all?"

"Well, she also asked how much we get from Welfare, are our bills all paid up, are you workin' . . . you know, like that."

"Nosey old biddy. So, what'd you say?" Still casual.

"I said I didn't know much 'bout such things. I figured you wouldn't want me to say anythin' else."

"You figgered right enough." He went on eating.

"Daddy."

He ignored her.

"Daddy."

Something in her tone caught his attention. "What the hell you want now?"

"I know what you been doin' to Carol Ann, an' I know it ain't right. It just ain't right for daddies to do that to their little girls. An' you are fixin' to stop it."

He stood up without taking his eyes from her face. "Just who in the hell do you think you are talkin' to, girl? I will do what I want,

20

when I want, with who I want, an' ain't no one gonna make me do different. You listenin' to me, girl? Your smart mouth has just earned you a good whippin'!" His hand went to his belt.

"No, you ain't gonna whip me. You are gonna leave me alone. You are gonna leave Carol Ann alone, too, an' all the children. No more messin' with her an' no more hittin' on any of us. Or I will tell all I know to the school nurse. She'd be very interested an' so would the Welfare Department."

His face turned beet-red and his eyes widened with rage. "You are gonna wish you'd never been born, girl!"

She stood very still. His belt was in his hand. She wanted to run, but the wolf image came back to her and instead she took a deep breath and straightened her shoulders.

"I mean it, I will tell." Her voice was firm now, sure.

"You don't know jack shit. But you are gonna learn somethin' right now!" He snapped his belt loudly. "There ain't gonna be nothin' left of you girl, 'ceptin' a greasy spot!"

She stood her ground. "I know you got more money than Welfare gives you. I seen those men come here late at night—I seen you take money from them. An' I know that messin' with Carol Ann ain't a Christian thing to do. I know enough to know you are gonna do what I say about this."

His jaw tightened, his knuckles showed white against the dark leather. He slapped the belt against the table with all his might.

"You are gonna live to regret this day, girl!"

"You just think on what'd happen if'n I told." She remembered it was her father she was threatening. "I reckon I'll go on up to bed now. G'night, Daddy."

~~~~~~~~

Since Christmas vacation, Kincaid had become a model student: doing her homework neatly and on time, finishing all the extra credit questions on every worksheet and quiz, working overtime to improve her academic standing. She was aware that her teacher still didn't like her, but she did what she could to stay out of Mrs. Meyers' way.

So it came as a surprise one day when the teacher once again kept her after class.

21

"I have graded all the tests, Martha. You had the highest score in the class, higher than Matthew, who is a straight A student. It is obvious that you cheated. Would you care to explain it to me now, or to the Principal?"

"I did not cheat, Mrs. Meyers."

A malicious smile lit the teacher's eyes. "Very well. Come along."

Kincaid was left in the main room while Mrs. Meyers went into the Principal's private office. In all this time, Kincaid had never actually had to meet with the Principal, only with the Head Secretary, but the Head Secretary and Mrs. Meyers were as close as two peas in a pod as far as Kincaid was concerned. Just now, the Head Secretary glared disapprovingly at her and pointed to a bench against the wall.

"I declare, we're gonna have to put a plaque on that bench with your name on it."

Suddenly, the door opened and her teacher smiled coldly.

"You may go in now, Martha."

Kincaid sat down in a big chair facing the Principal's big desk. She felt very small and her throat was very dry.

"Well, Kincaid, you're becoming rather famous. Your name has come to my attention often this year. Now, you know Mrs. Meyers believes you cheated on this test. She says that you say you didn't. Now, what's the truth? Did you cheat?"

"No, ma'am." She slowly shook her head.

"Well, how did you get the highest grade in your class, then? I've seen Mrs. Meyers' records of your past work. It does seem a right far stretch."

Kincaid quickly decided that the truth was her best defense. "I been studyin' more."

"It would seem to be a rather recent decision on your part. Mind telling me why?"

"I didn't like the idea of stayin' back a year with Mrs. Meyers."

"Your grades aren't very good, but they are passing. What made you think you'd be held back?"

"She said I would be."

"Just what did she say?"

"Uh, she said she was gonna allow me the pleasure of her company next year as well as this year."

"She said it just that way?"

"Yes'm."

"You haven't gotten along well with Mrs. Meyers this year, have you?"

"No, ma'am."

"Want to talk about it?"

"No, ma'am."

"I don't know what to say, Kincaid. You've done right well up until this year. Your brother got into some trouble a few times, but not you, nor Carol Ann. This just doesn't seem like you."

She remained silent.

"Well, I believe I understand. So, Kincaid, do you think that your grades are going to continue to improve?"

"Yes, ma'am, I do. I'm aimin' to pass."

The Principal stood up. "Good. Perhaps I'll see you again then, under more pleasant circumstances, perhaps handing you an honors award at graduation." She walked Kincaid to the door.

Her smiled changed abruptly. "Mrs. Meyers, may I have just one more moment of your time, please?" she said rather sharply.

As Kincaid passed, both Mrs. Meyers and the Head Secretary glared at her.

~~~~~~~~

She was again awakened by angry voices. This time, only her father was shouting. The front door slammed. A car drove away. Her father stomped up the stairs and slammed his door. Amid much cursing, there was also a lot of thumping and banging. She had finally fallen back asleep when he burst into her room.

"Kincaid? Kincaid! Wake up now, I gotta talk to you." He shook her roughly and sat down on the edge of her bed.

"I'm awake, Daddy." She leaned over to switch on the lamp.

"No! Don't turn that on! They might be watchin'."

"Who?"

"Never you mind that. Just listen to me now. I gotta leave here, go away for awhile. This here's all the money I can spare—I'm leavin' it with you to take care of the young'uns." He stood. "I'll come back for y'all when I can."

"This has somethin' to do with those men who come here, don't it?"

His face had a sly, closed look. "You just take this money an' do like I say. I'll be back soon." He turned to leave.

"But Daddy, what if they come lookin' for you?"

He looked at her for a long moment, shrugged his shoulders, and left the room in silence.

"At least say good-bye to the little ones," Kincaid called after him. But she knew he wouldn't. She also knew he wouldn't be coming back; gone was gone for good. Hadn't her mama already proved that?

~~~~~~~~

"When will Daddy come home?" Patty was only three. "Is he gonna bring Mama with him?"

"No, Patty, he's not bringin' Mama," Kincaid said patiently. "But, he said he'd be back real soon."

"Shit, Kincaid! Don't lie to the kid! He ain't ever comin' back an' you know it!" Bobby exploded. He grabbed his jacket and slammed the front door behind him.

The noise scared Patty more than anything else and she began to wail. Kincaid glared out the window at her brother's retreating figure. Scooting closer, she pulled Patty onto her lap.

"It's all right, Pattycake, ever'thing's gonna be just fine."

She turned to the others. "Y'all better scoot now, you don't wanta be late for school. An' not a word 'bout this to anyone, y'hear? It's gonna work out, I'm gonna think of somethin'. I'm talkin' to you, too, Jimmy Joe! Now, turn off that TV an' git!" She swatted his behind.

"Yeah, yeah, yeah." Jimmy grabbed his lunch sack and kicked the screen door open.

"Yeah, yeah, yeah," echoed Billy Ray, who, still in his pajamas, was building a road for his truck with a deck of cards.

Carol Ann hung back. "We're gonna be separated, we're gonna have to go to homes, aren't we?"

Kincaid sighed. "Oh, Carol Ann, I don't know. We have some money . . . Now go on to school, I gotta have time to think."

"It's not right to separate families." Carol Ann was working up to a good cry.

"Yeah, well, it's not right for parents to abandon their kids, either, but I guess it happens sometimes."

"Do you think we been bad, real bad, like maybe we sinned somethin' awful an' didn't know it?"

"What could we have done that was so bad? An' anyhow, I think it's only sinnin' if you know what you're doin' an' just go ahead an' do it anyway. Now, go to school." Kincaid gave her sister a hug and a push toward the door. "Go on, dammit! I'll probably have a plan all figured out by the time you get home."

Kincaid went to the phone. "Hello?" She coughed a couple of times. "This here is Martha Kincaid. Yes, ma'am, I'm feeling right poorly. Got a bad sore throat an' a terrible cough." She coughed again for good measure. "An' a real high fever. My daddy says I shouldn't come to school today. No, he's not here right now, he went to the drugstore after some cough syrup. Yes, ma'am, I'm gonna stay in bed an' keep warm. I might be out most of the week, though. Oh yes, ma'am, my daddy's takin' me to the doctor's this afternoon. Yes, thank you, ma'am."

She turned back to Billy Ray, still playing with his cars and Patty, whose face was all screwed up, deciding whether or not this called for more bawling.

"I know what let's do, let's read you two a story."

Patty brightened. "A story? In the daytime? Oh boy!"

"Oh boy," Billy Ray echoed, not even looking up.

~~~~~~~~

Kincaid counted carefully. It still came out the same: not nearly enough. She rubbed her eyes. Maybe if she got a job . . . Yeah, but who'd take care of the kids? Grimly, she dialed the phone.

No answer. Maybe Grandma was outside.

She stuffed the money back into her pocket and went to finish last night's dishes. Later, she called again. Still no answer. She left a note for Carol Ann and the others and walked with Patty and Billy Ray over to Grandma Kincaid's.

The house was shut up tight and yellowed newspapers littered the porch. Leaving the kids to play in the yard, she went next door and knocked on the screen.

"Hey, Mrs. Sutton."

"Why, hey, Kincaid, c'mon in! Mighty good to see you! How's your family gettin' on?"

"Right well, thank you. Mrs. Sutton, do you know where my grandma is?"

"Why, child, didn't no one tell you? She took bad sick a few weeks back an' had to go to the hospital for a spell. I'd have thought they'd have told you, bein' kin an' all. Well, anyways, then I heard they took her up to that old nursin' home . . . Rosemont, that's the place. I expect she's still up there. They say she was pretty bad off. I sure am sorry to have to be the one to bear bad news for you, Kincaid."

"Well, I appreciate you tellin' me, Mrs. Sutton." She pushed open the screen but turned back abruptly. "D'you think she'll get better? Get well, I mean?"

The old woman smiled kindly. "I 'spect so, child. They wouldn't have let her from the hospital if they'd thought there was any danger. Why don't you get your daddy to drive you up there? Ease your mind an' probably do her a world of good, too. She thinks mighty highly of you, you know."

"Yes'm. Thanks again, Mrs. Sutton."

"Well, don't make yourself so scarce, y'hear?"

Kincaid went back to her grandmother's house and sat down on the wide blue-grey steps. Hugging her knees to her chest, she stared at the snowball bush beside her, all leafed out with tight, tiny flower buds that would soon burst into giant blue globes. Blue was her grandmother's favorite color—but her grandmother wasn't here to see it.

Kincaid got up and began collecting all the papers, all the trash from the porch and carried it around back to the garbage can. She took the broom from the back porch and after sweeping there, went to the front and swept it. Now her grandma wouldn't have such a mess to clean up when she finally got to come home. Returning the broom, Kincaid caught a glimpse of the rabbit cage where Thumper had spent the winter. On impulse, she pulled it out from under the back steps and cleaned it out, too. When she put it back, she left the wire door propped open, just in case. You never knew when some little animal might need a home.

~~~~~~~~

"Hello, Mammaw Wilson? This here is Kincaid . . . "

They made the rounds: a week with their other grandmother, a week with Uncle Frank and Aunt Wilma, a week with Aunt Sally and Uncle Carter, two weeks with Aunt Bessie, and finally on to Uncle Doyle and Aunt Elizabeth's, Charley's parents.

Kincaid worked overtime to keep everything together, to keep everyone happy, to keep them from being a bother. She went to bed every night listening to the others snore around her while she worried, trying to think of a way out.

Then late one night, when she just couldn't get to sleep, she got up for a drink and overheard her aunt and uncle arguing.

"Don't anybody ever get along?" she wondered.

"It's the only way, Elizabeth. They've been here three weeks now an' we can't afford to keep them any longer. We can't send them back to Mother's—she cannot handle six children, not at her age. An' they've stayed with everyone else. No one can afford to take in six growin' kids, not with their own families to care for."

"But there must be another way, Doyle."

"Don't you think I feel for them? They are my sister's children, after all. But a man can only go so far . . . It's a terrible situation but I honestly can't see another way out."

"If we kept just one or two, say Kincaid an' Carol Ann, maybe the others could take some. One or two wouldn't be like havin' six . . . "

"It wouldn't work Elizabeth, it would just be prolongin' the inevitable."

Prolonging the inevitable. Is that what she had done, Kincaid wondered. She thought she'd found a way to keep her family together, only to find them once again unwanted and pretty much uncared about.

Well, maybe there was something wrong with her. Everything she did always messed up, even when she tried to do good. Maybe that was why her parents left them, maybe she was the problem. And in that case, how could she ever fix it?

She went back to bed and stared at the outline of the old live oak tree silhouetted on the window shade until she fell asleep.

None of the kids were outside when she got home from school the next day and there was a strange car in the driveway. A Ford. Uncle Frank hated Fords, but Uncle Carter swore by 'em. She wondered absently whether Uncle Doyle had an opinion on Fords.

She let herself in quietly and set her books softly on the phone table. She stood in the entry way, listening, while around the corner in the living room, a strange woman said, "You have no idea of the father's whereabouts? Is there anyone else who might have more information? And the mother, in all this time, no word? What was her maiden name? Can you give me a description . . . "

Suddenly Kincaid knew she hated Fords, too. At least this one— it made her stomach hurt. She walked woodenly to the room she had shared with Charley and Carol Ann. Carol Ann sat on the floor holding Patty tightly and rocking the crying child. Charley sat quietly beside them. No one spoke when she came in.

"Charley, would you please go find Jimmy an' Billy Ray, an' ask 'em to come here? I'll go on an' talk to Bobby, but I expect he's already packed."

Charley couldn't meet Kincaid's eyes as she silently left the room.

Chapter Two

"Martha, we've found a foster home for you, dear."

"My name is Kincaid," she mumbled, staring at the floor. If she squinted just right, the dots on the tile looked a little like a dragon. Then the rest of the woman's words sunk in. "Will we all be together?"

The woman behind the desk fiddled with her pen.

"Well, no. We don't have any foster parents who can take so many children at once. But all our parents are good people; you'll all be well taken care of, I promise you that."

"Families should be together," the child insisted. "It's not our fault there's so many of us."

The woman dropped her pen and came around the desk and knelt beside Kincaid.

28

"Of course it's not your fault! Nothing that's happened has been your fault. And I feel just the same as you Martha, about families. But there are things we can do, and things we can't."

"My name is Kincaid," she repeated. If she turned her head to the right, the dragon changed into a mountain with trees. "What'll happen to my brothers an' sisters?"

"We've already found a home for Patty and Billy Ray, together. And a home for you." She stood up and walked back to her desk. "By tonight or tomorrow morning, we'll have placed Bobby, Carol Ann, and Jimmy."

"Patty an' Billy Ray are gone?"

"Not yet. Would you like to say good-bye?"

Kincaid nodded miserably. "How long will we have to live separate?"

"I won't lie to you, Martha, this is most likely a permanent situation."

"My name is Kincaid." And if she tilted her head, the mountain and trees became a hand with its fingers spread. "Will we ever get to see each other again?"

"We'll make arrangements for it, okay? Now, about your foster parents: Their names are Walter and Jean Henderson. They moved here two years ago from California and they have been wanting to adopt a child for a long time. They've never been foster parents for us before, but we're very pleased to have them in the program. They're good people Martha, very nice. I think you'll like them."

She squinted and tried to find the dragon again.

~~~~~~~~

Walter helped her lift her box of things into the trunk of a shiny green Chevrolet. The trunk had green carpet in it, clean carpet with no spots. Even the spare tire was clean. Kincaid's box, raggedy and stained, looked out of place surrounded by so much cleanness. But it was all she had and it didn't take up much room.

Walter walked around and opened the rear car door for her but she hesitated, turning back to the ugly red brick building, half-expecting her family to be there, to rush to her and beg her not to go. But they didn't. So she got in. Sliding across the seat, she imagined Carol Ann, tears streaming down her face, pressed up against a window with Billy Ray and Patty, their two tiny hands just barely reaching over the sill, straining to wave goodbye. Sitting up on her knees, her eyes searched row after row of windows as Walter started the car and drove away. The building got smaller and smaller behind them until they turned onto another road and she could no longer see even a tiny speck of red. For awhile, her eyes latched onto the white lines on the road— dash, dash, dash, dash.

Finally, she turned around. Hands clenched in her lap, eyes shut, she tried to take a nap. But she wasn't sleepy. She squinched her eyes tighter and did her times tables. She got all the way through twice and was back to her fives before the car stopped and the motor shut off.

She sat very still and kept her eyes closed. But that didn't help. Walter came back and opened the door for her anyway. So she opened her eyes and scooted out, standing up not on loose gravel but on a driveway of clean, unbroken concrete. She went to the trunk for her things but Walter hefted the box instead and she was left to follow up the flagstone path behind him, hands in pockets, uncomfortable and embarrassed.

Jean took her on upstairs, to her room—a room almost as big as her living room used to be, with a bed and a dresser and a mirror and a desk and a chair, all just for her. And in the bathroom, a towel hung just for her. And Jean told her there was a bike in the yard just for her.

Then Jean left so Kincaid could "unpack and settle in." The door closed and Kincaid dutifully reached for her box. The first thing she pulled out was Horatio, the raggedy lime-green gorilla that Bobby had won for her at the county fair years ago. She looked around the room—she looked at the gorilla. Slowly, she put Horatio back in the box and closed the flaps. This was a room for someone called "princess" or "kitten." Her stuff would just junk it up. She flopped across the bed, arms dangling, and her fingers traced patterns in the soft plush carpet: a dragon, maybe. Or a mountain with trees.

Supper was not what she was used to, either. First off, they called it dinner. And it began with salad: greens with tomatoes and vegetables in a bowl. Raw. She picked the tomatoes out with her fingers and ate them but as for the rest... She wiped her hands against her jeans and stared at the tablecloth—blue and white checks made up of teeny tiny blue and white dots.

30

"Try the salad dressing, Martha. Plain lettuce is rather . . . well, plain." Jean passed a small bowl.

"My name is Kincaid," she said, dumping a spoonful of creamy dressing on her greens—white, molten lava sliding thickly down rich green mountainsides.

Jean and Walter looked at each other. "Kincaid?"

"I'm called Kincaid." She noticed there were two forks beside her plate, a little one and a big one. What, didn't they think she was old enough to use a regular fork? She took the big one and mixed her dressing around.

"Kincaid it is, then," Walter smiled, wiping his mouth with his napkin and returning it to his lap.

Kincaid glanced over to Jean; Jean's napkin wasn't on the table either. She looked at her own napkin, unused, beside her plate, and quickly slid it down onto her lap. Then she noticed they were both using little forks to eat their salad. She set her fork back beside her plate and picked up the little one. Not that she cared what they thought. And anyway, maybe they hadn't noticed.

~~~~~~~~

The house was dark and quiet. In the distance, a church bell chimed the hour: two a.m. Kincaid lay on top of the covers, unable to sleep. She got up quietly and went to the window. Opening it, she leaned far out over the sill, deeply breathing the faint scent of jasmine in the cool, night air. Below, the street light glinted off the bicycle in the backyard. Her bicycle. Her backyard. Her room. Yeah, for how long? The social worker had said permanent. Kincaid snorted. Permanent—what was that? Until Walter and Jean got tired of her, like her parents had, like everyone had. Until she messed up.

She looked around the neatly manicured lawn, felt the soft carpet beneath her feet. Hers . . .

And where were her brothers and sisters tonight? Were they sleeping, dreaming of a place like this, while she claimed it for her own?

She whirled from the window, turning to stare at her silhouette against the wall. No, this place wasn't really hers, anymore than the silhouette was really her. It was a trick—people didn't really live like this, only in storybooks, or on TV . . . Her breath caught. She had wished it . . . but wishes didn't really come true. She turned back and stared out the window. No, she didn't belong here. It was only prolonging the inevitable, whatever that was. She slammed the window and went back to bed.

As she pulled the sheet up a little voice whispered: What if it was real? What if it might be hers? What if . . . She yanked the pillow over her head and started her times tables.

~~~~~~~

Sunday morning they got all dressed up and went to church. Sure was a different kind of church than Mammaw Wilson's—no Hellfire and Damnation, no sinners burning for all Eternity, no shouted Amens from the congregation. It was more like talking than preaching. Even the singing part was quiet.

Walter and Jean seemed to like it.

Kincaid didn't. She was bored. And her collar was too tight. The starched lace on her slip was scratchy. Her new shoes had eaten her socks and the wrinkles were uncomfortably stuck under her toes. And her stomach growled so loudly the lady in front of her turned and stared.

God, what if every Sunday was like this? There were a lot of Sundays left in her life. She sighed. The lady turned around again. Kincaid stuck out her tongue.

~~~~~~~

Sunday supper was fancy. Fresh flowers graced a lovely white linen tablecloth, set around with beautiful matching dishes and crystal stem ware and real linen napkins folded into flowers beside each place. Kincaid had never seen such elegance. She spread her napkin on her lap and secretly, guardedly watched Jean and Walter, determined not to embarrass herself again. She ate slowly, carefully, remembering to take only small bites and chew with her mouth closed.

Suddenly, midway through the meal, she spilled a whole glass of grape juice. She watched, unable to move, as the purple stain quickly spread.

"It's okay, dear," Jean said, although Kincaid could see she was upset. "Accidents happen."

Jean's niceness was the last straw. Kincaid jumped up, knocking her chair over.

"Sure, accidents happen—I was an accident—I come from a whole family of accidents! That's what ever'body thinks. That's what you think, too, ain't it?" she yelled. "Well, y'all don't have to keep me here—send me back! Go ahead, 'cause I hate it here, anyway!" She stomped up to her room without looking back.

She was lying across the bed drawing random designs in the carpet with her fingers when Jean knocked gently and came in to sit beside her. Jean reached out to stroke Kincaid's hair but paused, fearing her touch would not be well received.

"I'm sorry I ruined your tablecloth," Kincaid said quietly into the silence.

"That really is all right, Kincaid. What is absolutely not all right is your thinking we don't want you here, that we would send you away for an old tablecloth."

"But I don't belong here! I been nothin' but trouble my whole life. My brothers or sisters shoulda come here, not me. I'm the reason our Mama an' Daddy run off, it's all my fault. I'm all the time actin' up an' gettin' in trouble. I guess Mama just couldn't stand it no more. An' Daddy left 'cause I . . . well, anyhow, it's on account of me." She wiped away the flower she had drawn.

Now Jean did reach out and stroke her hair. "Oh, honey, it is not your fault."

"Yes, it is! I wished it! I wished it at sunset! But I only wished it 'bout me. I was selfish an' didn't think 'bout anybody else."

"Kincaid, please believe me, it's not your fault. And you belong here just as much as anybody else. Why, when Mrs. Curtis told us about what happened to you children, we asked for you. We did."

"Why?"

"Well, at first, never having done this before—being parents, I mean—an older girl seemed easiest. And you seemed as if you needed the love we had to share. You know, when it comes right down to it,

I'm not exactly sure why we chose you, but I am sure it was right! We want you here, Kincaid. We chose you."

Kincaid drew a tree with many branches in the carpet. "You'll get tired of me soon enough."

"Yeah, probably. In a couple hundred years. But before that, you'll probably get tired of us."

Kincaid's hand stopped. The little voice was back: what if... So okay, what if? She rolled over to face Jean.

"I never been 'round so much niceness before, I don't rightly know how to do here. I'm always afraid I'll mess ever'thing up."

"And we've never been parents before, we'll probably make a few mistakes, too. How about if we all learn how to do this together? With a little patience, a little time . . . "

Time. Kincaid's face clouded. How long until something really messed up, went wrong?

Jean reached out and stroked her hair again. "We can do it, you know, together. If you want to."

Kincaid could tell she meant it. The little voice inside her screamed "yes!" And suddenly how long didn't matter. It was hers right now and she did want it; for as long as she could have it, she wanted it: the lawn, the carpets, the bike, the niceness, everything! Even the salads. She smiled for the first time in weeks.

Jean smiled back. Then she straightened up and looked stern. "All right, young lady, now that we have that out of the way, you march right downstairs and help Walter clean up that mess. Then you will apologize to both of us for that rude outburst."

Kincaid nodded and jumped up, still smiling. She stopped at the door. "Y'know, my middle name is Jean. Martha Jean."

~~~~~~~~

The Fourth of July—Kincaid had been looking forward to, and dreading, this picnic for days. She hadn't seen her brothers and sisters for a very long time. Patty and Billy Ray were too young really to talk and she hadn't heard from Bobby or Jimmy at all. And the phone calls from Carol Ann . . . well, Carol Ann always cried and complained. But Kincaid was worried. What if none of them were happy? What if she was the only one who was?

34

She lugged the heavy picnic basket out for Walter to pack in the car.

"Thanks, honey," he smiled at her, taking out a handkerchief and wiping his face.

All the way back into the house, Kincaid kept thinking that no one had ever called her "honey" before. Her mama had called her "squirt," and "punkin" when she was little, but that just wasn't the same. When Walter called her "honey," it sounded just like Kathy Anderson's daddy calling Kathy "kitten" or "princess." It sounded really good.

In the kitchen she announced to Jean, "It's pretty hot out there. I'm gonna take Walter a big glass of iced tea."

Jean smiled. "That would be nice, Kincaid. It is pretty hot today."

Walter was appropriately appreciative. He gulped the tea down quickly and sighed. "That was great! A person can get mighty dry out here in this heat." He laughed and winked at Kincaid as he mopped his face again. "On the inside, that is."

He pointed in the direction of the garage. "If you bring me that old inner tube, I think I can squeeze it in. I thought your little sister— Patty?—I thought Patty could use it to splash around the lake. What do you think?"

He was asking her opinion? He was! He really wanted to know what she thought. She ran back with it, breathless.

"I think she'll like it."

"Good." He slammed the trunk. "Now, I hope Jean doesn't have anything else she wants to take—I couldn't fit even another napkin in there." He grinned and held out his hand. "Let's go get her before she finds something she forgot."

~~~~~~~~

"So, Carol Ann, are they good to you? What are they like? Are you happy?"

Carol Ann shrugged. "They're okay. They're nice enough. They got two kids of their own, a boy an' a girl." Carol Ann pointed. "That's them over yonder. We go to movies, an' on picnics, an' sometimes they even play games with us. I got me some new clothes. But it's different. You know. It ain't family. How you gettin' on, Kincaid?"

"I got my own room. An' a bike. An' Walter's all the time sayin' funny things, y'know, jokin' 'round. An' Jean is great, too. Right now, we're refinishin' an old wardrobe together. It's gonna be mine when we're done. An' I have a cat. That's her name, too, Cat. She's black an' white an' she followed me home . . . "

"Home? What do you mean, home?" Carol Ann's eyes widened. "You like it there," she accused. "You like it better'n your real home."

"I don't like it better," Kincaid hedged. "Some parts are, y'know, fun. But I don't like it better."

"You do! You like them better'n your own family!" Carol Ann wailed. "Oh, Kincaid, how can you just leave an' forget about us?"

"Forget about you? I ain't forgotten anyone. It's just . . . oh, Carol Ann . . . " Kincaid shrugged. "Hey look, there's Bobby sittin' on that table over yonder." She hurried over, leaving Carol Ann to follow.

"Hey, Bobby! Whatcha sittin' way over here by yourself for?"

"Bobby?" Carol Ann touched his arm when he didn't respond. He responded then by jerking away.

Kincaid shook her head. "What are you bein' such a pissant for? We just wanted to say hi."

"Beat it," he answered sullenly.

"What the hell's wrong with you?" Kincaid's voice was sharp.

"Look, I didn't wanta come to this stupid picnic. They made me. But even if I have to be here, y'all can just damn well leave me alone."

"Fine by me." Kincaid turned to go but Carol Ann grabbed her arm.

"Kincaid wait," she pleaded. "Bobby, we haven't seen you for so long! Please don't act this way. We're your family!"

He looked at her coldly. "Family? Family be damned! We ain't never been no goddamned family, Carol Ann. That's all been in your imagination! We're just a bunch of misfits that got stuck together, accidents of birth."

Carol Ann began to cry. Kincaid sighed and shifted her weight from one foot to the other.

"C'mon, Bobby, knock it off. We just wanta know how you been keepin'. What're your new folks like?"

"Which ones?" he asked scornfully. "I been to three homes already, an' number four ain't far off."

"Bobby!" Carol Ann was shocked.

36

He shrugged. "What do I care, it's just some place to hang my clothes. If I can find a place . . . "

"Well, are these folks nice?" Carol Ann tried again.

"Nice?" He mimicked her voice. "They get paid for my room an' board. They can afford to be nice, they're makin' plenty off it."

Kincaid made a face. "Bobby, you are such a jerk." Turning to Carol Ann she said, "You can stay here if you want, but I'm goin' swimmin'." She didn't wait for an answer.

Sniffing, Carol Ann slowly followed her to the pond.

"Lookit me! Lookit me!" Patty was splashing around in the shallows holding on to the inner tube Walter had brought. At first, Kincaid thought Patty was calling her, but when a young woman with a baby in her arms and Billy Ray in her lap responded by waving, Kincaid realized that Patty was trying to get her foster mother's attention.

Well, Patty was happy.

And Jimmy was throwing mud at several sun-browned boys his own age, too busy to answer her greeting. She took that, too, as a positive sign.

She waded into the lake, mud squishing between her toes. So the little ones were taken care of anyway, even if Bobby was still off by himself, sulking, and Carol Ann just sat on the bank with that hang-dog expression on her face. So why did she feel so guilty? She relaxed and leaned forward, letting the warm water take her weight. Anyway, what else could she do for them? She shook her head as if to clear it and began to swim, hard, concentrating on keeping her splashes small, like the swimmers on TV.

Suddenly she was struck by a thought: She could tell them about wishing! Maybe it wasn't too late. She hurried back and stood dripping while she told Carol Ann about magic wishing, only leaving out the part about where her own wishes had led them.

Wide-eyed, Carol Ann protested, "But wishes don't come true, only in fairy tales!"

"Maybe they don't—but what've you got to loose?"

Slowly her sister nodded. She screwed up her face and squeezed her eyes really tight. "I wish we were a regular family again, with Mama an' Daddy an' ever'one at home, just like it used to be!"

"Carol Ann!"

"What? You said I should wish for what'd make me happy! Ain't that right?"

"Yes, but . . . " Kincaid shrugged and turned away from the questions in her sister's eyes. "Carol Ann, it ain't even sunset yet. An' I'm goin' to get some ice cream, 'fore it's all gone."

She watched her feet as she walked back to the picnic table where some grown-up was handing out little paper bowls of freshly cranked ice cream. The bowl was red, white and blue. Kincaid studied the neatly pressed crinkled rim trying hard to find a pattern in the crinkles. Maybe wishes didn't come true. Or maybe some of them didn't—if somebody else wished the opposite. Maybe.

~~~~~~~~

"Now, I want you to remember to write. Often." Jean straightened Kincaid's collar.

"I will. I promise I will!"

Walter took Jean's hand. "Will you let the child get on the bus?"

"Well, she's going to be gone for a whole month!"

"I'll be all right Jean, honest."

"I know you will, honey, but I'm going to miss you."

Hugs all around and Kincaid boarded the bus for Camp Winahoe. A tired-looking man stood by the door clutching a clipboard and put a check beside her name. He sighed and signaled the driver to close the door.

"She worries," Kincaid explained proudly.

The man just nodded and waved her toward an empty seat. As the bus started up, he slumped down in a seat behind the driver and closed his eyes. The noise level began to climb and the driver leaned back and said something to him. With what seemed like supreme effort the man, whose name tag proclaimed "Dave" in large red letters, stood and forced himself to look cheerful.

"Okay, Campers! We are on our way to a fun summer! Let's start it out right and show some of that great Winahoe Spirit! Let's all sing!" His voice cracked on the word "sing."

His enthusiasm was not in the least contagious, except to a couple of six-year-olds sitting up front. Sometime after the second off-key verse of "She'll be Comin' Round the Mountain," the rest of the campers mutinied. From somewhere in the back came a soft strain of "Ninety-nine Bottles of Beer on the Wall." Voices blended, energies combined, until the singers were singing at the very top of their lungs, feet were stomping out the rhythm, and the bus was swaying along down the road.

"Hold on! Wait! Stop that!" Dave tried desperately to regain control. "That is not an appropriate camp song! Let's all get together here! Let's sing 'The Ants Go Marchin'!'"

But no one heard him, or if they did, they didn't listen. He sat down again, rather dejectedly, Kincaid thought. He obviously was not enjoying the song—he just didn't seem to have that old Camp Winahoe Spirit.

~~~~~~~~

Kincaid tiptoed out of the cabin. The night was so quiet! And so dark she tripped on a rock and stubbed her toe.

"Ouch!"

"Shhhh!" a voice warned and a hand grabbed her arm.

"What the . . . ?" Kincaid was about to let fly with her right fist when the hand suddenly let go.

"Be quiet!" The voice ignored its own warning. "Who are you, anyway?"

"Kincaid," she whispered back, peering into the darkness around her. "Who the hell are you?"

"Sharon. I remember you—we sat at the same table at supper. Whatcha doin' out here, Kincaid?"

"I was goin' to the bathroom—say, what business is it of yours, anyway? What are you . . . " A sudden noise caught her attention. "What was that?"

"Shhh! Oh, shit, I hope I haven't missed it! Come on." She grabbed Kincaid's arm again. "An' be quiet!"

"Hey, wait, I still gotta go . . . "

"Not now! Hurry, I don't wanta miss it!"

"Miss what?"

"Just come on!"

Winding through the dark shadows with skill, Sharon clearly knew where she was going. The sounds Kincaid had heard earlier now became the murmur of voices, and Sharon pulled her to an outcropping of rock and crouched low, yanking on Kincaid's arm to pull her down beside her.

"Oh, Arlene, you are so soft." The man's voice was squeaky. "Now, please say now."

"Oh, Davy, yes!"

It was so dark Kincaid couldn't see a thing. She heard a zipper slowly moving, soft moans and movements, but she couldn't see what was going on. Evidently, neither could Sharon—she let go of Kincaid's hand and crept closer; a twig snapped loudly.

"What was that?" Arlene sounded terrified.

"Nothin'," Dave mumbled.

"It was! Somebody's over there! Somebody's watchin' us!"

"Arlene!" He seemed as if he were about to cry.

"Somebody is over there, I tell you!" She was getting hysterical.

Movement. A zipper. "Okay, hand me the flashlight! I'll go take a look."

Kincaid and Sharon were off. They made enough noise that Dave had no difficulty following them until they split up, going in opposite directions. Then, his inability to make a decision to follow one source of sound lost him the chance of following either. The girls kept running until they were certain they were no longer being pursued and met up behind the archery range, collapsing on the straw.

"Jesus H. Christ!"

"Wow! That was close!" Kincaid's heart was pounding.

"Shit, it was so dark! I couldn't see a thing! I never counted on it bein' so dark. An' then, I had to go an' step on that stupid twig! I been watchin' this romance for two summers now, waitin'." She looked at Kincaid slyly. "You ever seen anybody do it?"

"Do what?"

Sharon snorted disgustedly.

"Oh." Kincaid caught on. "Not exactly." She tried to block out the ugly pictures her memory so readily called to mind.

"What does that mean? Either you have, or you haven't." She shrugged. "Well, I haven't. An' I been waitin' two years to watch these two do it." She sighed. "Two years of waitin' shot to hell!" She kicked the bale with her heels.

Kincaid scooted closer and put an arm around Sharon. She tried to think of something comforting to say when she realized that her hand was resting against the small roundness of Sharon's breast. Her heart pounded even harder.

Sharon didn't appear to notice. "Well, that's it. It's all over," she sighed.

Kincaid's face flushed but her hand remained still—if she moved it now, Sharon would surely notice. She swallowed hard and tried to make her voice sound normal.

"There's still two whole weeks, maybe Dave will try again."

"I don't know, Arlene's bound to be awful skittish now."

"I heard there might be a staff party Saturday, up at the main lodge. Maybe he'll try it then."

"I don't know . . ." Sharon suddenly sat up, looking long and hard at Kincaid. "I never told anybody 'bout this before," she said slowly. "An' I don't even know you—how can I be sure I can trust you?"

"I won't tell anybody, Sharon, I promise." Sharon looked skeptical. "I'll swear if'n you want me to."

Sharon stood up. "I want you to do more'n swear. I want you to take a blood oath."

"You mean, like signed in blood?"

"Will you do it?

Kincaid swallowed hard, then nodded slowly. "I'll do it."

Sharon smiled and leaned back, hands behind her head. "Well, that's okay then. I just wanted to make sure."

"I don't get it. Do you mean I don't have to take a blood oath, now?"

"Naw . . . So long as you're willin' to, I guess I can trust you." She jumped to her feet. Reaching back, she grabbed Kincaid's hand and pulled her up, too.

"I guess we're partners, now." She pumped Kincaid's hand up and down.

"Yeah," Kincaid agreed, shaking hands and trying to shake the feelings her memories had evoked.

"Well, I guess we better get back before they miss us."

Kincaid's hand tingled all the way back to her cabin.

~~~~~~~~

Kincaid woke early, sunlight streaming across her face. Silently, she raised the window by her bunk. The heavy sweet scent of dewy pines seemed to tease her, to call her outside. Dressing quickly and quietly, she slipped out the cabin door without waking anyone and tiptoed down the hill to the road.

The road forked. To the right lay the archery range and the stables, and beyond that, the lake. She didn't know where the left path lead, so that's the one she chose. Soon, the path dwindled to a small trail, winding deeper and deeper into the woods. She breathed in the rich morning air, the clean, damp smell adding to her sense of adventure as she wandered farther and farther from camp.

The woods were anything but silent. Crickets chirped from the cool shadows, jays squawked as they flitted from tree to tree, and squirrels chattered at the jays. And a sweet humming . . .

Humming? More like a vibration . . . but sweet, clear notes, flowing, blending, separating, merging. Not machine-like, but it wasn't exactly human, either. It reminded her of something, but she couldn't quite remember what.

She looked around and saw nothing unusual. Perhaps in the clearing up ahead . . . yet when she got there the source of the sound was still a mystery.

And the humming continued . . .

Her hand brushed against a bush and she jumped back, startled. Cautiously, she repeated the movement, with the same results: The humming seemed to get louder when she touched the leaves. She tested it again and again, checking out bushes, weeds, trees—all the same. The plants were humming! Each plant hummed a slightly different note, the tone of each leaf changing with the intensity of the sunlight striking it.

From inside her came an answering note, swelling and ebbing, keeping pace with the singing of the plants. She sang, too, immersed in the power of the music.

A twig snapped. She whirled to face the sound. Not twenty feet away, blending in so well with the landscape that she might have missed them, stood three mule deer, staring at her. She froze, not even daring to breathe for fear of startling them. After an eternity, they relaxed, big ears waggling to catch any sound, and began again to nibble the young green leaves nearest them, venturing slightly closer as greener leaves beckoned them.

A mosquito landed on Kincaid's cheek and, unthinkingly, she swatted it. In an instant, the deer were gone. Sadly, she scratched the bite and realized the music, too, had faded. She reached out tentatively, but the plants no longer responded to her touch. But they had . . . hadn't they? Or had she just made it up, like the play-pretend games of her childhood?

The camp wake-up bell echoed hollowly through the trees. She ran all the way back and met up with Sharon coming out of the bathroom with towel and toothbrush.

"Where you been?"

"I went for a walk."

"A walk?" Sharon sounded incredulous. "You got up before seven o'clock in the mornin' to go for a walk?" She yawned and shook her head. "Boy, are you nuts!"

When Kincaid didn't answer Sharon looked at her sideways. "You sure are actin' weird. What's with you, anyway?"

Kincaid shrugged and fell into step with her new friend.

Sharon shook her head disgustedly. "So don't tell me. See if I care."

"You ever . . . hear . . . things?"

"What things?"

"Uh, y'know . . . music . . . "

Sharon snorted. "Yeah, ever' time I turn the radio on. What are you talkin' 'bout?"

Kincaid shrugged again. "I don't know. When I was a kid I used to pretend that trees an' bushes made music . . . I was just thinkin' on that . . . "

"Uh huh. Trees an' bushes, huh? Talkin' to you? Girl, you should wear a hat when you're out in the sun."

"It was just a game I played."

"Uh huh. Well, this mornin' I hear pancakes callin' me from the mess hall," Sharon laughed. "An' they are makin' beautiful music." She flicked her towel at Kincaid as she ran on ahead. "So, I better hurry up an' get dressed. Meet you there!"

Kincaid managed a smile for her friend but she still felt confused. She had been pretending, hadn't she?

~~~~~~~~

"See, I told you they wouldn't come. It's over. I blew my chances."

"Well, it was good to check.

Sharon shrugged. "So, now what do we do? I'm wide awake. I know, let's go swimmin' in the lake! I bet the water's real warm!"

"We'd get caught. An' besides, my suit is in the cabin, under my bunk."

"We won't get caught . . . who's to see? An' you don't need a suit, we'll go skinny-dippin'!"

"I never did that before."

"Well, then, it's high time you did. Come on, Kincaid, let's have us some fun!"

Kincaid was glad for the darkness as they undressed but even so, she kept her back to Sharon until they both were in the water. A luxurious feeling of freedom enveloped her as she relaxed into the warm darkness.

"This is great," she sighed.

"Yeah," Sharon agreed. "Glad I thought of it."

"Say, I'll race you to the divin' platform," Kincaid challenged.

They both swam hard and fast to the big wooden structure anchored in the lake's center. Kincaid touched several seconds ahead of Sharon.

"Hey, no fair! You're too good! You on a team or somethin'?" Sharon pushed wet hair back from her face and climbed onto the platform.

Kincaid stayed in the water, holding on with one hand. "No, nothin' like that. I just swim a lot. The city pool's near my house an' I go 'most ever' day." She looked up and caught a glimpse of Sharon's body shining silver in the moonlight, her eyes drawn to the place where her hand had touched warm softness. She wondered how it would feel to touch there now . . . Her face suddenly hot, she shivered and quickly turned away.

"You cold?"

"No," she said slowly, "it's just, well, don't it bother you that we're out here like this?"

44

"Like what?" Sharon dangled her feet into the water, making little splashes.

Kincaid swallowed against the funny feeling in her stomach. "You know . . . naked!"

Sharon snorted. "Heck, no. Me an' Clarissa, she's my best friend back home, we take showers together all the time. Naked don't bother me none. Does it bother you?"

"Yeah, kind of. I never seen anybody my age naked before. An' I sure ain't been naked in front of anybody."

"How 'bout your brothers an' sisters?"

Kincaid shook her head. "An' I never even looked at them 'ceptin' when they was really little."

"Wow," Sharon said seriously. "Now that is shy."

Kincaid shrugged. "Jean says I'll grow out of it. I guess that's what moms always say when they don't know what else to say."

Neither of them spoke for a while.

When it became clear Sharon was not getting back into the water any time soon, Kincaid took a deep breath, and staring straight ahead, finally pulled herself onto the floating deck. Sharon was now lying on her back, hands behind her head, watching the clear night sky . . . like a beautiful silver statue, Kincaid thought. She couldn't help but stare. Sharon turned her head and smiled and patted the space beside her. Kincaid lay back, too, listening to the frogs and crickets and smiling in the dark.

"Look!" Sharon pointed. "A fallin' star! Make a wish, Kincaid, quick!"

Sharon's encouragement was unnecessary. Kincaid was already wishing the summer would go on forever, that the magic of this night would never fade.

~~~~~~~~~

Kincaid sat self-consciously staring at the blackboard. Around her, the other seventh-graders laughed and chatted loudly, catching up on each other's summer activities. No one spoke to her; no one even really looked her direction, so involved were they with their friends. She thought about Sharon.

It was a relief when the homeroom teacher came in and handed out their class schedules and locker assignments and census cards to fill out.

But then the bell rang and she was pushed and shoved along the crowded hallway until she got thoroughly turned around. She got lost on the way to her first class. It wasn't until the second bell rang and the hallways cleared that she managed to find the right hall and the right room number. And, of course, the only seat left was in the first row directly in front of the teacher's desk. The room was deadly silent and everybody stared at her as she made her way to the front—where she tripped over the slightly extended chair leg and fell into her seat with a plop. Someone giggled. Her face flushed, she stared at her notebook, the blue canvas running in diagonal lines from corner to corner . . .

~~~~~~~~

She closed her history book and rubbed her eyes. No one should have to do homework on Saturday. Scooting her chair nearer the window, she stared out in amazement at the big white flakes floating down. She hadn't even noticed it was snowing and already the backyard was covered! She watched as familiar sharp lines and angles became softened into gentle curves, as individual feather-light flakes danced and swirled by the window, caught in the updrafts of wind against the house. Was it just last winter that Carol Ann had dragged her out of bed and they had all built a snowman . . . ? What was Carol Ann doing right now? How was Bobby? Were they any closer to being happy? Kincaid shook her head to clear it. She couldn't do anything about that anymore. That was then, this is now. A strong whiff of hot chocolate called to her from the kitchen. On each step of the stairway she repeated, "That was then, this is now," until immersed in the rhythm of the chant, she forgot why she'd begun it.

Jean turned from the stove with a cup in her hand as Kincaid walked in.

"That was good timing: I was just about to bring this up to you." She passed it to Kincaid. "When I was young we always had hot cocoa when it snowed."

46

"I didn't know it snowed in California." Kincaid blew over the chocolate and watched the surface turn darker and crinkle into the skin that she liked so much.

"I was born in the Midwest, not all that far from here really, and I moved to the West Coast to go to college. And actually, it does snow in California—in the mountains and in the northern parts. That's why I like southern California so much. I can drive up and play in the snow all I want and then go home where it's nice and warm and take a hot shower and get all dry again. The best of both worlds."

A sudden shout from the living room drew their attention.

"Walter's watching skiing," Jean explained, pouring another cup of cocoa and indicating with a nod that Kincaid should take it out to him.

"Thanks," he said absently and set it on the coffee table, never taking his eyes off the screen. "Giant slalom. That last guy caught the flag with the tip of his ski and just went flying! Carried him off on a stretcher." He shook his head. "And he'd been in first place all along."

Kincaid put her cup beside his and sat down on the sofa. "Do you know how to ski, Walter?"

"No. I'm a California kid. Swimming, a little surfing . . . that's my style." He grinned at her. "In fact, I won a few medals back in high school for swimming."

"You did? Would you teach me?"

"From what I've seen, you're doing all right. But sure, I can give you a few pointers."

"Today? Will you go to the pool with me today?"

"Is your homework finished?"

"Well . . . almost."

"Okay, I'll make a deal with you. Finish your homework and I'll go with you today." His eyes took on a sudden glint. "And when report cards come out, I'll go with you to the pool one day for every A. Deal?"

"Deal!"

~~~~~~~~

Jean was in the kitchen icing Christmas cookies when Kincaid burst in waving a little white piece of paper.

"Straight A's! I got straight A's, Jean!"

"That's great, Kincaid! I'm really proud of you. Your hard work paid off, didn't it?"

Kincaid reached toward the cookie tray. "I can't wait to show Walter!"

Jean swatted her hand. "Just one, now. I'm saving these for the Christmas party. By the way, is there anyone you want to invite? From school?"

"Naw," she said, sneaking a couple more cookies.

"I saw that. You're sure there's not someone . . . "

"No, there isn't. These cookies are great! D'you think I have time for a swim 'fore supper?"

"Kincaid! It is the dead of winter!"

"The pool's indoors, Jean. An' it's heated. An' I'll dress warmly an' wear a hat. Please? I wanta practice a little 'fore Walter goes with me on Saturday."

Jean shook her head in resignation. "Dinner will be ready at six. And make sure you do wear that hat."

Kincaid grabbed another cookie on her way out. "Don't tell him, now. I wanta surprise him!"

~~~~~~~~~

They waited together in her room as the hands of the clock on her dresser inched closer to twelve. Suddenly, Kincaid threw her two handfuls of confetti into the air and cheered, adding her voice to the raucous chorus that could be heard from Jean and Walter's party guests downstairs.

"Happy New Year, Jean! Happy New Year, Walter!"

"Happy New Year, Kincaid!"

Walter poured grape juice into three long-stemmed glasses and handed one to her and one to Jean before picking up the third and raising it high.

"To the New Year! May it be joyous and prosperous and bring all of us closer to one another!"

They clinked glasses and drank deeply, while strains of "Auld Lang Syne" filtered up from below. And Kincaid wasn't the only one to have to wipe her face hastily before goodnight hugs.

The house was unusually quiet. Jean wasn't in the kitchen to tell Kincaid not to slam the door and supper hadn't even been started. Something was wrong.

"Jean! Jean, where are you?" Fear made Kincaid's throat tight.

"We're in here, dear."

Uneasily, Kincaid grabbed an apple and hurried out to the living room. Jean and Walter were sitting on the sofa. Nothing unusual in that—except it wasn't time for Walter to be home from work yet. She set her books on the stairs and hurried back into the living room.

"Have a good day, dear?" Jean asked.

She nodded, looking from one of them to the other.

No one said anything for a very long time. Kincaid just stood there. She noticed a nick in the coffee table she'd never seen before. And a stain on the carpet next to the left side of the couch.

Finally, Walter cleared his throat. "We might as well get on with it. Kincaid, I've been transferred back to California."

Blood roared in her ears. Her stomach felt as if she'd been dropped into a bottomless pit. She stared at a scuff mark on her shoe. It was over. They were leaving. She'd known it wouldn't last, but so soon . . .

"The thing is this," Walter went on. "It hasn't been quite a year since you came to us . . . and there are rules . . . "

Yeah, rules. They had to send her back. Of course they did. Her other shoe wasn't scuffed.

"It has to be a full year, you see, without any contact from your parents . . . We were waiting for the year to be over before we brought it up, but now, with the transfer . . . Kincaid, we haven't had the chance to talk with you about this, but we want to adopt you." He reached out and took her hand.

Her thoughts whirled frantically. She shook her head, totally confused. "What?"

Jean spoke up. "We're not perfect, Kincaid, I'm sure we'll make lots of mistakes, all parents do. But we do love you and we want you to be our daughter very much."

Kincaid's thoughts crowded one on another, so many, so fast she had trouble sorting them out. She shook her head. "You're not sendin' me back?"

Jean took her other hand. "No, Kincaid. We want you to stay with us, always. But it's really up to you. What do you want?"

What did she want? What did she want? She pulled on their hands, tugged them to their feet and hugged them, a great big three-way hug.

Tears glistened on Jean's cheeks and Walter's voice was thick as he continued, "But remember I said there were rules. We have to finish out the first year and then the adoption proceedings can take up to another year. And we can't take you out of the state until it's all completed."

Kincaid looked confused. "But, the transfer . . . "

"Walter is going on ahead, honey. He'll find us a nice home and when everything is signed and sealed, he'll come back and get us."

"But that means you'll have to be gone a long time . . . "

He moved back and reached for both of her hands, his eyes shiny. "Dads have to do hard things sometimes, but daughters are worth it."

The lump in her throat made it hard to swallow. "I guess this means I'm Martha Jean Henderson, now."

"You can be anything you want to be!" He held her close.

"Good, 'cause I want to be your daughter." And she pushed hard against his sweater so no one could see her face.

~~~~~~~~

It wasn't Mrs. Curtis who came to talk with them about the adoption. Mrs. Dodd had taken over their case and Mrs. Dodd looked as if she'd just eaten a sour persimmon. She took Martha alone into the living room and made herself comfortable on one end of the big sofa. She patted the space beside her to indicate Martha should sit down, too. Martha sat at the far end, on the edge.

"Now, then," Mrs. Dodd said. "We'll just have ourselves a nice little chat, shall we? I'm goin' to ask you some questions an' Martha, I want you to be very truthful with me. You understand the importance of tellin' the truth, don't you? That's right, you do. An' you know you call tell me anything because I'm your friend an' I want to help you.

That's why I'm askin' questions, so I'll know the best way to help you. Okay? Now Martha, do you know the Hendersons have asked to be allowed to adopt you? How do you feel about that?"

"Good."

Mrs. Dodd opened a notebook and licked the end of a freshly sharpened pencil. "Just 'good?'"

"Well, yeah. I mean, I want 'em to."

"You want them to adopt you? You know they come from 'way out West, an' they plan on movin' back there. An' you'd have to go with them. Is that really what you want?"

Martha nodded.

"You'd have to leave your whole family behind. I mean, your real family. Probably never see them again. Now is that what you want?"

Martha shrugged away the sudden image of Carol Ann bawling her eyes out. "I want 'em to be happy. I want 'em to have good homes."

"What about your mama an' daddy? Don't you miss them?"

Martha picked at a loose thread on the sofa cushion. "Not really."

"You don't miss your mama an' daddy?" Mrs. Dodd stared at her hard.

Martha wrapped and unwrapped the thread around her finger. "They never liked me, anyhow." She watched Mrs. Dodd's pencil flying over the paper. "Jean an' Walter like me."

"But you still love your mama, right?"

Martha's finger was turning all red; the thread was too tight. She unwound the thread and examined the tiny little lines it left on her skin.

"Martha?"

"She run off."

"Are you angry that she left you?"

Martha searched her feelings. "No."

"You're not the least bit upset at her?"

Martha shrugged.

"Well then, what about your daddy, you love him don't you?"

The thread broke and Martha stared at the frayed end. There were a lot of teeny tiny threads all twisted together to make just one single thread. Martha wondered if each of the tiny threads were made up of bunches of even tinier threads.

"Then, are you angry at your daddy?"

Mrs. Dodd's pencil scribbled frantically even though Martha hadn't said anything.

"Martha, tell me the truth now, don't you really want them, your real mama an' daddy, to come back an' get you?"

Martha's voice was just above a whisper. "No."

"You don't ever want to see them again?"

"No."

"Martha, I don't believe that. I think you just think you don't want to see them again. All children get angry at their parents sometimes, just like parents get angry at their children. But that doesn't mean they don't love each other." She closed the notebook and laid her pencil on the coffee table.

A new number two pencil, Martha noticed, with a whole eraser.

"Thank you, Martha. I think I have enough information now. You may run along an' play. I'll just speak with Mr. an' Mrs. Henderson for a minute."

Mrs. Dodd called them and Walter and Jean emerged from the kitchen carrying a tray of coffee and cookies—Martha's favorite cookies, but she didn't take one. She couldn't even look at them. For some reason, she felt as if she'd done something wrong and she scooted upstairs before anyone could say a thing. But she waited on the top landing, out of sight, but not out of hearing. She fiddled with her shoes, making bunny ears with her shoelaces.

"I'll get right to the point," Mrs. Dodd said firmly. "The child is confused, withdrawn, an' very troubled. I haven't had the chance to read all of her chart, but from what I've seen today, I don't believe this would be a good match. I'm sorry. Perhaps in California you will find a more suitable child."

"Wait!" Jean protested. "What do you mean, 'suitable?' We want to adopt Martha."

"We happen to think it is a very good 'match,'" Walter added.

"Mr. an' Mrs. Henderson, this happens all too often with foster families. They get too close, lose their perspective, lose sight of their real goals. You want a child, I can sympathize. But not this child. This child needs . . . well, I believe she needs her family, her real parents. An' I am goin' to do ever'thing in my power to locate them an' see that she goes home where she belongs."

52

"I don't understand. Mrs. Curtis seemed to think there'd be no problem after we waited the required length of time . . ." Jean sounded scared.

"She belongs with us." Walter's voice was firm.

"We shall see." Mrs. Dodd sounded equally as firm.

"Isn't there someone else we could talk to?"

"I am Martha's social worker, Mrs. Henderson. I am also the one in charge of deciding when and where to transfer such cases. Now, you must realize this is nothin' personal. I just want what is in the best interest of the child."

"So do we."

"Good. That's what we expect from foster families."

The front door opened and closed. Martha could smell the rain.

"Oh, Walter, what will we do?" Jean sounded really scared.

"I don't know, honey. But I do know that what's right is right. And it's right for Martha to be with us."

Martha retied her shoe and trudged heavily back to her room. Pulling the chair over to the window, she opened it and breathed deeply of the cool, wet air. She watched tiny drops land on the window ledge and combine into bigger drops. What's right is right. Was it right for her parents to abandon her? Was it right for her to abandon her brothers and sisters? Was it right for her to be happy? Mrs. Dodd was right about one thing: she was confused.

She looked around the room—it really was hers now, really felt like hers. She snorted. Yeah, right. She should of known better. Things like this never happened to people like her, not really. It had just been pretend and she had forgotten . . . She dropped to her knees and reached under the bed, pulling the old, tattered box into view. She'd never unpacked it. Swallowing hard, she drew it closer. Then all at once, her hand closed into a fist and smashed into the side of the carton, sending it flying back under the bed, out of sight. She threw herself upon the bed and, staring at the ceiling, did her times tables over and over until she finally fell asleep.

~~~~~~~~

Two depressing weeks and dozens of phone calls later, Mrs. Curtis was again her social worker. Martha was afraid to believe it, but it was true. And Mrs. Curtis asked her just two questions. Was she happy? And did she love Jean and Walter enough to be their daughter?

The first question was no problem but the second . . .

"I don't rightly know what love feels like I don't think. But I sure like 'em a lot. An' I want 'em to adopt me."

Mrs. Curtis smiled at her. "Many of us are unsure what love is, Martha. But I can tell you one thing, when Walter and Jean look at you, that light shining in their eyes is most definitely love. And I don't think we could find a better family for you anywhere."

To Walter and Jean she said, "It would be easier if both of you could be here, with Martha and within the state. It's highly irregular to proceed in this way, but since you are willing to make sacrifices and work to make this happen . . . Well, I'm willing to go to bat for you."

~~~~~~~~~

Jean and Martha drove Walter to the airport. Martha carried his briefcase for him through the long lobby, up the escalator, and to the row of blue plastic seats closest to Gate Six. The waiting area overlooked the runway and Martha watched the planes take off and land while Walter and Jean sat nearby, holding hands. She didn't want to look at him. Finally, they stood up and called her.

Walter took his briefcase from her, "I'll be back for holidays. And I'll write often."

"I'll work hard an' be good."

"I know you will, honey. And Mrs. Curtis said she'll push things just as fast as she can. It won't be long, I promise." He hugged her and kissed Jean and disappeared down a long corridor.

They waited at the window as his plane taxied down the runway, picked up speed and jumped at an impossible angle into the sky. When they could no longer see even a speck against the clouds, they walked back the long way they'd come, back to the parking lot and the car.

Martha stared out the window as Jean drove them home. He said he'd be back soon. But so had her daddy.

~~~~~~~~~

"Finished with your homework?" Jean looked up from the sofa as Martha passed by on her way to the kitchen for a snack.

Martha nodded.

"Good. Because my favorite old movie is on TV in just a few minutes and I was about to invite you to watch it with me. Harvey is a giant, six foot white rabbit and no one can see him but Jimmy Stewart."

"You really like old movies, huh?"

"Lots of them. This one is really funny."

Martha sank down beside her. "Can we make some popcorn at the commercial?"

"You bet."

~~~~~~~~

Dearest Martha,

After work last night, I hurried to the beach to watch the sunset—pink and orange and grey and at least six shades of blue. And the waves crashing against huge sandstone rocks!

I can't wait to show you the ocean. It isn't warm enough yet to swim, but even at that, early in the morning you can see dozens of surfers out on their boards waiting to catch a big one.

California is beautiful, Martha. Not like the South, but with a beauty of its own, subtle, harder to define.

I miss you. I love your letters. Please send more. Time will pass and before you know it, you'll be here, watching sunsets with me.

Love, Walter.

~~~~~~~~

She ended seventh grade with a four-point-o average. But she didn't feel much of the thrill of success—Walter wasn't there to keep his end of the bargain. Still, she spent most of the long summer days at the pool, honing and refining her skills, concentrating especially on the techniques Walter had shown her.

She came home one evening to find a black Ford in the driveway. Her stomach got all tight and her mouth suddenly tasted like cotton. She tried to sneak upstairs but Jean heard and called her into the living room. Mrs. Curtis stood up when Martha came into the room. Jean also stood and she was smiling. No one said anything for a moment until a movement from the far corner of the room caught her attention.

"Hello, Martha." Walter stood beaming at her.

She looked from one to another of the grown-ups, disbelief still in her eyes, a grin widening on her face.

Jean nodded. "Yes, Martha. We're a family now! The three of us!"

Part of Martha wanted to fly to each of them but something else kept her from it. A nagging little voice whispered "How long? How long?" She swallowed. That was then, this is now. What's right is right. She looked at Walter. He was her father now. No. He wasn't anything like her father. He had proved that "gone" wasn't always "gone forever." He had come back, just like he had promised. And Jean—she'd stayed even after Walter left, stayed with her, helped her with homework, cooked supper every night for her, watched old movies with her. That was then, this is now.

She turned back to Walter. "I got straight A's for the whole year. Now you'll have to teach me how to swim in the ocean."

He hugged her close. "A deal is a deal."

~~~~~~~~

The goodbye scene with her brothers and sisters was pretty much what she expected. Carol Ann cried and carried on, afraid that Martha would go off and have so much fun she'd forget them. Patty, now almost five, took her cue from Carol Ann. Billy and Jimmy hugged her with no apparent feelings about her leaving. Bobby sat sullenly ignoring everyone.

Time seemed to drag. No one seemed to have much to say.

She took Patty onto her lap. "I'll send you some pretty seashells from the ocean, Pattycake. An' I'll take pictures to send to the rest of y'all," she promised.

Billy Ray became interested. "Will you see Flipper?"

56

"Well, I'll just bet there are dolphins in the Pacific Ocean. Would you like me to send you a picture if I see one?"

Billy nodded emphatically.

"Are you gonna learn to surf?" Jimmy's interest, too, was caught at the thought of oceans.

Martha laughed. "I'll just have to wait an' see 'bout that, but I'll let you know if I do." She turned to her older brother. "Well, Bobby, it's gonna be a long time . . . "

He continued to ignore her.

"Okay, well, let's all gather 'round Bobby then, 'cause I want a picture of y'all to take with me. Walter, would you take a picture of us, please?"

After posing for several pictures, which had given them all something to do, everyone just sat around again, staring at their shoes. Finally, Walter called her aside.

"Say your last good-byes, Martha, their families are here."

Carol Ann had been close enough to overhear. She looked stricken. "Martha? You lettin' folks call you Martha now? Seems like you've turned your back on your family for sure!"

"Carol Ann . . . "

Carol Ann shook her head vehemently. "Your name is Kincaid, no matter what you call yourself. You're Kincaid, that's your real family name!"

One by one, they left. Carol Ann, still crying to beat everything, managed to convey great disappointment with life in general and disapproval of Kincaid's life in particular. She vowed to write every week.

Patty had a different slant on things. "Bye, Kincaid. Send me pretty shells. An' if Flipper has babies, please send me one of them, too."

"Maybe you could send me a bottle of ocean water," Billy said, thoughtfully. "An' maybe some sand. I could make a little beach here."

"Send me a picture of your surfboard," Jimmy said. "An' tell Mr. Disney I like his cartoons, an' could he put Mickey Mouse on weekdays, after school."

Bobby headed for the door without having said one word, but Martha stopped him.

"I want you to know I'm gonna miss you." She shrugged at his continued silence. "Well, bye Bobby." When she let go of his arm, he turned and walked stiffly away. But not before she saw a tear form in the corner of his eye.

"Well, hell," she thought. "Well, hell."

~~~~~~~~

"I'm real happy to see you, Kincaid." Her grandmother sat up straighter on the bed. "I been missin' you children somethin' fierce. How y'all gettin' on?"

"We're all doin' fine, just fine." She wet her lips and swallowed hard. "Daddy up an' left us, Grandma, just like Mama."

"I know. We don't get out much here, but news does get in. I know, it's a sorry mess. I had hoped when he married your mama he'd straighten out some, but . . . I'm just sad you children had to suffer. Anyway, I heard y'all were sent to nice homes. How they treatin' you, Kincaid?"

"Real good. You'd like them, Grandma. They adopted me, all legal-like."

"Well, what are their names?"

"Walter an' Jean Henderson."

The old woman nodded. "So, I guess you'll be Martha Jean Henderson from now on. Well, no matter what name you carry, you're still my granddaughter an' you tell them that if they don't treat you right, they'll have to answer to me."

Martha toed the little throw rug beside the bed. "Grandma, Walter got transferred to California and we gotta move. Right soon."

"So, this is a good-bye visit."

She nodded miserably. "Grandma, I'm ashamed I haven't come to see you before this."

"Why, I'm not upset with you, child! I understand you been goin' through some rough times, yourself. Just glad to see you now. Don't look like we got much time for regrets, Kincaid, so let's make the most of what we got left."

She held her arms out and Martha flew into them.

"Oh, child, I am gonna miss you for sure."

Chapter Three

To Martha, California meant Mickey Mouse and Donald Duck, cowboys riding tall in the saddle on sure-footed painted ponies, sagebrush and cactus, grizzled old prospectors leading long-eared pack mules. And oceans. Waves crashing against rugged cliffs, palm trees swaying in cool tropical breezes, sweeping expanses of sand, brilliant white sails against a deep blue backdrop.

She wasn't prepared for skyscrapers, freeways, and traffic jams. Not a cow nor a cowboy in sight. The few palm trees Jean excitedly pointed out as they drove away from the airport in Walter's new car, were short, stubby little things. And everything—even the sky—had a dry, brown cast far from the crisp, sharp colors she was used to. To Walter and Jean California might be beautiful, but for Martha it was going to take some time.

They drove practically forever, freeway to freeway, with hundreds of cars barrelling past them at incredible speeds, before they at last exited off into a residential section. They turned this way and that and Martha noticed streets were not in blocks here, but in circles, arcs, curves. Finally, the car stopped in front of a low, squat stucco house. Martha's mouth dropped open. She quickly closed it, along with her eyes, hoping against hope they were just visiting someone before going on to their new home. The sound of a big truck rumbling to a stop nearby caused her to open her eyes; the moving truck had parked right in front of them and already the movers were beginning to unload boxes. Jean and Walter jumped out of the car to open the house and raise the big garage door.

Jean called to her from the house, enthusiastically waving for her to get out of the car, but Martha was in no hurry—she could see more than enough from where she sat. The house was seriously ugly. First off, Martha hated stucco. She'd never seen it before, but one look was quite enough. And it was a strange brown color that clashed horribly with the bright pink flowers on the bushes under the front windows. And there was no porch. And no trees. The tiny patch of brown grass out front sported one equally tiny stick that might someday be a tree.

Martha shook her head. All this way for a new start . . . to this. She swallowed hard as Jean purposefully made her way back to the car.

"Come on in, honey. While they unload, let's you and me go exploring, see what we can find!"

Martha let herself be led from the car and up the short walk. While Jean oohed and ahhed over closet space and the breakfast nook and the built-in oven, Martha struggled to suppress her feelings. They were so happy, why should she spoil it for them?

When at long last the final box had been unloaded and the moving van was just a rumble in the distance, Walter suddenly slapped his hands together with a whoop.

"Surf's up!" He grabbed a suitcase with one hand and Jean's hand with the other and danced her down the short hallway, leaving Martha open-mouthed amid the boxes in the living room.

"Hurry, Martha, your suitcase is already in your room—get into your bathing suit! The waves are waiting!"

Martha shrugged and slowly walked the length of hallway to her own small, square room. She was in no hurry to get to the beach, either. It was probably not so great anyway, and so what? What did she care about the dumb old ocean? The beach probably didn't even have any palm trees.

In the car, Jean again pointed out landmarks and objects of interest but Martha couldn't seem to focus. She wasn't interested in old missions or pretty skylines. She leaned back and closed her eyes and automatically began her times tables.

She smelled the ocean before she could see it. Tangy but sweet, it pulled her head up, made her strain for a first glimpse—and that first glimpse took her breath away. She got out as soon as the car stopped, threaded her way through the crowded parking lot and all the sunbathers sprawled across the sand, never once taking her eyes from the blue-green wonder, hardly feeling the burning sand against her feet.

She walked straight into the water, the chill bubbles swirling and bursting against first her ankles, then her legs, across her belly, and finally, over her shoulders. She wiped hair and water from her face and saw that her fingers were all puckered. She licked her lips and found that they, too, were wrinkled and they tasted salty. Completely unafraid and at home, she relaxed, letting the waves push her back and forth, up and down. Her arms floated up to the surface and she laughed, embracing the whole ocean, acknowledging and submerging herself in an energy and power far greater than her own. Her heart filled to overflowing and she suddenly felt like singing.

Her body stiffened and she sank. Choking and sputtering salt water, she frantically sought to upright herself until her feet at last found the bottom and she could take a deep breath. That was just a game she used to play: singing with the trees, talking to animals, singing the sun up. Pretend. Kid stuff—and she wasn't a kid anymore. That was then, this is now. That was then, this is now. She leaned back and let her feet rise to the surface. Floating, she stared at the clouds: a giant flower, a dog's head, a doughnut. She let the waves carry her back in to shore.

~~~~~~~~

"James Granger?"
"Here."
"Ellen Harman?"
"Here."
"Martha Henderson?"
"Here," she drawled.
A snicker.
Martha sighed and clamped her jaws tight.

~~~~~~~~

She walked through the noisy cafeteria line in silence. She chose the least crowded table, the farthest chair and ate quickly, looking at no one. Then pushing her tray aside, she pulled out her not-quite-finished homework. Voices buzzed around her but she paid no attention; nobody was talking to her.

A body suddenly plopped into the seat next to hers and leaned close, a finger pointing to Martha's English book.

"I said, if that's homework for Mr. Bennett's class, you don't have to worry—he's giving us all another day on it."

Martha looked up uncomprehendingly.

The girl beside her continued. "I had English last class, and well, since you have the same book, I just thought . . . "

"Hey, Ellen!"

The girl stood and waved towards the other end of the table. "Yeah, I'm coming!" Turning back to Martha, she smiled. "Gotta go. See ya."

"Uh, thanks," Martha called after her. But her voice didn't carry over the all the shouting and laughing and scraping chairs.

~~~~~~~~~~

Martha shoved open the wide metal door and was greeted with the sharp, no-longer-unpleasant smell of chlorine and the familiar pat-pat of bare feet slapping wet concrete. But today there was an unfamiliar tension in the air. Today the splashes were not random background beats to the usual deafening roar but individual, singular reports that drowned out the subdued and muffled voices. Today was swim team tryouts.

She draped her towel over the back of one of the many chairs that lined the walls and sat down on the cold, hard deck to warm up, just like Walter had taught her. Imagining her muscles as soft, loose rubber . . .

A pair of dripping legs stopped in front of her.

"Hi!"

Martha looked up to see the girl from the cafeteria, the one who also had Bennett for English.

"Hi." She went back to her stretches.

The girl flopped into the closest chair. "You're trying out, huh? Me, too. I didn't make it last year but I've been practicing. It's a great way to meet some really cute guys, y'know? By the way, I'm Ellen Harman."

"Martha Henderson."

Ellen nodded. "I know. We're in the same homeroom. You just moved here, huh? I like your accent. Your dad in the Navy?"

"No."

"Girls, thirteen to fifteen, ready!"

Ellen stood. "That's us! Wish me luck."

Martha nodded and got up slowly, hanging back a little, letting several other girls get in line behind Ellen before she stepped in herself. She kept her head down, staring at the tiny lines and cracks in the discolored concrete as she inched her way to the pool. Muscles loose and warm . . . Taking a deep breath, eyes on the water before her, she stepped onto the starting block.

"Name?"

"Martha Henderson."

"Stroke?"

"Freestyle."

"Up and back."

The whistle blew. She jumped. From a long, shallow dive she began her stroke underwater, before her body broke the surface. A neat, tight turn, making the most of her glide, no energy wasted, and she was back, pulling up on deck. She looked expectantly at the assistant coach.

He looked at his stopwatch. Then at her. Then back to the watch.

"Coach! Hey, Coach!"

Martha tried to catch his eye but he only looked at the watch. Then the watch was passed to the coach whose face split into a wide grin. He looked at Martha. Everyone in the now-quiet room was looking at Martha.

"So what team you been swimming for, kid?"

"Never swam for a team before."

"Okay, so who's your coach?"

"My dad."

"Come on, kid, help me out a little here. Who's your dad?"

"Walter Henderson."

He looked annoyed. "Never heard of him." He stared at her a moment longer, then shrugged and turned back to the assistant coach. "Won't Prescott just die?" he chuckled. "Thinks he's got this year's trophy all sewn up . . . " They both laughed and moved away.

"Wait! Did I make it?"

"Huh? Oh yeah, sure, of course you did. Are you kidding?" He grinned and winked at her. "Just stick with me, kid, and I'll make you a star!" He laughed again and grabbed his whistle.

Martha walked back to the chairs for her towel. Ellen sat waiting for her.

"Congratulations."

"Thanks."

Ellen shook her head. "You made it look so easy. How'd you do that?"

Martha shrugged. "I don't know. Just did. How'd you do it?"

"I didn't. Again. And I've been practicing a lot." She sighed. "Guess some of us have it and some of us don't." And for a moment, she looked and sounded just like Carol Ann.

Martha busied herself with her towel. Still without looking at the other girl, she asked, "What'd you think about while you were swimmin'?"

"Huh? I don't know . . . if I was going to make the team, if I was swimming fast enough . . . What did you think about?"

"Well, I imagined I was a dolphin, flyin' through the water faster an' faster. An' I was racin', an' saw myself touchin' the edge first, 'way before anybody else."

"Do you think that makes a difference?"

"Don't know. But my dad says that's how the judo experts break all those bricks an' things; they imagine their hand goin' through 'em an' comin' out the other side."

Ellen stared at her thoughtfully for several seconds then jumped up and hurried away without looking back.

Martha shrugged again and headed for the locker room to change. She had just finished packing her gear when the door banged open and a very excited Ellen slid to a stop before her.

"I made it! I did what you said and I made it!" She held out her dripping hand.

Martha hesitated, then took it. "Congratulations," she smiled.

~~~~~~~~~

"But Martha," Jean protested, "everyone will be wearing a costume—it's a Halloween dance!"

"Then ever'one else can look stupid. I'm not. I won't go if I have to dress up, I just won't go!"

Jean leaned back wearily. She shook her head. "Well, if you feel that strongly about it . . . I'm certainly not going to force you to wear a costume. I just don't understand . . . "

64

Martha didn't understand, either. But just thinking about going to the dance at all, her stomach got all tight and achey. She felt trapped. She thought about telling Jean that it was against her religion—it was true that Mammaw Wilson would've had a conniption fit if she'd known—but that wasn't it. She'd never really held with all those old Southern Baptist rules and she didn't want to lie to Jean, not even to get out of going to the stupid dance. So she was stuck. But she'd be damned if she would be double-stuck and make herself look ridiculous besides.

Everyone else was wearing a costume. Martha looked as out of place as she felt but at least, she told herself, she didn't also look stupid. They might stare but they couldn't laugh.

The general flow of movement was towards the gaping doors of the gym that had been enthusiastically remodeled to look like castle doors on a haunted house. She hung around outside, glancing at her watch, trying to appear as if she were impatiently waiting for someone until her waiting became conspicuous and people began to look at her funny. She inched through the door.

Inside, the light was dim and the air was close and steamy—it smelled like a gym after all. She edged away from the door and bumped into something.

"Excuse me," she mumbled before realizing it was the refreshment table.

A young masculine voice snickered.

She fled to the back corner where she stayed for nearly an hour watching the wild gyrations of the crazily costumed dancers. She figured she had two hours to kill before she could go home.

"Martha!" Ellen appeared out of the crowd as a long-tailed, long-fanged tiger.

"Uh, hi."

"Great dance, huh?"

"Oh, yeah."

Ellen's hand was grabbed by a tall, one-eyed pirate. "See you later," she called back over her shoulder.

Martha's eyes followed Ellen back to the dance floor, watched her dance with one partner after another, laughing and smiling and having a good time. She watched for another half hour before she left.

Not one boy had asked her to dance. No one had even spoken to her except Ellen. She walked home slowly; her feet and legs ached from standing all that time.

She opened and closed the front door very carefully but Jean heard her anyway.

"How'd it go, sweetheart? Did you have a good time?"

Martha nodded. "I'm gonna grab a hot shower an' put my feet up for a spell."

Jean grinned. "Danced 'em off, huh? I'm glad you had fun. I knew you would once you got there."

Martha trudged up the stairs her heart as heavy as her feet. She hadn't exactly lied to Jean, but . . .

~~~~~~~

She threw her books into the locker and slammed the door. A weekend with no homework! She gave the dial a spin to make sure it was locked and turned around—into Ellen.

"Hi! I was hoping to catch you before you left school. I wanted to ask you . . . " Ellen began and then stopped. She twirled a strand of hair with her finger.

Martha's throat got tight. Carol Ann used to do that same thing when she was nervous. Martha shook her head to clear it. That was then, this is now.

"Well, I wanted to know if . . . Well, you see, my parents aren't too happy about me being on the swim team and they don't like me going alone to the pool to practice . . . and I thought . . . I wondered if maybe I could go with you. You know, sort of practice partners." She twirled harder.

When Martha didn't answer right away, Ellen stared at her anxiously. "So, what d'you say?"

Martha took a deep breath, then shrugged and nodded. "Yeah, okay."

Ellen sighed with relief. "That's great! I gotta go now, my mom's waiting for me—but I'll call you tonight. Thanks, Martha!"

~~~~~~~

Thanksgiving wasn't the same in California. No sharpness to the air, no pretty leaves, no hint of winter. Just warm, blue skies, a day like every other.

They went to Walter's family for breakfast and to Jean's family for dinner. It was tradition, they said. She'd get to meet all her new aunts and uncles and cousins, they said. They even said it would be fun. But Martha wasn't so sure. Her throat was all tight and her stomach felt jumpy and even doing her times tables on the long drive over didn't help.

Evidently, nobody in Walter's family was ever hungry at breakfast, which was good, because there wasn't much to eat, just some fancy stuff Martha had never tasted before: croissants and imported cheeses, thin little cookies they called biscuits, and teas that smelled like apples and oranges and even one that was green and tasted like warm water.

The men laughed loudly and talked about business. The women talked quietly about clothes and shopping and their children. And the children—they looked like little grown-ups in their suits and ties and fancy dresses. They stood around in groups, just like their parents, their backs to her, conversations stopping when she walked by. They sure didn't seem like her cousins.

She sat down in a folding chair that had been shoved back into a corner out of the way and counted things: how many chairs' legs in the living room, how many slats in the venetian blinds, how many tiny sandwiches on how many fancy trays in the living room. She ran out of things to count so she got up and wandered around. How many steps to the front door, how many cars parked on the street... Finally she wandered into the backyard where she found a large white dog who was as happy to see her as she was to see him. He dropped a soggy, dirty ball at her feet. She grinned and picked it up.

A little later, Jean stuck her head out the sliding glass door. "Oh, there you are. Where are the other children? Well, come on and say good-bye, it's time to . . . Martha Jean! Just look at your dress! It's ruined, simply ruined!"

Martha pushed the dog away and tried to brush the dirt and grass stains off her new clothes.

Jean came out and quickly closed the door behind her. "What were you doing out here, anyway? Playing with that filthy dog?"

"He's more fun than those stupid kids," Martha muttered.

"What? Oh, I just can't believe it. We'll just have to go home and you'll have to change, that's all there is to it. And we'll probably be late for dinner . . . "

The evening didn't improve. Everybody in Jean's family looked at her funny, too. When Jean introduced her, folks said hi, but nobody smiled. And these kids wouldn't play with her, either. The boys, playing baseball in the backyard or riding skateboards, ignored her. The girls sat around showing off their new dresses and talking about boys, but whenever she approached they stopped talking and just stared at each other until she left. Then they giggled. Some of the little girls were playing jump rope but they didn't want her to turn.

She found Jean. "I wanta go home."

"We just got here, Martha. Dinner is almost ready."

"I want to go home."

"I know it's difficult meeting all these people, making new friends, but it's important. Go introduce yourself to the children and have a good time."

"There's nothin' fun to do here. I want to go home!"

Several people turned to stare.

"Lower your voice Martha! We are not going home. End of discussion."

"Well, I'm not stayin' here another minute! I'll hitchhike home if'n I have to!"

"I said keep your voice down! And since you are so unhappy in here, you may go out and sit in the car until I come to get you. Now. And I will expect you to behave yourself at dinner, young lady!"

Clamping her jaws, Kincaid stomped off. But not quickly enough to avoid hearing one of Jean's relatives sneer, "Cliche or not, my dear Jean, blood will tell."

~~~~~~~~~

"That one next!" Martha pointed to a big something covered by a sheet, too big to wrap or fit under the tree. She drew off the sheet and found a trophy cabinet made from black walnut, with hooks for ribbons and shelves for trophies. A big grin lit her face.

"Walter made it for you, honey."

"Oh, Dad!" She ran right to her room and brought back her ribbons, two red second places and one blue first place.

"It looks a little bare," she said sadly.

"Don't you worry," Walter beamed, "you'll fill it up!"

~~~~~~~

"Don't you think you're overreacting, honey?" Jean asked as they set the table. "Get down, Cat." She tilted the chair. The cat protested indignantly but jumped down. Jean turned back to Martha. "It can't be as bad as all that."

"Mom! I go to talk to a woman 'bout babysittin', she asks me how old I am, I say 'I'm fixin' to be fourteen,' an' she says 'Oh, you're from the South,' an' launches into a twenty minute—I am not exaggeratin' here—a twenty minute speech on how warm an' kind my people are! We never did talk 'bout her children! An' the other day, at practice, I was discussin' strategy for the next meet, an' Brenda just said, 'uh, huh,' an' called on Cheryl. Well, Cheryl up an' said exactly the same things I said, exactly, an' Brenda thought *she* was brilliant!"

"Well, you must realize people naturally notice anything out of the ordinary, like accents or disabilities or . . . Anyway, I'm sure they didn't mean to hurt your feelings."

"Yeah, right. Yesterday, I tried talkin' to Ellen 'bout it, an' she says, 'Oh, Martha, I just love your accent. I could listen to you talk for hours!'"

"Honey, she meant it to be funny."

"Well, it's not!" Martha plopped into a chair. "When people look at me, they see me. When I open my mouth, they hear Southern, an' that changes ever'thing! They can't hear what I say, 'cause they are too busy payin' attention to how I say it! Some folks think bein' Southern is the same as bein' stupid. Some folks think Southern accents are cute. Either way, they don't hear me at all. Nobody takes anything or anyone seriously with a Southern accent."

"Give it some time, sweetheart. It won't be long until you lose that accent now that we're in California. It'll be better soon, you'll see."

"I don't know. Maybe."

Something woke her. A shadowed figure stood at the foot of her bed, but strangely, she wasn't a bit scared.

"I didn't mean to wake you," said a familiar voice.

"Grandma? How'd you get here?"

"I wanted to see you again. To give you this." The old woman took a small beaded pouch from around her neck and held it out to Martha. The beads seemed to glow in the moonlight. Martha reached out to take it, but her hand passed right through it, as through a moonbeam.

"So that's how it is," the old woman said sadly. "Well, it will be waitin' for you, Kincaid. An' when the time is right, you will remember. You are a spark from an old fire an' you will remember."

"Grandma, I'm real glad to see you. I've missed you so much. I'm sorry I haven't written more, but . . . "

"It's all right, Kincaid. That's all past now. No need to worry 'bout anythin' like that. I just needed to see you once more, is all. Now, you lay down an' go on back to sleep."

"Hold my hand, Grandma, like you used to when I was little."

Martha felt a feather-light touch against her skin and the old woman began to sing, soft and deep, a lullaby she remembered from long ago.

When Martha woke, the sun was bright and warm through her window. She grabbed her robe and raced through the house looking for her Grandma. She found Jean in the kitchen. Munching a piece of toast, she slowly made her way back to her room to get dressed. That dream had been so real!

~~~~~~~~

Martha yawned and closed her notebook. "I think I'll go on to bed now, Mom. G'night." She leaned down and hugged Jean.

"Goodnight, sweetie. Walter will be sad he missed saying goodnight to you."

"No, I won't because I'm home at last," Walter said from the doorway.

Martha whistled. "You sure look mighty spiffy."

70

"Why, thank you, my dear." He loosened his tie and sank into his favorite chair. "I am sure glad that's over."

"Did your boss like your presentation, Dad?" Martha stifled another yawn.

"I think so. At least, he didn't say he hated it."

She yawned again. "I gotta go to bed." She walked around the sofa to Walter's chair when a strange, queasy feeling washed over her and she stopped before she touched him. He smelled sickly sweet, like liquor. Like her daddy. In a quick flash, she saw herself bending down to kiss her daddy goodnight, waiting for Carol Ann who always had to sit in daddy's lap, her legs wrapped around his waist, to hug him goodnight.

Martha shivered. That was then, this is now, she reminded herself fiercely. But she couldn't make her body bend to hug Walter.

"G'night, Dad." She waved and turned to leave.

"Hey, don't I get a hug, too?"

"Uh, yeah, sure." But her reluctance was clear.

"Wait a minute, Martha. You don't have to hug me if you don't feel like it."

She looked at him questioningly. He smiled and winked.

"Thanks, Dad." At the door, she called back, "I love you."

He looked a little sad. "I love you, too, sweetheart."

In her room, she pulled back the covers slowly. From under the bed, two furry black legs stretched, and Cat appeared, purring loudly. Holding her closely, breathing in the musky animal scent, Martha lay for a long while, just staring at the ceiling unable to sleep.

~~~~~~~~

"I don't think so, Ellen. I have a math test next week an' . . . "

"Come on, Martha, it's Friday night! We'll catch the early show so we won't be out late. You already know Cheryl and you'll like Bonnie, I promise. I mean, I've known them for practically eons!"

"I don't think so . . . "

"Martha, there is more to life than school and swimming. And I want you meet my other friends. It'll be fun. Please, Martha . . . "

"Well . . . "

"Great! We'll pick you up at six—Cheryl's mom is driving us. Bye!"

"I gotta ask my mom . . . " But Ellen had already hung up. Martha shrugged. It didn't matter, she knew what Jean would say anyway.

~~~~~~~~

She was undressing, getting ready for bed when she discovered it: a smear of scarlet, bright against her white panties. It had finally happened. The curse, the monthly, the monthly visitor, a visit from Aunt Jane, being on the rag, falling off the roof, her time of the month, her period, menses, menstruation, menarche had arrived and with it the ability to create life, give birth to a new human being. Not that she wanted to, but the power of it, the possibility, awed her.

She removed the rest of her clothes. Standing before the mirror she looked at herself, really looked at herself for the first time. Sliding her hands down this strange, new body, she claimed it as her own. She had breasts! No longer little flat, brown circles, they more than filled each cupped hand. When had they grown? Her hips, not angular and slim any more, were round, curved. When had that happened? Then, nestled between her legs, she found a forest of thick curls and inside that, slickery wetness. Surely these changes had not occurred over-night. How had she not noticed before?

She studied herself a long time.

Slowly slipping her nightgown over her head, she was acutely aware of how it brushed against her nipples, her hips, her thighs. Suddenly, pulling her robe close around her, she padded down the hall to the living room.

"Mom, can I talk with you?"

~~~~~~~~

The letter was from Carol Ann. Martha pulled out her dresser drawer, about to throw it in with all the other unopened letters, when something stopped her. She opened it.

Dear Kincaid,

I have some sad news to tell you. Grandma Kincaid died last Friday. They said it was a stroke, whatever that is, and it was good she went quickly. Daddy did not come to the funeral. We still have not heard from him.

How come you never answer my letters? Even if you are real busy, I think you could take a few minutes out to write to your own sister.

Yours truly,
Your loving sister Carol Ann Kincaid

Martha stuffed the letter back into the envelope and tossed it in the drawer. Leaning back against the bed, eyes closed, she could hear her Grandma's lullaby sweet and clear. That dream had been so real.

Chapter Four

"Hold still, Martha, I'm almost finished."

"This stuff stinks."

"Honestly, I can't believe you've never worn make-up before."

"And I can't believe you talked me into going to this stupid dance. Ow! Okay, that's it. Stop already!"

"Well, I'm done anyway." Ellen moved away from the dresser so Martha could look in the mirror. "What d'you think? Great, huh?"

Martha stared at her reflection for only a moment. Then she reached for a tissue and silently began to wipe her face.

"What are you doing?" Ellen yelped.

"This isn't me."

"Of course it's you! The new and improved you. Martha, there is nothing wrong with dressing up and looking nice!"

"I look just fine how I am."

"Of course you do but . . . " Ellen sighed. "Oh, Martha, you make everything seem so difficult." She reached for a jar on the dresser. "Here, you'll never get it off that way. Use this."

A half a box of tissues later, Ellen tried again. "Will you at least wear some lipstick? This is the first Senior dance."

"Drop it, Ellen."

The doorbell rang. Ellen jumped up. "There's Mark. How's my hair? Are you ready? Let's go."

"I still think you and Mark oughta go alone, Ellen. I don't have a date and I don't even want to go."

"You never want to go. I think you'd be content to stay at home until you're forty. But I am looking out for you, my friend. An old maid you will not be!"

That remark should have tipped Martha off but it didn't. As they came down the stairs, she was surprised to see another boy waiting at the door with Mark.

"Who is that?" she hissed.

"He's someone Mark knows . . . "

"You didn't? Please say you didn't fix me up with a blind date?"

"He's a nice guy, Martha!"

"Oh, shit! I can't believe you did this to me."

In the car, Martha sat as close to the door as possible. Ellen tried several times to start a conversation but Martha ignored her and sat staring out the window, counting cars.

They got out of the car in silence, walked into the dance in silence, and found a table in silence. The nice guy waited until Mark and Ellen headed for the dance floor before he disappeared into the crowd, on the pretense of going for punch. Martha waited until she was sure he wasn't coming back before she went to the refreshment table herself.

Bonnie and Cheryl were already there, munching and talking.

Martha poured a glass of pink punch. "Well, are you having a good time? Where're your dates?"

For some reason both girls looked embarrassed.

"Oh, they're around," Bonnie said casually. "Where's yours?"

Martha groaned. "So, everybody knew but me?"

Cheryl looked sympathetic. "No, I think she just told us."

"Some friends. You could've at least warned me."

Bonnie chuckled. "What and miss seeing the man of your dreams—according to Ellen?"

"The man of whose dreams?" A boy with close-cropped blonde hair leaned over and took a potato chip from the small mountain on Bonnie's paper plate. He reminded Martha of someone, but she couldn't quite remember who. "Do I know him?" he continued.

74

Bonnie swatted his hand. "Watch it. Martha, this is Andy Stephens." She grinned. "My date."

Andy choked on a chip. Another boy, also grinning ear to ear, came over and whacked him on the back until he stopped coughing. "Hi," Andy managed to croak out.

"And this is Steve," Cheryl said, pointing to the second boy. He nodded but kept a watchful eye on Andy.

"So, where is this guy, Martha?" Bonnie continued as if nothing had interrupted their conversation.

Martha shrugged. "*Gone With the Wind.*"

Andy looked at her closely for a moment, then a mischievous glint lit his eyes. "Well, at least you're not in too much of a *Frenzy* about it."

She looked surprised, then smiled back. "He was headed *North by Northwest* the last time I saw him."

Andy chortled. "Maybe all the way to the *South Pacific.*"

They stared at each other and began to laugh uproariously.

"Okay, what's going on here?" Cheryl demanded.

"The meeting of fellow punsters." Andy stuck out his hand. "I am truly glad to meet you, Martha."

She took his hand thinking to shake it but instead he bowed over it. Out of the corner of her eye she saw Ellen watching, nodding in approval.

~~~~~~~~~

Martha took a deep breath. She stared at the sofa arm.

"I've done a lot of thinking about this and I feel it's the right thing for me," she explained. "By graduating in January, I can start at the community college after the semester break, which is the perfect time for oceanography classes. And scuba diving is only offered in the spring semester."

"You don't want to graduate with your class?" Jean asked.

Martha forced herself to look up. "Not really. It's just not that big a deal to me. I've spent almost twelve years learning what someone else decided I should know—I'm ready to study what I want to know."

"And you're sure about quitting the swim team?" Walter asked.

She nodded. "I've loved it lots and I've enjoyed filling the trophy case, but it takes up most of my free time. I want to get a part-time job, save some money."

Walter looked up. "You need more money?" He reached for his wallet.

Martha held out her hand to stop him. "No, Dad, it's not about money."

He fiddled with the arm of the sofa. Martha watched his fingers.

He looked up. "It's just that . . . well, I know we never talked about it, but I had hoped that trophy case would hold some Olympic medals someday . . . "

She swallowed hard and stared at the stain on her shoe. "I used to think about that, too, back in junior high. But, I don't think I have the discipline or drive or whatever it takes to focus so exclusively on one thing. I mean, you have to give up your whole life . . . but it's great to know you think I could have made it. That means more to me than any old medal." She jumped up and hugged him.

"Well," he smiled, "it seems as if you have put a great deal of thought into this. I'm really proud of you, Martha—how you think things through. Jean and I will want to talk this over, of course, but it seems to me you've made good, sound decisions for yourself."

She hugged him again.

~~~~~~~~

Martha sat smoothing the warm sand in front of her and watching Andy and Bonnie and Steve and Cheryl toss a frisbee around. They had asked her to play but she had declined. She didn't much like frisbee—it all seemed so pointless. Then she remembered how she and Bobby used to throw plastic Crisco lids to each other across the yard all the time, playing like they were flying saucers.

Bobby. It was Bobby he reminded her of. Until now, she hadn't noticed how much Andy looked like Bobby: kind of tall and lanky, same brown eyes, same crooked smile. She shook herself. That was then . . .

"Martha, pass the hot dogs," Ellen called from across the fire pit.

As she reached for them, Andy took a flying leap to make a catch and landed with a spray of sand in the middle of the picnic blankets.

76

"Still want 'em?" Martha asked. "They're covered with sand now."

Mark, sitting on the blanket beside Ellen, grinned. "I like 'em that way—toughens 'em up. Puts hair on my chest."

Ellen giggled. Martha got busy wiping sand off her towel.

"So, you're not going to congratulate me on a great save?" Andy teased. He tossed the frisbee back to the others and leaned back on his elbow, staring at her.

She didn't say anything but her face flushed.

"Ellen tells us you're a hot-shot swimmer."

She still said nothing.

"Y'know, a conversation means more than one person talking, Martha."

"I'm sorry," she mumbled. "I'm not very good at conversations, I guess."

"Well, you're great at bad puns and that counts for a lot. And I'm sure you'd like to get to know me. I'm a nice person. I don't even bite. And anyway, I've had all my shots."

She smiled shyly and nodded. "Me, too."

"See? I knew we could be friends. Ellen also said you're looking for a job. It just so happens Steve and I do boat cleaning and repair and if you're interested . . . "

Across the fire pit, Ellen was watching and smiling. Martha wanted to throw something at her.

~~~~~~~~

"What's that smell?" Martha crinkled her nose.

"Okra and onions," Jean answered. "I decided to make a real Southern dinner tonight: okra, green beans, fried chicken and honey-ham, mashed potatoes, and even iced tea. What do you think? Sound good?"

Her stomach got all tight and her mouth went dry. A Southern dinner. "Uh, yeah. But I, uh, I'm not so hungry tonight. I think I'll just skip dinner and go on to bed, if you don't mind."

"But Martha . . . "

She watched her feet as she walked through the living room and up the stairs. One step, two steps, three steps, four... She really didn't feel so good. Her stomach hurt.

~~~~~~~~

The phone rang.

"No, I am not going to the dance, Ellen," Martha said firmly. "No, you cannot get me to change my mind. I'm going to the movies with Bonnie and the gang. Look Ellen, leave me alone about this, okay? I do not like dances, I never have any fun at dances and I am not going to this one. Yeah, well, why don't you ditch Mark and come along with us? Yeah, I didn't think so. Y'know what, Ellen? You're no damn fun lately, either!" Martha hung up, loudly.

~~~~~~~~

How did it work out, Martha wondered, that she ended up sitting in the middle, the guys on one side, the girls on the other? Instead of sitting next to Andy, Bonnie was sitting on the end, on the other side of Cheryl. And instead of being with Cheryl, Steve was on the other side of Andy. Maybe they were all fighting. Maybe. Uncomfortably, she recalled a recent conversation with Ellen.

"He likes you, Martha."

"Great, I like him, too."

"No, I mean he LIKES you."

"Well, that's too bad, because I'm not available. Besides, he's seeing Bonnie."

"Martha! What are you waiting for? He's really cute. And anyway, he's not serious about Bonnie. I can tell."

What if Ellen was right? Martha shifted in her seat, keenly aware of sitting in the dark, Andy's leg just inches from her own. She liked Andy, but not that way. She wasn't even sure what "that way" was. And she wasn't sure she wanted to know.

The movie started. She stuffed her hands in her pockets and scooted as far toward Cheryl as she could and stared at the flickering images on the screen.

~~~~~~~~~

Jean laughed. "You go horse-back riding and all you can talk about is a baby cow."

"Well, the horses were nice, too. But, Mom, you shoulda seen him, he was so cute! His hair was all soft and curly! And his eyelashes—Ellen would die to have eyelashes that long! And he licked me. I've never been licked by a baby cow before. This big, pink tongue . . . and he smelled so good, like warm hay."

"I'm glad you had a good time, sweetheart.

"Oh, I did. I had a real good time." Martha took a deep breath. "Mom, I want to be a vegetarian."

"What?"

"I've wanted to for a long time, but I couldn't figure out how to spring it on you. I just don't think it's right to eat animals. They think and have feelings just like we do. If you'da seen that baby cow, you'd know what I mean. He was so little . . . so sweet. He just wanted to be loved and touched. But he's a Black Angus, and he's gonna end up as someone's steak dinner. It's not right. Besides, primates aren't supposed to eat meat, our intestines are too long to digest it properly."

"Oh, Martha, where do you get these crazy ideas? What do you suggest we eat, then?"

"Vegetables."

"Just vegetables?"

"Sure. I like vegetables, and you're always saying how good they are for us."

"Yes, but you need more than just vegetables alone. You need a balanced diet that includes things like protein."

"Mom, this is important to me. I know it may seem crazy at first, but there are lots of vegetarians in the world. There must be a way to do it."

Jean shook her head. "But, honey, I don't know anything about that. I don't know how to cook that way. I wouldn't even know where to begin . . . "

"I'll go to the library after school and find some cookbooks. Please, Mom, can't we at least try?"

Looking at her daughter's face, Jean bit her lip and nodded. "But, I don't know what your father will say."

"He'll say: 'Martha Jean, where do you get these crazy ideas?'"
She laughed and grabbed an apple on her way out of the kitchen.
"Thanks, Mom."

~~~~~~~

"So, where were you last night?" Martha slammed the metal
locker door.
"Oh, Mark got off early and wanted to go out. I meant to call you.
You're not upset, are you?"
"Why should I be upset? I got all dressed up because I thought we
were going out to eat and to a movie. I waited three hours for you,
Ellen! I missed supper. And when I finally did eat, it was cold. Cold
spaghetti is not tasty, Ellen! You could have at least called."
"Gee, I'm sorry, Martha. I didn't think it was any big deal. I
figured you'd understand."
"Big deal? Understand? We planned this over two weeks ago!"
"Well, it wasn't like a date or anything. And Mark is my
boyfriend! If Andy had called, you'd have gone out with him!"
"Andy and I are just friends, Ellen, but even if we were married,
I wouldn't break a date with you to go out with him. I wouldn't break
a date with you for anyone! It's not right!" It pissed her off even more
that Ellen really didn't seem to get it.
"Mark is my boyfriend, Martha!"
"Yeah, I know, and I'm supposed to be your best friend! We've
been friends since eighth grade, and you've only known him for three
months—but lately all I hear is "Mark this" and "Mark that." It's
nauseating, Ellen!"
"So, what did you want me to do, tell him I couldn't see him
because I was going out with you?"
"Yeah, as a matter of fact!"
"Yeah, right! You just don't say that to a guy, Martha! Not if you
ever want him to call you again. I happen to like Mark very much and
I'm not going to jeopardize my relationship with him by making him
feel unimportant in my life."
"Oh, I understand now," Martha said sarcastically. "We wouldn't
want to hurt his little feelings by telling him that your best friend of
four years is as important to you as he is. His poor masculine ego

80

couldn't stand such a blow. What bullshit! What about me, Carol Ann? What about my feelings? You're saying that he counts because he's a guy and that I don't because I'm a girl, and you want me to be understanding about the whole damn thing! Well, I don't feel very understanding. As a matter of fact, I don't understand you any better than you seem to understand me." She yanked at her towel and stomped to the pool. Diving quickly, she swam her laps furiously.

Ellen stood for a moment with her mouth hanging open, then slowly followed. "Carol Ann? Who the hell is Carol Ann?"

~~~~~~~

"Martha Jean! You failed biology! How could you fail biology? I thought you were doing well in that class." Jean looked shocked.

Martha shrugged. "I wouldn't dissect an earthworm."

"What?"

"The class had to dissect earthworms. I wouldn't do it and Mr. Jefferies got pissed."

"Watch your language, young lady. So, what was the problem? Why wouldn't you do your assignment?"

"Mom, every semester every biology class dissects earthworms. What could I possibly learn from killing another earthworm that I couldn't learn just as well from reading about the several thousand that already died?"

"I understand your feelings about animals, Martha, but an earthworm? I think that's carrying things a bit too far. Your intention may have been good, but it just cost you an F that you can ill afford if this is your last semester. You've put off biology until the very last minute, and now you must pass to graduate. Thank goodness this is only the quarter report. Now, what can you do to make this up?"

"Jefferies says I have to do the assignment. But I won't."

Jean shook her head. "Well, you'll have to talk to Walter about this. I just don't know what he'll say."

"Whatever he says, I'm still not going to kill anything."

~~~~~~~

"I just love being a senior, don't you?" Ellen asked cheerfully.

81

Martha said nothing. Ellen didn't seem to notice.

"I mean, here we are at the pinnacle of our lives. Twelve years of school almost behind us, our lives stretching out just ahead." She sighed. "But it's sad, too, y'know? Our childhood gone forever. A bittersweet moment of life."

Martha hated these melodramatic moods.

"To think of our childhood friends practically all grown up and going off in so many directions, each seeking their own fate . . . " She looked sideways at Martha. "By the way, how come you never told me you planned to graduate in January?"

"I didn't think you'd be interested."

"Why, Martha, how could you think that?"

~~~~~~~

"Hi, Martha. I was just in the neighborhood and I thought I'd stop by and say hi." Andy kicked lamely at the doormat.

"Uh, come on in. I was just doing some homework. Test tomorrow."

He followed her into the living room. "Yeah," he nodded. "Me, too. History."

"Mine's math."

They sat rigidly on either end of the sofa, looking everywhere but at each other.

"Want something to drink?"

"Uh, no thanks."

Silence.

"Great assembly the other day, wasn't it?"

"Yeah. Great."

Silence.

"So, you have a history test tomorrow?"

"Yeah." He suddenly turned to face her. "Look Martha, there's something I have to talk to you about. We haven't known each other very long, but . . . Martha, do you feel like we're friends?"

Martha stared at the coffee table, at the cover of her math book, at her scratch paper doodles, at her pencil. "Yeah."

"Me, too. I mean, I like you more than any girl I've ever known. Maybe it's because we like a lot of the same things, or maybe because you don't pretend around me—most girls aren't real around guys, y'know. Maybe it's because I feel as if I don't have to pretend to be someone I'm not for you to like me. I mean, it seems as if you like me for who I am, not just because I'm a guy and you're a girl. So I want to be honest with you, I want to tell you the truth."

Oh, shit. Her eyes fastened on the nick in the coffee table. It looked sort of like a tiny canoe poised on the edge of a giant shiny lake, forever falling . . .

Andy poked at a frayed place on his jeans.

"So, what does that mean?" Martha asked faintly, already sure she knew what that meant.

He scratched his ear and ruffled a hand through his hair. "Well, haven't you ever wondered why I never, uh, asked you out alone?"

She blushed. And then shrugged. "I thought you and Bonnie were . . . "

"Yeah, that's what I wanted people to think. But the truth is . . . Martha, I'm gay."

"What? But I thought . . . Oh, Andy, that's great!"

"It is? Huh! I sure never expected that reaction."

"Yeah, well, see I thought . . . well, actually Ellen thought . . . and I'm so glad you don't because I don't . . . I mean, I was afraid you wanted . . . and I didn't want to hurt your feelings but . . . "

"Oh!" Now Andy blushed. "I do like you, Martha, but not like that. Steve and I . . . "

"That's why all the double-dating, the group things! You and Steve . . . "

"Yeah. So no one has to know."

Martha's eyes narrowed. "What about Bonnie and Cheryl? Do they know, or have you just been using them . . . "

"No! They know about us. We've all been friends forever, that's why we started going out together in the first place. And then, people began to assume . . . and it's turned out good for all of us."

"How about Ellen and Mark?"

He shook his head. "I'd just as soon they didn't. It's not that I'm ashamed or anything—it's just that other people don't always see it the same way and we could get in a lot of trouble . . . "

"So, do your parents . . . ?"

"They don't want to know. I don't exactly fit the stereotypes so it's easy for them to pretend. And right now, it's easier on me if they don't."

They were quiet for a while. Martha stared out the window. When she looked back at him, Andy had crossed his legs and was playing with his shoelaces. He felt her glance and flashed a slow smile that made her throat constrict. Sometimes he looked so much like Bobby . . . but he was not Bobby. That was then.

"So, have you always been gay or is this a recent thing? I mean, if you'd made out with girls or something, would you have . . . "

He laughed. "You're kidding, right? It doesn't work that way, Martha. It's just a part of me, like having blue eyes or size eleven feet. And no, if I'd made out or even "done it," I would still be who I am."

She nodded. "Well, thanks for telling me, Andy. I'm glad you trust me."

"I figured, since you're gonna be working with us . . . And besides, it's kinda hard, keeping who you are a secret from your friends."

~~~~~~~~

"I just couldn't wait to show you!" Ellen shoved her hand in front of Martha's face.

"Very pretty." Martha glanced at the ring and turned back to her locker.

"Mark and I are now officially engaged! Isn't it wonderful?"

"You're planning a long engagement, I assume?"

"Well, we're going to finish school, if that's what you mean. We're planning a June wedding, right after graduation."

"Does Mark have a job lined up? I heard he was playing for State next year."

"He is. He got a football scholarship. And he's already got a job, he works at the Pizza Palace just off campus. Oh, Martha, you're being such a pain! I want you to be happy for me, to congratulate me. Please be happy for me, Martha!"

Martha stared at the vents in her locker door. Four slits at the top, six at the bottom. The paint was chipped on the bottom one. She couldn't look at Ellen.

"I think getting married so young is a mistake. And getting married to someone whose big ambition is to play pro-football and whose only source of income is as a part-time pizza maker, I think that's a bigger mistake." She closed her locker gently and turned to leave.

"You sound like an old lady, you know that? You're just saying all this because you don't have a boyfriend. You don't know what it's like to be in love! I'm beginning to think what's being said about you is true."

Now Martha did look at her. "What's being said about me, Ellen?" she asked quietly.

Ellen stuck out her chin defiantly. "Everyone thinks it's pretty strange that you don't go out. You don't go to the dances, you don't have a boyfriend, you don't even date! Well, people are beginning to talk about you."

"And what are they saying?"

"Some people are saying . . . that you must be a . . . well, they just think it's strange!"

Martha stared at her coldly. "Some people think all sorts of crazy things, don't they?" She held Ellen eye-to-eye until Ellen finally looked away. In the same tone she said, "Congratulations on your engagement, Ellen," then turned on her heel and walked away.

~~~~~~~~

"Steve is okay with this, isn't he?" Martha grabbed an arm load of tools out of Andy's van.

"Of course. As a matter of fact, it was his idea. We've talked a long time about hiring someone else. It just isn't good business to turn away customers because we can't handle it all."

"It's just that he doesn't talk to me much and I though that . . . "

"He's just kinda quiet. It's nothing personal, I know he likes you okay. So, what d'you say we get to work, partner?" He slung a long, braided extension cord over his shoulder and headed for the marina gate.

Suddenly, the latch on the toolbox Martha carried gave way, spilling tools all over. Martha tripped and sprawled face down amid the mess. Andy ran over and helped her to her feet.

"Knock, knock," he grinned.

She gave him a withering look.

"Knock, knock," he repeated.

"Who's there?" she asked sourly, brushing herself off.

"Andy."

"Andy who?"

"Andy to 'ave around, aren't I?" he laughed.

"Yuck, yuck. Why don't you really give me a hand and pick up some of this stuff?"

He bent down and picked up a screwdriver. "It may have been bad, but I gotcha!"

~~~~~~~~

"Isn't it just the scandal of the century?" Ellen sounded melodramatic again.

"What?" Martha absent mindedly took her jacket out of her locker. She hung it up again and reached for her books.

"Didn't you hear anything I said?"

Martha looked at Ellen directly. "No."

"Honestly! I'm beginning to wonder about you. You seem a million miles away lately. I was talking about Bonnie and Cheryl!"

"What about them?"

"They were caught kissing! Each other!"

"Yeah, so what? Besides, it's probably just a rumor."

"Cindy saw them—behind the bleachers during the fourth quarter of the football game! We're all changing tables in the cafeteria." Ellen looked smug.

Martha hated the tone in Ellen's voice.

"Are you upset that they were kissing, or that they weren't watching wonderful Mark make his famous fourth quarter touch-down?"

Ellen looked shocked and surprised. She started to say something but didn't.

Martha closed the locker loudly.

As they entered the cafeteria with their full trays, the long table that was their usual hang-out was empty of all but two. Martha deliberately headed in that direction.

86

"Martha!" Ellen hissed. "Martha, don't!"

"Hi!" she said cheerfully as she slid into her customary seat. "What's new?"

Cheryl choked on her food.

Martha went on, seemingly unaware of the confusion and comment her choice of seats was causing. "That civics test was the pits, wasn't it? I couldn't figure out number fourteen. Did either of you understand it? What did you put for seventeen? I don't think he covered that in class."

Bonnie looked at Cheryl. Cheryl looked at Martha. "Why are you sitting here?"

"This is where I always sit." Martha went on eating. "Besides, everyone knows Cindy stretches the truth sometimes."

"She isn't this time."

"So, not everybody knows that. Unless you tell them."

Bonnie and Cheryl looked at each other again. "Why are you doing this?"

Martha shrugged. "I like to sit with my friends. Andy told me about him and Steve weeks ago—I should've put two and two together then." She grinned. "That makes four, you know. As in, double-dating . . . " She waited, and shrugged again when they didn't get the joke. "Besides, I frankly don't give a good goddamn what they think of me since I'm outta here in January. Say, if you don't want the rest of your pie, can I have it?"

Bonnie wordlessly passed the pie.

~~~~~~~~

"To tell you the truth, Martha, I'm kinda relieved Ellen decided not to come along." Andy looked apologetic.

She shrugged. "Yeah, well, actually, I didn't ask her. With how she reacted to Bonnie and Cheryl, it was only obvious how she'd be about you and Steve. I just didn't think it would be fair to you guys, or to your friend, Keith. I mean, he's being nice enough to take us sailing, he shouldn't have to put up with her shit."

Andy nodded and tactfully changed the subject. "You said you've never been on a boat before?"

She shook her head. "I don't count the boat ride at Disneyland. Do you think we might really see a gray whale?"

"It's a little early still, but yeah, Keith said we might."

The cool morning haze still lingered over the water, making everything mysterious and magic. As they got underway, sounds were muffled but clear, and voices seemed to hang in the air. The coastline receded, then disappeared, and as if on cue, the sun popped out and the haze burned off to reveal a crisp blue day.

"Okay," Keith instructed Andy, "drop the mainsail." He nodded to Steve. "Loosen the jib line so the jib luffs—that means 'flaps' for the uninitiated among us. We'll use just the jib and the rudder to keep our position or in case we have to do any light maneuvering. I want to be as still and unobtrusive as possible."

"Anything I can do?" Martha was eager.

Keith shook his head. "First time out you're a passenger, next time, you're crew. But keep your eyes peeled. I've a feeling the Gray's are coming through early this year. I've heard them calling the past few days."

"You live that close to the beach?"

"I hear them here," he tapped his forehead. "Not here," he pointed to his ears and grinned at her obvious confusion. "Whales are telepathic, y'know."

She couldn't tell if he was teasing or if he was crazy enough to believe that, so she just smiled politely. "Why do Gray whales come here every year?"

"They don't come here. They pass by on their way south. They're headed for the warmer waters of Baja—Scammon Lagoon to be exact—to mate and calf. We just have the great good fortune to be on their route."

Martha leaned back and closed her eyes. Inhaling deeply, she released her breath slowly, trying to imagine the feel of gliding gracefully through the ocean, day after day.

Steve nudged her. "Look."

Off the starboard side, Martha noticed a thin column of mist slowly fading as it dispersed. Too far away to see the great back breaking the surface, huge curving flukes gracefully rose up high and sank.

"Will there be more?" Martha asked when she could speak.

"Most likely," Keith answered without taking his eyes off the water. "The first ones are usually females ready to calf and they seldom travel alone."

Martha watched eagerly now, trying to peer beneath the surface, hoping for a closer look. Another column of mist rose, near enough this time to hear the whew! of expelled air. Suddenly, a large, liquid grey eye was staring deeply into her two smaller ones. The whale came close—she could almost reach out and touch the barnacle-encrusted jaw. The whale floated for a moment on its side, intently watching Martha. A thrill went through her, a feeling unlike any other. She couldn't willingly take her eyes away from the whale's, couldn't speak, could barely breathe.

"She sees into me." Martha's thoughts had become as slow as her breathing. "She knows me, knows who I am, what I am."

The whale made a small high-pitched sound as if in answer to her thoughts, turned slowly and was gone.

Keith stared in wonder. "What a gift!"

She returned his gaze and took a deep breath unable, unwilling, to speak.

~~~~~~~~

"Damn, I'm tired!" Martha collapsed, leaning against the coolness of the shiny silver mast.

"Buck up, kid." Steve handed her a cold drink. "We'll be finished with this by dark."

"And think of all that lovely green money we'll get," Andy added encouragingly.

"Yeah," Martha snorted, "fat lot of good it'll do me if I die from exhaustion."

Andy laughed. "But it's Saturday night and that means . . . pizza! I bet a large pizza with everything—hold the meat—would bring you around."

"Oh, yeah. Who's turn is it to buy?" Martha rubbed the cold can against her sweaty face.

"Mine," Steve answered, then shook his head. "But I gotta get home early tonight—visiting relatives. Distant girl cousins. My mom wants me to take them out, show them around. I think she thinks I need a little practice to get the idea . . . "

Andy's eyes glinted. "Maybe I should go along to protect you. Or at least my interests."

Martha chuckled. "Yeah, you could double-date—the two of you and the two cousins. At least you've got lots of experience at that."

Steve screwed his face up and looked embarrassed. "Uh, I don't think . . . "

"Relax, we were just kidding." Andy punched him on the arm. "I don't want to get near your cousins—or your parents. So, Martha, it'll be just you and me then. I'll spring for the pizza if you get the drinks."

Martha nodded but Steve still didn't look happy.

~~~~~~~~

Martha fiddled with the salt and pepper shakers as they waited for their pizza. "So, tell me the truth, Andy, do you think there's something wrong with me?"

"Yeah, your ears are crooked. What the hell kind of question is that, anyway?"

Martha shrugged. "It's just that I feel . . . out of sync, sort of. I mean, everyone else seems to have sex on the brain and I . . . well, I don't have any interest, y'know?" She lowered her voice. "You think maybe I might be . . . gay?"

"Do you think you're gay?"

She shrugged again. "I've been different my whole life. I've never fit in, never really belonged anywhere. For instance, do you know I don't like the Beatles? I'm probably the only kid in America who doesn't own a Beatles album."

"What has that got to do with anything?"

"It's just one indication among hundreds that I'm different. I think there must be something wrong with me. I've watched how you and Steve are together, I've seen how you look at him. I've watched Ellen and Mark. I've watched my parents. Hell, I've watched everybody—it's all I ever do, is watch. And it's clear that I'm missing out on something."

He shook his head. "I don't know whether you're gay or not, but I'm sure there's nothing wrong with you. Maybe you just haven't found anyone you're interested in."

"But, it's supposed to be hormonal!"

A number was called over the loudspeaker.

Martha stood. "That's ours. I'll get it."

"What's wrong?" Andy asked, as she dropped the pizza down with a heavy thunk.

"Mark is sitting at that booth over there, nuzzling the neck of a girl who most certainly is not Ellen!"

"Oh."

"What really pisses me off is she thinks this ass hole is a saint! He's probably going out with every girl in town!"

"I think the saint knows you saw him—here he comes."

"No doubt to beg me not to tell Ellen."

"Hi Andy, hi Martha!" Mark said cheerily. "I just stopped by to offer some advice."

"You want to offer me some advice?" Martha was incredulous.

His smile widened. "Yep. I want to advise you not to tell Ellen about this."

Martha snorted. "I can see why you'd be worried."

"Oh, I'm not worried about me. It's you I'm concerned about."

"Oh, really?"

"See, if you told Ellen you'd seen me with another girl, well frankly, she wouldn't believe you. In fact, she'd be very upset with you for lying about me. She'd think you were jealous and trying to break us up. It could very possibly end your friendship and I know you wouldn't want that. So if I were you, I'd consider my actions very carefully." He winked at her. "Bye, now."

"What a jerk!" Andy exploded.

"He sure is! And he's right, too!"

~~~~~~~

"Wasn't it great of the Coach to get us these tickets to Ocean Park?" Seventh-grader Becky Palmer was thrilled to be going anywhere with the older members of the swim team. "And I'm so glad you could come even though you're not officially on the team anymore."

"Me, too." Martha opened the map she'd been handed at the entrance.

Becky looked surprised. "Haven't you been here before?"

"Yeah, I came a couple of summers ago, with my parents, but that was before . . . " Her voice trailed as she studied the map.

"I came last summer, with my sixth grade class. I had a blast!"

Martha folded the map. "So, maybe your memory is better than mine. What do you recommend seeing first?"

Becky gave the offhand question serious thought. After all, Martha Henderson was asking her opinion! "Well, there's a tide pool area where you can pick up stuff—sea cucumbers and sea urchins and starfish. And there's a boat ride. And a whale show. But what I like best is the open pool where you can feed fish to the dolphin. Sometimes, they even come close enough to touch!"

"Sounds good to me, too. See ya later!"

"Wait, I'll go with you!"

As they approached the pool, all Martha could see was a dense crowd of people, all in shorts, Hawaiian-print shirts, and caps that said "Ocean Park," some with souvenirs stuck into their pockets and often with cameras around their necks.

She and Becky tried to wedge their way through to see the dolphin. They had to settle for peering around a little boy whose mother was holding him over the edge.

"Touch 'im, touch 'im, Brian! Hurry, touch 'im!"

"Noooo!" Brian wailed. "Noooo!"

"Brian, Daddy's taking a picture to send to Grandma. Be a good boy now and touch the dolphin. Wanta feed him a fish? Here, take the fish."

"Noooo!"

"Oh, for godsake! Okay, I'll do it! Here dolphy, dolphy! Come get a fish! Touch 'im now Brian! Got that Roger? Roger?!"

"I'm all focused now, Denise. Have Brian feed the dolphin. Denise, why is Brian screaming?"

"Oh, for godsake!" The woman yanked the still screaming child off the pool's edge and shoved through the crowd. A bewildered husband followed in her wake.

"But, we could have bought more fish! I had the camera all focused!"

Martha and Becky quickly slid into the narrow space vacated by Brian. The pool was a large oval, maybe fifty feet long and thirty feet wide, but what Martha noticed first was that it, in her opinion, held too many dolphin.

"They're wild animals, they're used to the whole ocean and this pool is so small!"

"But that makes it easier to pet them," Becky explained.

Martha made a disgusted face and turned back to the pool.

A dolphin swam up to her, mouth open, but as she had no fish, he turned away. Beside her, a woman with long nails and several ornate rings made a grab, leaving a long, ragged scratch down his side.

"Why don't they just stay out in the middle where no one can reach them?" Martha thought.

The dolphin who had been in front of her a moment before came back to face her. He stared briefly at her, then slowly moved to the center of the tank.

Martha then noticed a small boy reaching over the edge with a long plastic sword. He enthusiastically hit the dolphin with it.

"God, they're only safe at the bottom," she thought.

Still facing her, the dolphin sank down to the bottom of the pool. A few moments later, he surfaced and swam over to float in front of her once again. He exhaled directly into her face, his breath smelling like the salty sea breeze with just a pleasant hint of fish. At first, she thought the air just happened to blow in her face, but then he moved to the right, in front of Becky and exhaled again. The expelled air hit only Martha. He circled the pool slowly and came back to stop in front of her. Listing slightly to one side, he looked directly into her eyes. The same intense feeling washed over her that she had experienced with the Gray whale that day on Keith's boat. Her own breath caught in her throat and her whole body tingled with the feeling of being absolutely understood, of being completely and utterly cared about for herself, just who she was. It reminded her of something . . .

Suddenly the people, the yelling, the poking no longer mattered. She was aware only of the dolphin, how they swam together, the sounds they made, their breathing, the smell of fish and saltwater. She was only dimly aware of Becky leaving to go see one of the shows, of people shifting around her.

At one point, she heard people shouting and laughing and became aware that she stood alone at the pool's edge, drenched, while two dolphin raced, creating waves that splashed up and over, soaking her again and again. She loved it—the water, the energy, the raw power of their bodies! She longed to be in there with them, to race, to play, to laugh out loud with the joy she felt. She pushed her hands far out into the water and as they rushed past, the dolphin leaned into her hands so that she stroked the length of their bodies on each pass. The merest touch filled her with such delight that at last she did laugh, never noticing when others stared at her strangely.

Becky found her still in the same position hours later.

"Come on! You forgot to meet at the clock tower at four. It's time to go. Coach says come now or walk home. Martha, come on!"

All the way home everyone laughed and shared the exciting experiences of their day. Martha sat alone, dripping onto the seat, staring out the window and seeing dolphin eyes.

Chapter Five

Martha leaned against the rough cinder-block wall while her college classmates milled around waiting for scuba class to begin. On the other side of the pool, a playful scuffle led to a loud splash and lots of laughter as a wide-chested young man was pulled from the water by his friends. She adjusted the elastic straps of her bathing suit and wiggled her bare toes in a tiny, cold puddle of water. A young woman with short, curly hair separated herself from the crowd and walked towards her. Martha recognized her as someone from her marine biology class.

"Hi," the newcomer smiled, "I'm Karen. I'm glad to see someone here that I almost know. And I'm sure glad I'm not the only woman in Bradford's class!"

"I'm Martha Henderson."

"Your first semester here, huh?"

"How'd you know?"

Karen smiled. "I saw your books in the locker room. Nobody takes Irwin's freshman biology class if they know better."

"That bad?"

"Worse. He's old, he's boring, and he hates women—thinks we should all be home having babies, not taking up valuable space in the science classes."

Martha shrugged. "It's the only regular biology class I could squeeze in and still take marine biology this semester. Do you know anything about this instructor?"

Karen shook her head. "I've heard she's tough. And I believe it since she's having us suit-up the first day! But you'll like Bradford's class—I had him last semester for physical oceanography. I also saw a western civ book in that stack of yours. Do you have Martin or Williams?"

"Williams."

Karen nodded. "She's good. She's well-traveled and shows slides, makes it interesting."

The instructor's arrival interrupted their conversation. Though not overly tall or pretty, Chris Palmer had a presence, an energy striking enough to attract everyone's immediate attention. She looked over the group and when her eyes landed on Martha, she smiled and nodded.

Martha was startled, confused at being so singled out. She didn't have much time to dwell on it, but she did have time enough to notice that Chris Palmer had the most beautiful lacy-blue eyes she'd ever seen. And she wanted her to smile again.

"Good afternoon, this is scuba class, otherwise known as Physical Education number one-fifteen. I'm sure you're all eager to get started, so we'll go over the boring part quickly. Pay close attention, as I do not repeat myself and mistakes are not tolerated in this class.

"Men: swimming trunks, not racing trunks. Women: one-piece suits." She held up her hand to silence the groans. "And anyone with hair past shoulder length is to have it tied back or in some way restricted. I know Hollywood makes it seem romantic to have long, loose hair floating all around, but in this class it's a safety hazard and we're not here to impress anyone.

"I grade individually on attendance, test scores, and class participation. I do not grade on a curve. Anyone missing a dive will drop grade, miss two and you're out. Any safety violation—I do mean any—and you're out." She glanced towards the still-dripping youth who had either fallen or been pushed earlier. "I tolerate no horseplay and no goofing around. My decisions are final and there are no second chances. Adds and drops, see me after class—which reminds me, as you leave the locker rooms, you will see a sign-in sheet and several stacks of handouts. Be sure to sign in—legibly—and pick up the handouts. You are responsible for knowing the information contained in them by next class. Okay, let's get on with today's work. You may have noticed . . . "

The same damp young man stepped forward with a bold grin. "So when do we actually get to dive?"

She looked him straight in the eye. "When I decide you're ready." She turned back to the others, no smile lighting her face now. "You may have noticed I'm big on safety. If not, you should have. Some people have labeled me a tough instructor. Well, I hope so, because in a few short weeks you'll be on your own, facing a much tougher instructor than I could ever be.

"The ocean tests us each time we come to her. Experienced or inexperienced, she challenges us each and every time, requires us to be all that we can be not only physically, but in our hearts and minds as well. Her tests are individually designed to find our hidden flaws and our inner strengths, and she waits to catch us off guard.

"In this class, we learn to plan for the unexpected. We find our own weaknesses and build them into strengths, *before* it becomes a life or death matter. Today we begin with endurance. For the next forty-five minutes you are to swim or tread water. No floating. If, at any point, you feel unable to continue, come out and do some light stretches. You are not being graded on this, but I expect you to do your best. Ready? Into the pool!"

Martha had worked on endurance often, but of necessity had concentrated on her speed. She worked now on pacing herself, realizing just how long three-quarters of an hour would be.

Fifteen minutes later she heard sputters and coughs and knew that some were already out of the water.

She flipped over onto her back to work another set of muscles. However, her backstroke wasn't very good even when she was at her best, so it didn't take long before she lost her sense of direction and bumped into another swimmer.

"Sorry," she exhaled, and rolled back over again swimming freestyle, becoming aware as she did so of the radically diminished number still in the pool.

Fifteen minutes more and it was down to her, Karen, and three others.

With ten minutes still to go, Martha's arms and legs felt leaden and her vision had narrowed to her immediate surroundings. She knew she was allowed to tread water, but it had become a matter of pride to finish her time swimming. The clock was not going to beat her.

Five minutes later she was swimming so erratically she again bumped into someone, unaware they were the only two left in the water. She swam on, her conscious mind exhausted by the effort of breathing, of keeping her body moving. Her world had become just the space her body occupied in the water. She never noticed when she became the last one in the pool.

The whistle caught her in midstroke. She leaned back, too exhausted to groan, and let the water support her. Her breathing was now deafening in her own ears. She could feel heat rising from her exposed skin. But she had done it—she swam the whole forty-five minutes!

Sometime later, she became aware she was chilly and slowly made her way to the side, gratefully accepting the hand that pulled her from the water and the big towel that felt so comforting around her shoulders.

"Good job." Chris Palmer led her back to the locker room that everyone else had long since vacated.

Martha sighed. "I'm not a distance swimmer, that's for sure."

"You did what you set out to do, that's all that matters."

The instructor took her directly to the showers. As Martha adjusted the temperature, Chris massaged protesting muscles in arms, shoulders, and legs until Martha's tired body felt as if it might someday belong to her again. She became aware once more of those lacy-blue eyes and warm hands on her calves.

Chris straightened up abruptly. "When you've dressed, come on down to my office."

This took longer than Martha expected. Getting dressed was no easy task with muscles that quivered like jelly. Walking became an exercise in will power.

Before she even got through the door, Chris handed her a tall glass filled with a yellowish liquid.

"Drink."

Martha sniffed it. "What's in it?"

Chris laughed and those blue eyes flashed. "You're not as bad off as I thought. Lemon, honey, salt, some trace minerals, and distilled water. Drink it." She motioned to the chair next to her desk.

Martha sat down and took a cautious sip, then drained the glass.

Chris refilled it. "I was pleased to see you in the class." At Martha's quick glance she added, "Becky Palmer is my little sister. Since I go to all the meets, I feel as if I've known you a long time. You're something of a hero to her, you know."

She hadn't known. "Becky's a good kid," Martha said sincerely, "and she's a heck of a good swimmer."

"I'll tell her you said that."

Martha stared at the glass in her hands, all at once uncomfortable. Was she getting the star treatment? People might resent . . .

Chris gently took the empty glass from her. "It's my job, Martha, to make sure my students are in good health before and after they come to class. All of them."

"Oh. Of course." Even though she hadn't wanted special attention, that answer disappointed her. She stood up. "Well, thanks for the help. I was really wiped out!" She stopped at the door. "Why did you have us do that today? I mean, forty-five minutes is incredibly long, and on the first day . . . "

"I've found it weeds out the curious from the serious. It also gives me an accurate idea of people's skill levels. And it challenges limits. I'm a firm believer in challenging limits."

Martha sighed. "I think I found one of mine today."

Chris looked surprised. "Really?" She shook her head. "I'm not so sure. Give it some more thought and let me know what you decide."

Martha smiled weakly and waved.

Karen was sitting on the grass just outside the gym. She stood up when Martha came out. "That was pretty impressive."

"I don't feel too impressive. I'm just glad I don't have another class right now."

"Wanta go for a soda or something?"

Martha shook her head. "I wanta go home."

"Another time, then. See ya Thursday."

Martha nodded wearily and headed towards the bus stop.

"Hey, wait! Do you need a ride?" Karen called.

"It's okay, the bus'll be here soon."

"C'mon, you can't tell me you'd rather ride the bus."

"I don't want to impose . . ."

"I wouldn't have offered if I didn't want to."

Martha smiled. "Okay, I would like a ride. Thanks."

"Anytime."

~~~~~~~~

Andy leaned back with a sigh. "I'll sand this later, it's . . . " he wiggled his eyebrows meaningfully, "launch time!"

Steve groaned.

Martha winked at him and grinned at Andy. "Oh, yeah?" She thought fast. "Well, canoe finish it quickly?"

"Yeah, the schooner the better, I always say."

"Andy, I never thought you'd sloop so low as to use old cliches."

"Uh, uh . . . "

Martha laughed. "Gotcha! So, whose turn is it to buy the pizza tonight?"

"Mine," Andy answered around a mouthful of sandwich.

"Uh, sorry guys, I gotta skip out early again tonight," Steve shook his head.

"Puns getting to you, huh?"

"No, that's not it. Family stuff, you know how it is."

Martha nodded. "But I'm not letting you off the hook, Andy. It's still pizza as usual."

"Yeah, well, next time maybe I'll have some family stuff going on, too. Then Steve can pick up the tab." He laughed but there was a slight edge to his voice.

Steve looked uncomfortable. Martha looked away. Neither of them said anything.

~~~~~~~~

Martha put her pencil down and rubbed her eyes. She glanced across at Karen, two rows over. Karen appeared so confident, so sure as she wrote down another answer. Noticing Martha watching her, she grimaced and held her nose, pointing to the test.

Martha nodded and looked away, suddenly embarrassed to be caught staring. Her heart raced and she felt her face flush as she turned her attention back to the test.

After class, Karen caught up with her. "What a pain! Where'd he dig up those questions, anyway?"

"You looked like you were doing okay."

"Yeah, but gone are the carefree days of my youth—I think I aged ten years over that one. I'm so far gone that only a large pizza will revive me. How about you? Feel like some pizza?"

Martha surprised herself by shaking her head. "Not today, thanks."

Karen looked surprised, too. "Okay, well, see you Tuesday." She waved and headed toward the parking lot.

Martha watched her leave, embarrassed again and confused. What was wrong with her? She liked Karen. And she sure liked pizza. Why had she said no?

~~~~~~~~

The first one into the Park, Martha stuffed her annual pass into her backpack and hurried over to the dolphin pool. For that hour or so each morning while the first shows still held the early bird tourists' attention, Martha was alone in a world of sunlight, saltwater, and dolphin.

For some time she had mostly watched, learning to distinguish one from another, male from female. Then, as she began to understand some of the subtle nuances of sound and movement that was their language, she became less hesitant, less shy. Now, she leaned as far out into the pool as she could, the rough concrete hard against her rib cage, her arms stretched out, hands cupped invitingly.

She spoke softly the names the trainers had given them, and it didn't seem unfitting that the trainers had named them after Greek gods and goddesses. Sadly, she didn't know their real names, the ones their mothers had given them, or even if she could have pronounced them.

They came one by one to be stroked and caressed, floating cradled in the arc of her arm. Wriggling in sensuous delight, they obviously took as much enjoyment from her touching as she received from touching them.

As he had done on so many mornings recently, Apollo swam up, mouth slightly opened, and tried to suck her fingers into his mouth. She instinctively jerked away. He moved aside, mouth closed, a look of sadness and entreaty plain in his eyes.

"Don't you understand fear?" Martha asked him miserably. "I'm afraid to do that. Part of me knows you won't hurt me, but I'm still scared. Why do you do this every day? Why is this so important to you?"

Suddenly, it was as clear as if he'd spoken words. Every day they opened their bodies to her, took pleasure in her touch and shared that pleasure back with her. Every day they trusted her, trusted her to be different than the other humans they came in contact with. It was her turn to open, to trust.

She smiled thinly. "Okay, but I'm still afraid, y'know."

He did seem to know. The next time he swam close, he opened his mouth wide, giving her time to place her fingers gently inside, enough time also to see his teeth had all been filed down to jaw level. He slowly closed his jaws around her hand and, releasing several short bursts of air, pop . . . pop . . . pop, gave the dolphin equivalent of a chuckle. Martha, too, giggled as he wiggled his tongue back and forth tickling her palm. She relaxed, really knowing he was not going to hurt her.

"What the devil are you doing?" demanded a groundskeeper. "Get your hand outta his mouth! Ya wanta get bit?"

"He doesn't have any teeth," was the first thing that came to Martha's mind.

"Teeth, hell! His jaws could crush your bones just like that!" To illustrate, he snapped his fingers. "Get your hand outta there!"

She decided against telling him this was a moment of triumph Apollo had worked towards for many weeks. She tried to comply, but the dolphin held her hand firmly.

"Listen, kid, you take your hand outta his mouth right now or I'm calling Security!"

She noticed the mischievous gleam in Apollo's eye. "This is no time to be cute," she muttered. "I'm about to be in real trouble." She tugged on her arm. Apollo chuckled.

"All right, that's it!" The man turned away.

"No, wait! Just a minute, he'll let go in a minute!"

"What? You mean he's holding you? That settles it! I'm getting a trainer." He eyed her suspiciously. "And Security."

The man left. The dolphin let go—and floated just beyond reach, eyes twinkling, waiting for Martha's reaction.

She wasn't laughing. She just stared at him, mouth ajar. Had that been a joke?

A small blue cart approached carrying a blue-uniformed man in hip boots.

"Any problems here?"

"No, sir."

He nodded approval of that answer. "Glad to hear it. Just one thing, though. Occasionally, a dolphin will take a playful little nip at someone and you know how people are, they misunderstand and think the dolphin is trying to hurt them. Gives dolphin a bad name, if you know what I mean. We try to discourage that sort of play. You'll remember that, won't you?"

"Yes, sir."

"Good. Have a fun day."

She looked back at Apollo. He was still there, watching her—she fancied he was smiling.

~~~~~~~~

Martha sat by the edge of the pool, waiting for class to begin. She stretched to the left, held it, then stretched to the right. She bent all the way forward and rested her forehead against her knees, feeling the gentle pull on her muscles all the way down her back. She had the strange sensation of someone watching her. Straightening up, she noticed Chris Palmer standing just a few feet away. Those intense blue eyes held hers for an instant with an energy that took Martha's breath away, then abruptly Chris turned and blew her whistle, calling everyone over to the side. Martha swallowed hard against the fluttering in her stomach and wondered what, if anything, that look had meant to Chris.

~~~~~~~

Karen poured half a bottle of ketchup over her fries. "So, what prompted you to graduate early and enter the hallowed halls of higher education?"

"I wanted to study oceanography."

Karen nodded and cocked an eyebrow. "Well, yes, I already figured out that much. But why? Why Martha does what she does is the mystery. And I'm dedicated to solving mysteries, you know."

Martha shrugged. "There's no mystery. I just wanted to, that's all."

Karen shook her head. "I'm a big Sherlock Holmes fan, watched all the old Basil Rathbone movies when I was a kid. There's always a motive, Dr. Watson, always a reason no matter how elusive or obscure . . . "

Martha smiled and relaxed. "Well, Holmes, let me put forth another mystery that only you can solve: What of Karen? What is she about and why does she ask so many questions of others while revealing so little about herself?"

Karen laughed. "Okay, but I expect a good story from you since I have to wait." She stopped smiling and poked at the ice in her glass. "Well, I have an older sister, Laura. She's deaf. Only, my parents didn't want a deaf child, so they just pretended she wasn't. They spoke slowly and expected her to lip-read. Lipreading is very difficult and not all deaf people can do it . . . Laura can't. So, when that didn't work, they sent her to a special school that promised to teach her to talk. She was born deaf, she's never heard a sound, but these people swore to my parents that Laura could learn to talk, which just played into their belief that she could be 'normal.'"

"When I was old enough to be interested in communicating, Laura and I worked out this great sign language system. It was the first time Laura had been able to talk to anyone. But my parents found out and quickly put a stop to it—so they thought. They had decided that if we signed, Laura wouldn't feel the need to learn to communicate 'properly.' Can you imagine what it was like—having to sneak to talk to my own sister?

"When I was in, I guess it was fifth grade, the special-ed teacher at my school taught me American Sign Language. And at night, we'd make a tent with the covers and by flashlight I would teach Laura what the teacher taught me.

"Then one day, Laura was about sixteen, she got really sick—extremely high fever, vomiting—and they rushed her to the hospital. Spinal meningitis. The doctor said if they hadn't brought her in when they did she probably would have died. See, if they had known Sign, Laura could have told them when she first started feeling sick."

"Why didn't she tell you?"

"At first, because she didn't want to get me in trouble. Later, she was too sick. But it worked out for the best. When my parents realized they'd almost lost their daughter, they decided signing probably wasn't all that bad. Anyway, that explains what I do. I'm an interpreter. And I'm going for my teaching degree so I can work with deaf kids."

"That's an incredible story. So how does oceanography fit in?"

Karen thought for a minute. "It's difficult to put into words . . . The oceans are so vast, the enormity gives me a sense of what it must be like to be deaf in a hearing world. When I'm skin diving, I can see the beauty in deafness, like the seaweed dancing or rays of light swimming—it's like signing music. Sign isn't words, y'know, but concepts communicated visually with movement and . . . well, words are a poor substitute." She leaned back. "So, what about you?"

Martha began uncertainly, with lots of shrugs and little eye-contact, putting her feelings into words for the first time. Encouraged by Karen's warmth and openness, she was soon leaning forward, gesturing animatedly.

"Wow! I'm impressed!" Karen said. "I've never even seen a gray whale, much less had one talk to me. You must be something special, Martha Henderson. If I hang around, think it'll rub off on me?"

Martha blushed.

104

She arrived early at the North Shore Marina to find the guys already there, pouring over a huge map spread out on the sidewalk in front of Andy's van. Seeing her, they hastily folded it up and Andy grinned a sheepish hello.

"What's up?" Now she was curious.

"Uh, nothing much. How about you?"

Martha just looked at them—the silence was not comfortable.

"Okay," Steve said finally, bringing his eyes up to meet hers defiantly. "Andy and I are kicking around the idea of refitting the van and traveling around some this summer. Kind of discovering America, you know, finding out what it's all about."

"Uh, huh. And who's going to look after business while you're gone? Were you planning on letting me in on this little secret, say, sometime before you left?"

Steve stuffed the map into his hip pocket and looked at Andy.

Andy looked at his feet. "Nothing's definite. We were gonna tell you just as soon as we had a real plan."

"Gee, thanks. Glad I didn't have any real plans for the summer."

"You don't, do you?" Andy sounded so eager, just like a little boy. So much like her broth . . .

She walked back to the van and yanked open the sliding door. "No, of course not." She grabbed a tool box and started down the ramp to the slips.

A dolphin floated by. She lazily reached out and stroked him.

"Hey Hermes, old buddy, how's it going?"

In answer, Hermes took a mouthful of water and squirted her. Not to be outdone, she cupped her hand and playfully squirted him back. He squirted her again. She squirted him. He rolled to one side and slapped the surface with his pectoral flipper, soaking her. Laughing, she used both hands to make a big splash, splattering water down his whole length. He turned away.

"Hermes! Don't be pissy, I was just playing! C'mon back!"

He stopped. With a quick nose dive, his flukes arched high into the air and, with a sharp flick of his strong muscles, they came down like a wide flat paddle sending water flying everywhere.

"You win!" Martha sputtered, wiping water from her eyes. Hermes chuckled and swam to the other end of the pool.

~~~~~~~~~

"Did you hear what happened?" Karen dropped her books on the cafeteria table with a loud plop.

"No, what?" Martha mumbled around a mouthful of food.

"All the frogs for Irwin's biology classes—almost three hundred of 'em—mysteriously disappeared overnight! So did the mice and rats for his special projects. Boy, is he pissed! I heard him yelling clear down in the Fine Arts building this morning. You have Irwin, don't you? Well, you won't be dissecting frogs this morning. Say," her eyes narrowed as she noticed Martha's bland expression, "you know something about this."

Martha calmly continued eating her sandwich. "How would I know anything about it?"

Karen nodded. "Okay, fine. But whoever liberated the lab ought to know Irwin's out for blood."

Martha nodded and peeled an orange. "Wanta come over tonight and study for Bradford's test?"

Karen snorted. "Sure, as long as three hundred frogs aren't likely to jump out at me if I have to use the john."

Martha smiled serenely. "You don't have to worry about that."

~~~~~~~~~

Martha put down her biology book, her notebook, and her cookie and went to answer the door.

"Ellen!" Martha realized guiltily that she hadn't given Ellen much thought lately, hadn't even called her.

"I need to talk to you." The desperation in Ellen's voice broke through Martha's self-recriminations.

"Let's go up to my room."

Ellen collapsed on the bed. "Martha, I don't know what to do, who to turn to!" She swallowed hard. "I'm pregnant."

Martha sat down heavily on the floor.

"Have you been sick? Sometimes a fever . . . "

Ellen shook her head.

Martha pulled a slipper from under the bed and picked at the inside fuzz. "Does Mark know?"

Again Ellen shook her head. "I've been afraid to tell him."

"What'd your parents say?"

Ellen picked up Martha's pillow and hugged it to her. "Martha, I can't tell them, they'll disown me. I've been thinking of running away—but there's no place to go. I just don't know what to do."

Martha rolled the fuzz into a little ball and stared at it.

"I went to the Clinic, y'know, and they were real nice. They talked to me about my options and I decided to, uh, get rid of it. Y'know, an abortion. I was laying on the table, my feet in those awful things, a white sheet over me, in this ugly white room. They tried to make it pretty, but it was ugly. And it was cold. I'd already talked to the counselor and everything, I was sure I wanted to do it, but when I looked around that room, it was like . . . I couldn't go through with it. I felt so guilty. I mean, it's a real baby—MY baby. My parents are going to disinherit me, Mark's going to hate me, but I can't do it. I just can't and I'm so scared . . . "

Holding onto the pillow so hard her arms shook, Ellen soaked it with her tears while Martha made a bigger ball of fuzz and rolled it tighter and tighter.

Finally, Ellen sat up, wiping her face with her hand. Martha silently handed her a box of tissues.

"I'm sorry to come here and dump this on you. I just needed someone to talk to . . . " Ellen dabbed at her eyes. "Martha, things aren't turning out at all like I planned."

"So, what're you going to do?"

Ellen sniffed and tightened her lips. "I don't have a lot of choice, do I? I guess I'm going home, throw myself on their mercy." She shrugged and smiled thinly. "Hey, what's the worst they can do? Throw me out, right?"

Martha nodded and stared at the newly made bare spot inside her slipper.

~~~~~~~~

Chris hefted the heavy metal cylinder to her back, showing them how to properly position the tank, how to adjust the straps. Martha watched Chris's arms, her shoulders, her hands—the ease of long practice making her movements graceful.

"You're drooling again," Karen observed dryly.

"What?"

"Nothing." Karen shrugged and sighed. "Are you ready to practice?"

Martha nodded and picked up her tank, trying to make her hands move as smoothly as Chris's had.

~~~~~~~~

"Wait a minute," Martha said, holding up a jar. "Let me get this straight. This species of fish was thought to be extinct fifty years ago. Last year, a local marine biologist caught this one but instead of letting it go to mate and reproduce, he killed it—thereby practically insuring the extinction of an obviously endangered species. Is there something wrong with this picture, or what?"

"Miss Henderson, what you fail to understand is . . . "

"What I fail to understand, Mr. Bradford, is how we learn a life science by studying dead things."

"Live things very seldom allow us to put them under microscopes, Miss Henderson."

"That's just the point, Mr. Bradford. I question whether that's necessary. So much research has already been done—we have detailed drawings, x-rays, photographs, even movies of practically every species that has ever lived, I don't see why we can't use available resources and leave the poor animals alone."

"Thereby learning nothing new. You would have us back in the Dark Ages, guessing about the nature of things based only on the information we already possess."

"Isn't that what we do anyway?"

"Miss Henderson, an inquiring mind can be a blessing—or a curse. If you are serious about continuing in this field of science you will, at some point, have to rethink your position in this matter. At the

very least, you will learn to keep your opinions to yourself—
beginning now. If we may return to our work . . . "

Martha's face flushed—not from embarrassment this time. She
took a deep breath and counted the number of chairs in the room, the
number of chair legs, the number of people wearing tennis shoes.

Sometime later, she became aware of Karen watching her. She
pretended not to notice. After class, Karen waited at the door.

"I'm glad you spoke up. I never thought about that before."

"A fat lot of good it did."

"Maybe more than you know. At least, people will think about it."

Martha shrugged. "Maybe."

~~~~~~~~

She couldn't concentrate on her homework. She went out to the
hall, picked up the phone and dialed Ellen's number. Ellen's father
answered and said she didn't live there anymore, he didn't know
where she was, and he didn't care. He hung up on her. She stared at
the receiver for a long time until the dial tone became a piercing
whistle. Then she hung up and wandered into the kitchen where Jean
was preparing dinner. She bit her lip, and facing Jean, took a deep
breath. But then changing her mind, she slowly released her breath
and instead, grabbed an orange from the bowl on the table. She stared
at it for a moment, then replaced it and turned around and left the
kitchen. Upstairs in her room, lying across the bed, she stared at the
bare spot on her slipper.

~~~~~~~~

After her last class, Martha went back to her locker for her gym
clothes. She found her suit was there, but not her towel, and thinking
she must have left it by the pool, she headed that direction.

She had assumed that at this late hour the pool would be
unoccupied and was surprised to see someone swimming laps.
Whoever it was was good, Martha could see that. Tight turns, tiny
splashes, and concentrating hard enough not to notice her standing by
the door. Freestyle, breast stroke, back stroke, and then butterfly. As
the swimmer rose high on the down stroke, Martha could see the wide

shoulder muscles ripple with power. It took strength and skill to make the butterfly look that graceful. Martha couldn't stop staring. Then the swimmer pulled out of the pool on the far side, back turned to Martha, and walked over to the diving board. It was Chris Palmer. Standing on the platform, Chris noticed Martha watching her. In silence she paced to the end, jumped high into the air, and performed a near-perfect jack-knife, entering the water with very little splash. Martha felt her heart pounding, her blood racing.

Chris surfaced and swam over to the side and got out. She picked up her towel and walked over to Martha, a faint smile in her eyes. She said nothing, just stood there—probably not as long as it seemed to Martha. Embarrassed, Martha dropped her gaze. But that only made matters worse—her eyes fell to Chris's chest, erect nipples straining against wet nylon. So round . . . so hard. Martha's breathing became strained.

"Can I help you with something?" Chris finally broke the silence, eyes twinkling.

"Uh, uh." Martha swallowed. "My towel. I was looking for my towel. I think I left in here . . . somewhere . . . maybe . . . "

Chris swiveled her head and seeing no other towel around, indicated the one she held. "Is this it?"

Martha stared at it and nodded.

"Sorry, I didn't know. I'll take it home and wash it, how about that?"

Again Martha nodded. "Uh, thanks." She turned and not quite ran out the big double doors.

~~~~~~~~

Andy pulled up the emergency brake and motioned for Martha to get out. They were parked at the end of a narrow dirt road about twenty feet from a cliff edge, overlooking a long, deserted beach. The sun was just setting and the sky was a patchwork of pink, blue, and orange highlighted against billowy white clouds.

"It's a magnificent sunset Andy, but we could have seen it closer to home."

"Look just beyond the crests." He pointed to a large group of what appeared to be dolphin jumping into the building waves and riding the crests almost to the beach.

"They're bodysurfing!" she laughed. "They look black. I thought all Pacific dolphin were grey."

"They're not dolphin." Andy was pleased to know something Martha didn't. "They're porpoise—Pacific Whiteside. Their markings are very similar to killer whales." He held up his hand to forestall her protest, remembering she hated the name "killer."

"Sorry. I mean, they are similar to Orcas."

She smiled at his correction. "Do they play here often?"

"Anytime I've been by here at dawn or sunset, I've seen 'em. Here." He handed her a pair of binoculars. They watched until it was too dark to see.

On the way home she asked, "So you never did tell me, where was Steve today?"

"One of those family things . . ."

"His family's been doing a lot lately, huh? Must be hard for you."

Andy shrugged and didn't answer.

~~~~~~~~~

"And so, class, if we graph the answers to questions A-G like so, what we get is . . ."

Freckles. Karen had a cute spray of freckles across her nose—and the hint of a dimple when she smiled.

"And her hair always smells so good," Martha murmured.

Someone giggled in the now quiet room.

"What was that, Miss Henderson?" The teacher was looking expectantly at her. In fact, everyone was looking at her.

Her mouth tasted like cotton. She knew she was blushing.

"Uh, uh, nothing. Excuse me."

The instructor turned back to his diagram on the board. "Now, if we compare graph one with graph two . . ."

She stared straight ahead and tried to focus her attention where it belonged. God, what was wrong with her, anyway?

~~~~~~~~~

111

Ordinarily, nothing could have dragged Martha to Ocean Park on a weekend. She was absolutely repulsed by the tourist throngs so eager to snap pictures of the kids with a "killer" whale, no doubt intending to paste them in family albums along side the ones of the kids with Mickey Mouse. But this Saturday it was raining, a fine, cold February drizzle into which few but the dedicated were going to venture.

The dolphin were active, swimming in groups of two's and three's, too busy with each other to have much interest in Martha. From her close acquaintance with them, she understood that sexuality was not a weighty issue in their lives, their sensuality being an obvious part of everything they did. Sexuality was simply pleasurable, and dolphin were big on pleasure. Martha had learned more about how she believed sexuality should be expressed in people's lives from watching dolphin than from all the lectures and discussions she'd been subjected to by well-intentioned adults.

Strangely enough, watching them didn't embarrass her as had the rare occasions when she'd accidently seen dogs or cats mating. Perhaps it was because they weren't embarrassed or ashamed, or perhaps it was their easy acceptance of her passive involvement, but however it came about, she enjoyed watching their play, loved the electric energy that crackled on a day like today.

Apollo floated by on his back, pushing a small plastic lid around with his erect penis. He pushed it toward Martha who stood absent-mindedly dribbling the cold water through her fingers. He retracted his penis and rolled over to breathe. Swimming close, he leaned into her hands, listing to one side so she could reach his chest and belly. Startled, Martha felt the brush of his penis against her hand and jerked away. He looked at her quizzically and opened his mouth wide.

She shook her head. "I think this is going to take considerably longer than touching your tongue!"

He waited a while, seemingly to offer her a second chance, then returned to his solitary pursuit of the plastic lid, making a game of it, hooking the rim over his penis, pushing it high out of the water, then suddenly retracting his penis back into his body so the lid fell with a soft plop.

A well-dressed couple with a blonde, blue-eyed little girl in tow leaned over the pool. "Hurry up and touch one, Debbie, I want to get out of this rain," the man complained.

"What is he doing, Mommy? What's that pink thing?" the child innocently pointed.

Without a word, her parents took her hands and led her away.

"The dolphins are tired now, sweetheart, we need to let them rest."

"But, what was that pink thing? Was it a fish?"

Martha felt certain they would never tell her.

~~~~~~~~

The sudden coldness shocked her and the bubbles from her own entry momentarily disoriented her as she groped for the tether that trailed from the starboard side of the cruiser. Becoming accustomed to the shifting patterns of sunlight filtering down through the translucent grey-green, Martha realized something of what Chris must have meant when she said diving could be a total experience of self. A peaceful solitude as tangible as the surrounding water isolated each thought for individual examination and contemplation. She became acutely aware of minute details. Her blood pulsed in harmony with the life-rhythms of the ocean. Her breathing, loud in her own ears, matched the undulations of a kelp forest far below. She had a sense of herself as a small but infinitely important spark in a vast life-force, a harmony of interdependence with all living things.

Another student jumped into the water and startled her back to a more pragmatic level; it was time for class.

Once back on deck, Martha stayed slightly apart from the others, savoring her experience, not quite comfortable with the boisterous energy and loud voices. No one seemed to notice.

Then, from behind, she felt firm, warm hands on her shoulders. "So," Chris asked softly, "how was it?"

Somehow, Martha was not surprised by her instructor's question. She turned around and met the woman's eyes directly, openly. "It was incredible . . . it was . . . some people might call it a . . . religious experience."

Chris nodded, her eyes shining just as brightly as Martha's. "I tried to give you as long as possible before letting the others go in."

"You knew it would be like that?"

Again Chris nodded.

"It's like that for everyone, then?" Martha was both relieved and disappointed.

Chris shook her head. "No, Martha, not everyone. A very few. But I knew it would be for you. And I'm glad." She reached out and gave Martha's hand a squeeze, then turned away.

"Wait! How . . . ?"

"I just knew. You see, I had a . . . religious experience too, on my first dive. And Martha . . . the best part is, the feelings never fade, they're renewed with each dive. It just gets better and better." She winked at Martha and went to oversee the stowing of the gear.

Martha picked up her tank and followed.

Karen came up and touched her arm lightly. "Sometime I'd like you to tell me what happened to you down there. It's in your eyes, you know."

Martha smiled and nodded, still unwilling to put words to her experience.

~~~~~~~~

She idly scooped up water, dribbling it from one hand to the other. It had been a very busy morning at the dolphin pool but with the afternoon heat, the number of tourists had decreased and now she stood alone. The dolphin, well fed, swam slowly. Nothing held their attention for long. Hermes swam over and halfheartedly opened his mouth.

Martha shook her head. "What would you do with a fish if I gave you one?"

Hermes slowly floated away and just as slowly dove to the pool's bottom. He returned, carrying an uneaten fish. His mouth just under the surface, he squirted the fish toward her.

She grabbed it and offered it back to him. "Now hold on to it, silly."

He worked his pectoral fins and used the gentle current to move back a little and squirted it to her again, right into her hands.

114

"Oh!" She caught on and tossed it back to him.

He moved back a little more and sent the fish to her again. She returned it.

He moved back only a fraction this time, but his aim was off and the fish floated just out of Martha's reach. When she didn't immediately return it, he lost interest.

"Hey, I was just getting the hang of it!" Martha splashed at his retreating figure. He didn't return, but floated slowly, effortlessly away.

She went back to playing in the water, trying to aim her squirts more accurately, but not trying too hard.

~~~~~~~~

Martha squinted to see in the growing darkness. She was exhausted and there was still so much to do! "So where the hell is Steve tonight?" she growled.

"He's busy," Andy said curtly.

"Yeah, these days he's always busy. Funny how that is."

Andy threw down the sander. "Just what the hell is that supposed to mean?"

"It means he's off more than he works! It means Saturdays are our busiest time and we need him here!"

"Yeah, well, what do you think I can do about it? He's with his family, for chrissake!"

"Yeah, right. Every Saturday."

"What are you saying? You think he's seeing someone else, don't you? Well, you're wrong! He's with his family, that's where he is! Steve wouldn't lie to me. I can't believe you think he would."

Martha felt sick. "That's not what I meant, Andy. I just meant I think he's goofing off. That's all."

"Well, he's not." Andy picked up the sander and thumbed it to high.

~~~~~~~~

Ellen held up a glass and looked questioningly at Martha.

"Right side of sink, first shelf." She pointed with her chin, her hands full of dishes. "Cat, get out from between my feet!"

"This place is cute, Martha." Ellen put the glass away in its new home and unwrapped another. "And really, it's not much smaller than mine and Mark's."

"So, how are things going with you two?" Martha collapsed amid the boxes scattered around the kitchen floor. Cat ran right over and pushed her head into Martha's face.

"Oh, pretty good I guess." Ellen nodded to herself. "It's good. I don't get to see much of Mark these days, what with football practice and his double shift at the Pizza Palace. And of course, he has to keep his grades up to play in the games."

"Not to mention to avoid the draft."

They were quiet for a long while, only Cat's purring breaking the silence.

Ellen shrugged and stared at the pattern on the tile. "Actually, it's not so good. Not that it's bad . . . it's just not what I expected, y'know? He hardly ever talks to me anymore. We used to have so much fun, but now . . . And he hates the baby already. The first time I felt it kick I called him right up at work and he said, real sarcastically, 'Oh, how wonderful.' Whenever I want to buy anything for the baby, even diapers, he says we can't afford it—but he can always afford beer for his football buddies.

"Remember family planning class? I got an A in that class. Greg Fulton and I were partners. We organized the wedding, chose china patterns, picked out furniture to match our color scheme. I even learned how to keep to a budget. Mrs. Mitchell said we turned in the best report of the whole class. So, I had everything all planned out. I thought it would be like the class, like they said it would be . . . " She sighed. "But it's not like that, Martha, not at all.

"And no one calls, none of the old crowd. When I call them, they're always too busy or studying or doing entrance exams or something. It's like I don't fit in anymore. Or maybe they're just avoiding me, I can't tell. But it's hard, y'know?"

They were silent again.

At last, Martha looked up. "So, Ellen, where did General Washington keep his armies?"

"What?"

"Where did General Washington keep his armies?"

Ellen shook her head uncomprehendingly. "Valley Forge?"

"Huh, uh. In his sleevies!"

Ellen stared at her.

"Come on, Ellen, lighten up! Maybe you oughta go back to school, get a degree in something."

"Martha! I'm six months pregnant!"

"So, start after. But at least decide what you want to do with your life and then go after it. Don't sit around waiting for someone else to hand it to you."

Ellen shook her head. "College isn't for me. I hate school."

Martha shrugged.

She glanced at the clock. "Oh, shit! I'm supposed to be at the Half Moon Marina in five minutes!" She jumped up, dumping an indignant Cat to the floor. "I'm sorry Ellen, I completely forgot! I gotta run! But call me. Come by anytime." Martha grabbed her car keys and ran to the door.

"We're still getting together to do laundry Monday night, aren't we?" Ellen scrambled up after her.

"Sure, it's a date. Remember to lock up when you leave. See you."

~~~~~~~~

The morning was extremely hot and dry and reminded Martha that without man-made irrigation most of southern California would be a desert. Even the occasional breath of wind was arid, carrying with it the smell of sun-softened blacktop. She leaned against the pool's edge lazily dribbling water through her fingers. The glare off the water made her eyes ache, so she kept them half closed and downcast. Everything felt melted and slow.

Gradually, Martha became aware of a change in energy, tension in the air, a taut, stretched feeling. She looked around, yet nothing seemed out of the ordinary. The dolphin still languidly circled the pool. Hermes still napped alone out in the middle. A handful of people halfheartedly tried to entice the dolphin to come close. But there was a difference—Martha could feel it.

Suddenly, abruptly, Hermes lunged forward. He raced straight ahead at full speed and smashed into the concrete wall. Martha felt the impact in her own body—every muscle hurt, her head ached, and her lungs burned. Reeling, he turned and headed for the opposite wall. The other dolphin circled the edge more quickly, trying to form a barrier between Hermes and the wall. But again and again he found the gaps between them and rammed his soft flesh against the unyielding cement. Again and again, until his blood stained the water and his flesh hung in ragged strips.

Martha's held breath exploded. "What are you doing? Stop it! Stop it! Hermes! Listen to me! Listen to them! Stop! Whatever is wrong, we'll fix it! I swear to you, we'll fix it! Just stop! Oh, Hermes, don't! Please don't!" But she knew he couldn't hear her anymore.

She ran to the booth beside the pool and shoved through the line of people waiting to buy fish for the dolphin. Ignoring their complaints and shouts of "Hey, kid, get in line!," she pounded on the glass to get the attendants' attention.

"Call a trainer! Call a trainer, quickly! Hermes is trying to kill himself! Oh, hurry! Please hurry!"

The attendant informed her that dolphin often played roughly.

"Please don't argue with me—there isn't time! Just call a trainer! Hurry!"

She ran back to the pool. The dolphin now formed a tight circle around their friend, in front, beside, underneath. But it was no use. Hermes just ran over them. Again and again he smashed himself.

She ran back to the booth. Yanking the back door open, she grabbed at the phone.

"Hey!" The attendant tried to snatch the phone back.

"If you won't call, I will! He's dying!" Martha jerked the phone savagely. "He's killing himself and they can't stop him! Don't you understand—he's killing himself!"

"All right, all right! I'll call a trainer!" Clearly, he thought she was crazy.

Martha ran back to the pool. There was a calmness amid the desperation now. The other dolphin had withdrawn to the pool's center where they watched and waited, accepting Hermes' decision. As Martha stood by, powerless to stop him, Hermes continued his insane pounding until finally, with a plaintive little squeak, he released his last breath. His limp, battered body floated in a vertical position, leaning slightly backwards, jaws relaxed and above the surface, his lifeless eyes wide and staring.

Then, as Martha numbly watched, a woman stepped up and shoved fish into Hermes open mouth as his body floated near.

"Come on, swallow it," the woman laughed. "I won't give you any more until you swallow what you have."

The woman's smile quickly changed to an expression of annoyance. "Will you look at that, George? He's still begging for more with all that fish right there in his mouth! He won't even swallow it!"

She squealed with delight as she reached out and touched his flipper. "It's just like a wet inner tube, George! Oooh, look at his face! He must have been fighting . . . "

Martha vomited. She cleaned up as best she could at the drinking fountain, the cool water and abrasive paper towels helping to bring everything into sharper focus. Turning back around, she found everything just as it had been. But now the dolphin were humming. At least, it felt like humming—a vibration just out of the audible range seemed to fill the pool and spill over, traveling through her feet and hands to her very heart. She'd heard that sound before, or something like it, but just now she couldn't remember where; she could only listen and feel as it warmed and calmed her.

At long last the trainer arrived. With a look of annoyance, he went to the booth and used the phone. Martha hurried over. She asked what they would do with Hermes body.

"Oh, the vet'll do an autopsy, find out why he died," he answered without looking up.

Martha stared at him coldly. "I don't think you'll discover that by cutting up his body."

He looked at her now. "You're one of the regulars who come here a lot, aren't you?"

She nodded.

"Well, then, I'll level with you. Parasites are common in these animals. Parasites in the brain often cause abnormal, even bizarre behavior."

"Parasites? In a healthy body that you've been taking care of for several years?" She shook her head disgustedly. "I'm sure that will be found to be the 'official' reason."

Now his expression was severe. "Just what are you implying?"

"These 'animals,' as you call them, are confined in this little prison every day of their lives and you expect me to believe that parasites caused Hermes to commit suicide?"

The trainer snorted derisively. "Suicide? You people really get me! You come here, spend a couple of hours a couple of times a week, and you think you know everything. You live in some sort of fantasy world—you wanta make pets out of wild animals!" He shook his head. "If you'll excuse me, I have work to do."

"That's just it—they're not pets! And they're not wild animals, either! They're people!" she yelled at his back with sudden conviction, "with feelings and needs just like yours and mine! And you know he didn't die because of any parasites, either!"

A big yellow crane lumbered up and dropped a sling into the pool. Martha watched as they maneuvered Hermes' body into the sling and lifted it, dripping, from the tiny pool that had been his home for more than a decade. The crane rumbled away.

She turned back to the others. They still huddled together but the humming had stopped. They were closed to her now, as if she were a stranger. She waited a long time. Finally, not knowing what else to do, she picked up her backpack and went home.

~~~~~~~~

"So, will you come?"

"I don't know . . . what I've heard about women's liberation has really turned me off. I'm not into hating anyone or burning my bra."

"Do you believe everything you hear? You like me, don't you? I'm a feminist. Come on . . . it's just a rap group. We'll be talking about ourselves, not plotting to overthrow the government—we meet on Wednesdays for that." Karen's eyes twinkled. "What are you afraid of, anyway?"

Martha laughed. "I stopped taking dares a long time ago, Karen. Oh, all right. I only had homework to do anyway."

Fifteen women sat cross-legged or leaned against the colorful pillows that were piled everywhere on the floor. Some of the women were dressed in blue jeans and flannel shirts, a few wore long "hippie" dresses, and a couple of the older women wore polyester pantsuits.

120

Martha guessed the age range to be from mid-fifties to early twenties, and at nineteen she was almost certainly the youngest.

"Good evening," a tall attractive woman in blue jeans greeted them, "and welcome. I'm Barbara, the facilitator this evening. Tonight's meeting is open to new people, something we try to do about every six months and it will run as usual: Everyone gets a chance to speak—no one speaks twice before everyone has spoken once, no one speaks three times before everyone has spoken twice, and so on. Everything that goes on here is confidential, even to the names of the women present." She smiled warmly at each of them. "Tonight's topic is 'growing up female,' and since there're so many of us, let's keep the introductions brief.

"I'm Barbara," she repeated. "I was married for fifteen years, the classic stereotype of a suburban housewife. I drove the boys to Little League, my daughter to dance classes. I was vice president of the PTA four years running. Running—that's how I lived my life, running from the realization that I was miserable—because, I was miserable. Well, I'm an avid reader—an avoidance of reality you know—and one rainy day at the library I picked up some feminist stuff, quite by accident I assure you. Well, the more I read the more I saw ME in what I read. I didn't much like what I saw, but at least I began to see me, not Bob's wife, or Brian's mom, or even Edna's daughter.

"That was five years ago. I can't believe what a change there has been! I got rid of Bob," she grinned, "found a job that almost pays me what I'm worth, and began this CR group to help me sort out who I really am from who everyone has always wanted me to be. I think I've almost gotten that together now, but I still come here every Thursday night because I love the connection with other women, the closeness I feel here." She turned expectantly to the woman on her right.

"Well, I'm Melinda. I've been very happily married for four years, and we have a lovely daughter, Angela, who's three. Tom is away on business a lot and though I love Angela dearly, she's still only three. My friends are mostly mothers of young children and our conversations usually revolve around toilet training and tantrums and where to get the best deal on children's clothes. Some days I feel lost, like I don't exist outside of being a wife and mother. The other day, I even answered Tom's questions about our checking account in

121

rhyme, like Dr. Seuss. I think I need some time just for me and I thought I'd give this a try." She smiled shyly.

"I'm Rosa," the next woman said. "For me, growing up female was secondary to growing up Chicana in a white culture. Racism and sexism are all mixed up together for me. I'm also a lesbian, so there's that oppression to deal with, too. My lover keeps telling me that I should open myself to my white sisters, trust you more. So, here I am." She seemed embarrassed. "Wait. I don't mean 'here I am, prove I can trust you,' I mean, I think she's right and so here I am."

"I'm Karen. I'm also a lesbian. I'm here because I, too, like the connection with other women and because I never leave one of these meetings without feeling better than when I came in."

Suddenly, it was Martha's turn and she had no idea what to say—besides, she was busy assimilating the fact Karen had just said she was gay.

"Uh. I'm Martha. I thought I came to keep Karen from bugging me about it anymore, but now I realize that something has been missing in my life, too. Seems like I've always been takin' care of everyone else, an' when it's been my turn, when I've needed support, seems like ever'one has had tons of ideas on how to fix up my life, mostly leadin' to: find a boyfriend, get married, an' have lots of babies. Nobody seems to care that I want somethin' different for myself. Seems like I've had to struggle against ever'one to get where I am. Well, I'm tired of strugglin'. An' if'n I'm hearin' right, that's what y'all are sayin', too. I guess I came here 'cause I needed to."

She surprised herself with such uncharacteristic candor and was more than a little embarrassed by it, but she looked around and saw smiling faces and nodding heads. Karen was grinning.

Karen's grin lasted all evening. On the way home she said, "So, you had a good time, didn't you? Aren't you glad I talked you into it?"

Martha chuckled at the friendly teasing. "Yes, I am. But it did hurt my feelings a little that you haven't told me you were gay before this."

Karen glanced at her. "I'm sorry. I just wasn't sure what reaction I'd get. I haven't had very good responses coming out to women who aren't out themselves yet."

"Who aren't out themselves yet . . . who aren't out themselves yet," seemed to echo in Martha's ears. Did that mean Karen thought she was gay, too?

"And speaking of secrets," Karen went on, "you led me to believe that you were a native Californian. Why haven't you ever mentioned you're from the South?"

"Huh? What brought that up? It's not a secret, just an unimportant fact of my past."

"Perhaps you aren't aware of it, but when you talk about your feelings or things that are important to you, your accent sneaks out. I've noticed it before, but tonight it was particularly strong."

"Do I have an accent now?"

"No, it's gone now. Why do you do that? Suppress it, I mean?"

"I don't know. I guess . . . well, you know how Rosa talked about racism? Well, being Southern has an '-ism,' too, though I don't know what you'd call it. It's not the same as Rosa's '-ism' because I can change the way I talk and no one has to know I'm Southern, but it's definitely there." She smiled slyly. "I haven't had very good responses telling Californians that I'm from the South."

Karen grinned good-naturedly. "So, talk to me now. I'll try not to say anything too stupid."

They were in front of Martha's apartment by now and she opened the car door quickly. "It's really rather boring. Maybe some other time." She closed the door. "See you tomorrow!"

Once inside, Martha put her things away and drew a hot bath. Leaning back into the warmth, she reviewed the events of the evening—what had been said, what she said, what she wished she'd said. Finally, shaking her head as if to clear it, she closed her eyes and let her hand slide sensuously down her belly to the even hotter wetness between her legs. Rhythmically tightening and relaxing her thighs, the energy inside her rose higher and higher. Then, out of nowhere, Karen's words came back to mock her: ". . . who aren't out themselves yet."

"Oh, shit!" Martha stood up and grabbed her towel, uncomfortably aware that just a moment before she'd been building to an orgasm thinking about lacy blue eyes and how Chris's mouth turned up at one corner when she smiled.

~~~~~~~

123

"Andy! You look terrible!" She opened the door and he stumbled in. "What happened?"

He fell onto the sofa. "I've been up all night."

"It's almost noon; have you had anything to eat?"

He stared at her. "His number came up, Martha. He's been drafted. We stayed up all night deciding what to do."

"And?"

"He's going in."

"He could go to Canada . . . "

Andy shook his head. "He won't. He says he's a queer, not a coward. I told him I'd be proud of him; I even said I'd go with him, but he won't listen. I'll never see him again, Martha. He's going to Viet Nam." He buried his head in his hands.

She put her arms around him and held him close.

~~~~~~~~

"These are your final grades for my class," Chris smiled. "You'll be mailed your official grades in a few days, but I hate to keep anyone in suspense. It's been a pleasure, dive safely, and have fun!" On her way out she motioned to Martha. "Would you meet me in my office in a few minutes?"

When Martha arrived there was another student already with Chris, apparently complaining about his grade.

"Look," Chris sighed, "I call 'em as I see 'em. You've given no indication of skill growth—you came in a strong swimmer, you're going out a strong swimmer. You've done just what was required of you, never putting out an extra ounce of effort. Your test grades are C's. You are a C student in my book. But if you want to challenge my decision, the Dean's office is open until three-thirty." She pushed him out and pulled Martha in, closing the door on his complaints.

Sinking into her chair, she yawned and stretched as she leaned back.

"Just two more hours and I can forget about tests and grades and classes for another three months!" She turned to Martha and smiled. "Now, on to more pleasant matters. I usually spend the weekends of my summer vacation diving with a small group of old friends. This summer however, my diving partner is frantically writing her dissertation and gets hysterical at the merest mention of spending time on anything else. To the point, would you consider diving with me this summer?"

"Me? Be your diving partner for the whole summer?" Martha was incredulous.

"Perhaps you don't want to commit such a big block of your time. I can understand that. I was just hoping . . . "

"Oh, no, that's not what I meant! It's just—well, you're the instructor—you just taught me! I mean, this is only the last day of the class, I don't have any experience . . . "

Chris's lips became a hard, straight line. "Bullshit! You know how good a swimmer and diver you are. I wouldn't put my life in the hands of someone whose capabilities I didn't trust. I understand you lack experience—that's what I'm offering you—in return for your skill." She smiled suddenly, her lips now turning up at the corners. "So, if there are no other objections, what do you say?"

Martha suddenly thought of Andy. He might need her on the weekends . . . But a chance like this . . . She stared at the papers scattered across the desk. She counted them—ten, eleven, twelve— no thirteen, one was hiding under the others. She bit her lip and took a deep breath. "I say yes."

Chris grinned. "Okay. Our first dive is next Saturday and we sail out Friday night. So, how about I pick you up around three?"

All at once Martha looked stricken. "I don't have any equipment!"

"Diana, my partner, has graciously offered to loan you hers. So, next Friday at three?"

Martha opened the gym door to find Karen waiting.

"Well?"

"She asked me to be her diving partner for the summer!" Martha still couldn't quite believe it.

"And so wise of her to wait until today to ask you."

"What are you talking about?"

"Now you're no longer her student. Don't you get it?"

"I get that I'm going to be diving every weekend, all summer."

"With Chris!" Karen added with a knowing grin.

"What do you mean by that?"

Karen just grinned all the more. "Wanta go out for pizza?"

Martha shook her head. "There's an old movie on TV tonight that I've missed the ending of three times."

"What movie?"

"You've probably never heard of it. It's called *The Awful Truth*."

"Irene Dunn, Cary Grant, and Mr. Smith, who later became Asta in *The Thin Man* series in the '50s."

"Right! I can't believe you knew that."

"I told you, I'm an old movie buff. But my favorites are Katherine Hepburn and Errol Flynn. And of course, old Basil himself, Mr. Sherlock Holmes."

"Well, how about if you come over and we order pizza and watch the movie?"

"Sounds good to me."

Later that evening during a commercial, Martha repeated her question: "What did you mean about it being wise for Chris to have waited to ask me until today?"

Karen reached over Martha's legs for another piece of pizza. "Come on, Martha, think what it would do to her career if it got out that she was seeing one of her students socially. You, in particular."

"Why me, in particular?"

"Martha! Get serious! It's only obvious you have a heavy-duty crush on the woman!"

"I do not!"

"Okay, have it your way," Karen grinned. "But I wish a woman would look at me the way you look at her."

"Oh, yeah? And just how do I look at her?"

Karen put on an exaggerated look of longing, trying hard to keep from laughing.

"I do not!" Martha hit her with a pillow.

"You do!"

"Do not!" Again, emphasized with the pillow.

"Do too!" Karen grabbed another pillow and began to defend herself.

"Do not!"

"Do too!"

Soon, they were wrestling amid empty pop bottles and pizza boxes.

"You're stronger than you look," Karen grunted.

126

"Shoulda thought of that before you started this," Martha returned.

"I didn't start this, you did!"

"You did!"

"No, you did!"

"It's no fair making me laugh!" Martha wheezed.

"It may be my only chance!"

They were both sweaty and tired and laughing so hard that neither one could move well. Karen lay on her back struggling to push Martha off while Martha kept trying to pin Karen and stop her struggling. Their faces just inches apart, it seemed the most natural, reasonable thing in the world when Martha leaned even closer and kissed her friend. Karen stopped moving and leaned into the kiss. For a while, there was nothing else in the world for Martha except softness, a warm, wet softness wonderful beyond anything she'd ever imaged. Her tongue had just dared to reach out and explore this wondrousness when the phone rang. Her heart pounding, her breathing ragged, she rolled off Karen.

"Oh, great timing," Karen groaned. "Whoever that is should be shot."

Martha picked up the receiver. "Hello? Can I call you back in a little while, Ellen? Okay, okay, calm down. If you can hold on just a second, I'll be right back. It's okay, hold on." She placed her hand over the mouthpiece and turned to Karen. "This may take a while," she said regretfully. "She's just had a big fight with her husband, she's pregnant, he hit her . . . "

Karen stood up. Shrugging philosophically, she smiled. "I'll call you tomorrow."

"Promise?"

"You can count on it," Karen grinned and blew her a kiss.

Martha reached over and clicked off the television. "Four times," she sighed.

Chapter Six

When Chris pulled up in an old, battered Chevy pickup, it was not exactly what Martha had expected; a Jaguar XKE, an MG maybe, but

127

not a Chevy pickup. Martha threw her stuff in the back and climbed in, self-consciously sitting close to the door and staring straight ahead. She tried not to notice how Chris's hand looked cradling the stick shift, how the sunlight caught her hair, how her mouth turned up at one corner. She tried not to notice how her own heart pounded. She counted out-of-state license plates.

Chris, for her own part, focused on driving but every now and then glanced over at Martha, who continued to pretend not to notice. Finally, Chris reached down and turned on the radio. It was set to a classical station and she hummed along as if she knew the piece by heart. It wasn't until she pulled into the marina and parked that Chris spoke.

"Martha, if this is going to work, you're going to have to get past my having been your teacher. I assume that's why you're so uncomfortable. But then again, maybe it's not. And that's a problem. Between diving partners there needs to be very direct communication, no mixed messages, no confusion. We need to trust ourselves and each other. So, is there something we need to talk about?"

Martha shook her head. She took a deep breath and smiled. "I guess I'm just a little shy. I'll get over it."

Chris grinned back. "I guess you will."

Shouts and a horn honking raucously heralded another arrival. Chris jumped out of the truck and raced to the back. "Hurry! That's Barbara and Maureen! We've got to unload and get down to the boat before they do!"

Confused, Martha slammed the door and began cramming things into her arms.

As they grabbed, Chris explained. "Originally, we all agreed to meet at five. But then, certain people, who shall remain nameless, began showing up later and later, keeping some of us waiting longer and longer. So, we decided that tardiness should have its own just reward. Since then it's become a game, everyone arriving earlier and earlier, hoping to make someone else last. Because the last one aboard provides the evening's entertainment!"

They heard a trunk slam and Martha looked up to see two women, very much loaded down, running toward them.

Chris made one last grab. "Let's go, Martha! I didn't go into show biz for a very good reason!"

With much laughter and catcalls, Chris and Martha were chased to their destination: a well-kept twin-engine boat named Sea Nymph. "All right for you, Chris Palmer!" Maureen teased. "Just wait until you see what we have planned for tonight!"

"You'll be sorry we were the last aboard!" Barbara added and Martha recognized her as the Barbara from Karen's rap group.

The evening was cool and clear as they got underway, the sunset a wild array of pink and orange and gold and blue reflecting brilliantly off the shiny water, until the sun completely disappeared and their surroundings turned to black velvet. Martha sat in the stern, watching the night fall, listening to the steady sound of the engines, and trying to stay out of everyone's way.

Off the coast of Catalina Island, they dropped anchor for dinner. It was a potluck and Martha was embarrassed that Chris hadn't told her, but Chris dismissed it, saying she'd brought enough herself to feed a dozen women. And it was true that no one seemed to think anything of it. Still, Martha felt uncomfortable.

After the meal, Pat, who owned the Sea Nymph, brought out bottles of sparkling apple cider and they toasted to a grand and glorious summer.

"To dreams fulfilled," offered Helen, who was Pat's partner.

"To fantasies!" Barbara added.

"To a hot summer—in every sense of the word!" Maureen chimed in.

"These toasts are degenerating fast," Chris laughed, as she clinked glasses with Martha.

"So right," agreed a grinning Pat. "Which must mean we're ready for Barbara and Maureen. Show time, girls!"

The audience crowded aft while the two performers climbed atop the cabin in the bow. Arms interlocked and in bare feet, Barbara and Maureen worked up a fair imitation of a soft shoe routine. Moving into a tap dance, they set the little launch to rocking. Their finale, containing all the verses and choruses of "On Top of Old Smokey," with a few new ones made up especially for the occasion, could barely be heard over the laughter and hoots from the audience, which was just as well since neither Barbara nor Maureen could sing on key, or together in the same off key.

When the laughs died down, they leaned back and stared at the velvet night sky, talked of old friends, and brought each other up to date on their lives. They included Martha in their conversation, asked her questions—and she answered, and laughed at their funny stories. But mostly she was content just listening to them, letting their words wash over her as she watched the stars.

Later, in her bunk, the gentle rocking had almost lulled her to sleep when she heard their voices still on deck above her, speaking softly but carrying clearly.

"I think she's a nice kid, but I also think you ask a lot of rowdy old women. It could be a royal pain in the butt trying not to bruise her innocence and still have fun, if you know what I mean."

That was Pat—and they were talking about her!

"And are you sure it's safe? We all have careers to consider here," Helen reminded.

"Oh, I don't think we have much to worry about on that score," Barbara spoke up. "She's been hanging out lately with Karen Webster and seems rather receptive to Karen's advances. It's been sort of sweet watching them together. Reminds me of my early days."

"I have to admit I like her," Helen replied, "but don't you think she's a little young, Chris?"

"Maybe that's how Chris likes 'em—young and tender." Maureen's laugh was deep and throaty.

Chris chuckled. "Don't you ever think of anything else?"

"Not if I can help it."

"So, what has Diana said about all this?" Barbara asked.

Maureen laughed again. "Don't be silly, darling. Knowing Diana, I'm sure she said, 'Oooh, can I watch?'"

Everyone laughed.

But Helen persisted. "I'm just a little concerned, that's all."

"Well," Barbara said, "I think she'll be a pleasant, no, refreshing addition to our summer. And I'm going to bed now so I'll have some energy left for tomorrow. Good night."

"That's my cue." Maureen made it sound suggestive.

"You behave yourself," Barbara reminded.

"Aw . . ."

Martha lay awake in the darkness long after everyone else was asleep, their words replaying over and over in her mind. Most of her life she had felt very, very old. Here, now, she felt very young. Old may have been tiring, but young was scary.

The next morning she woke before anyone else to a breathtaking sunrise: a golden mist rising out of the water, becoming brighter and brighter until its center erupted into a glowing ball of orange, and the surrounding sky dissolved into pale blue, leaving the west a darker hue.

"You're up early," Chris yawned, coming on deck.

"I've never seen a sunrise on the water before."

"It can be spectacular."

"They're all really nice," Martha said. "Your friends, I mean. And I've met Barbara before."

Chris nodded.

"You should have told me about them, Chris—about your relationships. It wasn't fair, to me or to them."

Chris nodded again and looked away.

"So what did you tell them about me?"

"Just that you'd been in my class. And that you're a champion free-styler."

"That's not what I mean." She stared down at the water lapping against the side of the boat. "Why did you ask me to dive with you this summer?"

"Why do you think?" Chris countered.

Martha took a deep breath and slowly released it. Direct communication, the woman had said. Still staring at the water, she said, "I think because I'm good at what I do and because we share a love of the ocean. And because you're attracted to me."

Chris had nearly stopped breathing. "And why did you accept?"

Now Martha looked directly into those lacy blue eyes. "Diving is very intense for me—I can't be casual about it—and that makes diving with someone a rather intimate experience, at least from my side. According to Karen, it's obvious I have a 'crush' on you, though I prefer to think of my feelings in more mature terms: respect, caring, deep affection."

Chris returned her look and said nothing.

Martha sighed. "I know you have a lover and everything, and I don't want to screw anything up, but I thought maybe we should at least talk about it."

Chris smiled wryly. "You really took my direct communication speech to heart, didn't you?"

Martha blushed but did not drop her gaze.

"So, now it's my turn, right?" Chris ran a hand through her hair and for the first time Martha saw her look unsure of herself.

"Okay, here goes. Well, you're right about why I asked you to dive with me. Anyway, I think you're right. I'm not exactly sure what my feelings for you are, I've been denying them so long. I suppose I was hoping that some time with you might help clarify them. It's been difficult to admit, most especially to myself, that I have feelings for a nineteen-year-old student. I'm sorry to be so blunt, but there it is: I'm almost thirty and you're nineteen and that's a hell of a difference, Martha."

Martha turned to stare at the water again. She shrugged. "I've always been different, the odd one out. And I've always told myself belonging didn't matter to me. But now . . . I think maybe it does. Maybe I was just trying to belong to the wrong group of people. And I can't help it that I'm younger."

"And it shouldn't matter." Chris smiled and reached for Martha's hand. "So, now that we've been direct with each other, how about if we relax a little and just see where things go? No pressure, no expectations, no shoulds or shouldn'ts. Okay?"

Martha nodded and stared at her hand, tingling from Chris' touch. When she dared to look up, she saw Chris beaming at her. She grinned back, filled with a sudden dizzying lightness. Chris really liked her!

"Good morning," Maureen called loudly from the hatch. "Is there any chance of things moving in the direction of breakfast? Or has Chris gotten so flustered she's forgotten she's cook this morning?" Maureen leered at Chris and gave Martha a friendly wink.

Martha decided to ignore her embarrassment and winked back with a leer of her own.

Maureen hooted. "Well, kid, I think you'll fit in nicely with this crowd. Yes I do."

~~~~~~~~

"Yahoo!" Karen rode the wave on her body board as if she were riding a bucking bronco. Veering close to Martha, she reached out an

132

arm and stopped herself, knocking Martha over in the process, while the little board shot out from under her and followed the crest in alone to shore.

With a lot of laughing and slipping and dunking, they both finally got their feet underneath them, holding onto each other for support. Sputtering and wiping salt water from her eyes, Martha realized Karen was steadying herself with a hand against her breast. Karen suddenly realized it, too, and snatched her hand away. Then deliberately, looking directly into Martha's eyes, Karen reached out again, aware this time of her finger rubbing gently against Martha's hard nipple.

A hot current, like a flash of lightning, ran from Martha's breast to explode between her legs. Her heart pounded and she struggled to breathe as Karen's finger became more confident.

Then, a sudden shout close by abruptly reminded them they were not alone. Karen removed her hand. Martha shivered—all at once, the water felt cold. Karen sighed and taking Martha's hand, began the walk back to shore.

Martha's face was flushed and she would not look at Karen all the way back to the car. They drove in silence, Karen reaching out now and then to stroke Martha's cheek, but still she did not respond. When they got to Martha's apartment, Karen wanted to come in but Martha shook her head and reached for the door.

Karen stopped her. "Martha! Please talk to me. Are you mad at me?"

Again she shook her head.

"Then what?"

"I just need to be alone for a little while."

"But I thought you wanted it, too."

"I did." She scooted out of the car and ran up the sidewalk without looking back.

Inside, she went right to the bathroom and turned on the shower. Peeling off her bathing suit, she stared at herself in the mirror. Her nipples were hard again, but this time it wasn't from excitement. She had wanted Karen, wanted more than she had words for. But just underneath that wanting had been something else, something hidden, something unpleasant. She stepped into the stream of hot water and concentrated on pouring just the right amount of shampoo. She remembered the feeling of hot fire between her legs.

"One times one is one . . . "

~~~~~~~~

The room was filled with the sounds of dinner: clanks and scrapes and bowls being passed and set down with soft thunks. Martha concentrated on her meal, as uncomfortable tonight as she had been the first time she ate dinner with Walter and Jean. Now she knew which fork to use and where her napkin belonged, but she did not know exactly how a grown daughter visiting her parents for dinner was supposed to act. Judging by the silence, they were unsure, as well.

Walter cleared his throat. "So, how are you doing? Keeping up with your school work?"

She nodded. What could she say? How could she tell them about her life, about Chris—and Karen? They'd never even talked about sex except for that one time when she'd started her period . . . And now, not just sex, but lesbian. Oh, god . . .

"How's work going?"

"Busy. You know." She wanted to tell them. But not the two of them, together . . . maybe she could get Walter alone. No, maybe Jean. No, Walter . . .

Walter looked at her with misty eyes. "It's just so quiet around here without you . . . "

"We miss you, honey," Jean added. "We just want to know everything is going well for you."

"If there's anything you need . . . anything we can do . . . you're still our daughter, you know."

She nodded and smiled thinly. Not tonight. She couldn't tell them tonight.

~~~~~~~~

"Why the hell don't you look where you're going?" Andy growled.

Martha looked around quickly. "Sorry. I didn't realize you were there."

Andy grunted in reply.

About ten minutes later he snapped at her again. "Haven't you got that done yet? We don't have all day, y'know."

"Knock it off, Andy. What's eating you, anyway?"

"Nothing. Just get a move on. I wanta get outta here."

"Okay, fine. Just stop yelling at me, for chrissake."

They worked in silence for a few minutes. Then Andy reached into his hip pocket and took out a neatly folded piece of paper and handed it to her. "It's from Steve."

She opened it up and smoothed the wrinkles out over her knee. She hadn't read far before she looked up at Andy, her eyes studying his face. "Oh, wow."

He nodded. "This is the third letter. The first one wasn't so bad, the second one got worse. And now . . . "

"He's bragging about blowing 'gooks' away with his M-16 and playing smear-the-queer with the boys so no one will suspect him. Oh, Andy! What have they done to him?"

Andy looked away. Then his head bent and his shoulders shook. She reached out to him, but he held his body rigid, closed to her. She refolded the letter and sat where she was, not knowing what else to do.

~~~~~~~~

Karen set the candle down and lit it with a flourish. On her way back from the kitchen with chilled glasses and a bottle tucked under her arm, she flipped off the overhead light.

"I know what you're thinking and I just want you to know you're wrong," she said.

"I am?"

"Yes. You're thinking: 'Chilled glasses, sparkling cider, candlelight—this is a scene of seduction.'"

"But it's not?"

"No, it's not. I am a lesbian feminist—there are no roles or stereotypes in our relationships—they are all egalitarian. The word 'seduction' is not even in our vocabularies." She took the phone off the hook and put a pillow over it to muffle the noise. "I'm very politically correct, you know."

"I'm very glad to know all this," Martha grinned. "It's very reassuring."

Karen nodded. "A firm basis in correct political theory can be a comfort in times like these."

Martha leaned into Karen's arms and quivered at the feel of Karen's warm breath in her ear. "So, this is essentially a political act?"

"Oh, yes," Karen whispered. "Emma Goldman once said: 'If I can't dance, I don't want to be in your revolution.'"

"But we're not dancing."

Karen reached down and unbuttoned Martha's jeans. "Well, there's dancing and then there's dancing." She eased the zipper down slowly. Her hand stroked the tender warmth of Martha's belly, fingers straying lower and lower, gently tugging at Martha's tight curls, while her tongue circled Martha's ear, and sliding down her taut neck, came to rest in the tiny, soft hollow of her throat. Martha moaned. Karen moved her body down, her face rubbing against the softness of Martha's breast, her mouth making a small, round, wet circle as she sucked through the shirt, her teeth finding and pulling at the nipple straining to be touched.

All at once, Martha felt bad, as if she'd done something terribly wrong. It wasn't about Karen, it was something else . . . something awful. She didn't want to think of that now—she tried to ignore it, but it became stronger and stronger, drowning out all the good feelings. She shivered and struggled to sit up.

Karen pulled away and looked confused. Martha could only stare back, just as confused. And even though the room was warm, she continued to shiver visibly. Karen scooted in and put her arms around her.

"I don't know what's happening," Martha protested. "I just feel yucky. I don't know what this is about. I don't understand this."

Karen held her close. "Shhh. It's okay. Whatever it's about it's okay. I love you, Martha. We don't have to make love right now, we can wait."

"That's not it. I don't want to wait! I want you to touch me, but underneath I feel . . . yucky." She shuddered and closed her eyes against the feeling. One times one is one . . .

Karen touched her face tenderly, stroked her hair, whispered soothing words. Martha relaxed slowly and Karen continued to gently rock her until Martha fell asleep cradled in her arms.

~~~~~~~~

Martha folded a shirt and laid it aside. She picked up a pair of jeans.

" . . . and then Ed spilled his beer all over the couch! Of course, I had to clean it up—it wasn't half-time. Honestly, they're just like children! That's why it's so good to get out with you on Monday nights, even if it is just to do the washing . . . " Ellen's voice droned on.

Martha folded a towel. And another. What was Chris doing right now? When did she do her laundry—or did the gods just send her clean, folded clothes and magically whisk the old dirty ones away? She giggled at the image.

"What are you laughing at, Martha? I see nothing funny about two flat tires."

"Sorry."

"Well, anyway . . . "

All at once, Martha wanted to tell Ellen, to talk about the changes she was going through, about Karen. She needed to talk to someone.

"Ellen . . . "

Ellen didn't pause in her monologue.

"Ellen."

She still didn't appear to hear.

"Ellen! Shut up a goddamn minute and listen to me!"

"Well, you don't need to yell!"

Now that she had Ellen's attention, Martha didn't know where or how to begin. Her mouth went dry.

"Well, what did you want to say?"

Martha looked at her. Mistake. It would be a mistake. She shook her head. "Never mind, I'm sorry. So what happened after Kevin set off the fire alarm?" She picked up another towel and folded it.

~~~~~~~~

Martha's breath came hard. Her hand traced Karen's outline: shoulders, ribs, hips, thighs, inner thighs. Her hand slid into warm wetness, fingers seeking and finding dark, secret places. Hot and wet. Wanting. She slid closer, her fingers slipping inside the most secret of all places in rhythm to Karen's thrusting, her mouth muffling Karen's soft moans. She licked Karen's chin, her neck, each stroke of her tongue matching the stroke of her fingers as Karen rose to meet her.

Such a feeling of power! She exalted in it. She could feel her own thighs, moist and wanting. She moved closer still and wrapped those thighs around Karen's leg, riding hard, her excitement building as Karen's built, energy feeding energy until it exploded, showering both of them with silver light.

When she could move, Karen rolled over onto her elbow, her hand and mouth reaching, eager for her turn at that same power. But Martha stopped her—Martha could feel that feeling she could not yet name just under the surface, ready to wipe away what she'd just experienced. She pulled Karen close and they lay together, breathing deeply.

~~~~~~~~

Almost from the time she closed the truck door, Martha felt it: a subtle energy seemed to fill the cab, electrifying the air. At first she thought it was just residual energy, the result of her intense afternoon with Karen, but then she realized it was Chris. In class, Chris had always seemed self-assured, together, but now there was something else—a confidence; a sense of being centered in her own power seemed to radiate from her.

Martha looked at her more closely. She was wearing old faded jeans and a soft, sky-blue work shirt with the sleeves neatly rolled up, taut across strong muscles—swimmer's arms. Martha's eyes were drawn to the gentle curve of breast visible from Chris's partially unbuttoned shirt. Soft . . . round . . .

"What are you staring at?"

Martha jerked her head up, again looking straight ahead. "Uh, I've just never seen you in blue jeans before."

Chris chuckled. "I don't wear 'em much."

138

"How come?"

"Well, partly because they've become sort of a dyke uniform and also because my friends tease me, some half seriously, about looking so 'butch.'"

"I think you look good." Martha heard the words coming out of her mouth before she could stop them. She began to fiddle with the finger-sized hole in the knee of her own pants.

"Why, thank you. I like jeans. I like how I feel when I wear them. I think sometimes I worry too much about what other people are saying and doing. That peer pressure thing."

"Just tell 'em that blue jeans are part of your philosophy. Quote Thoreau. You know, that part about functional clothing."

"You've read Thoreau?"

"I gave up Golden Books a few years ago, Chris."

The woman's face reddened. "Sorry."

Martha leaned over and gently touched Chris's leg. "It's okay, I . . . " she broke off as she felt the energy arc from Chris's body into her hand, almost as if she'd been shocked. Martha stared at her hand as she rubbed it against her leg, still feeling the tingle. Their arrival at the marina saved her from having to say anything else.

Chris was talking away, taking equipment out of the back when Martha walked around the truck, removed the gear from her hands and kissed her. Startled, Chris hesitated only a moment, then returned the kiss with an intensity which surprised them both. But abruptly, she pulled back. "Uh, I think we'd better put a check on this." She leaned against the truck, taking a few deep breaths.

"I'm sorry." Martha became very busy picking up equipment.

Chris stopped her. "Don't be silly. I'm the one who's sorry. But there are others besides ourselves to consider."

Martha was unsure whether Chris was referring to Diana or to the women standing on deck waving energetically for them to hurry. She was afraid to ask.

They were met halfway to the boat by Pat and Helen. Pat reached out to take Martha's load and Helen explained, "You've been volunteered to come with me to get ice."

"Oh, sure," Martha agreed, her eyes following Chris and Pat down the slip toward the boat.

"Getting ice is usually Diana's job," Helen continued as she took Martha's arm and hurried her up the ramp to the parking lot. "There's an ice machine here at the marina, of course, but it only has crushed ice and we need two or three big blocks. Diana found a place close by and she always makes sure to pick some up on their way here. You've never met Diana, have you?"

Helen seemed to be stressing Diana's name pretty hard. "No, I haven't. But she sounds really nice. I'm looking forward to meeting her."

Helen nodded and opened the car door for her. "Yes, she and Chris have been together a long time. A lovely couple. Oh, their relationship isn't without its difficulties, but it's basically stable. Chris talks about non-monogamy from time to time—almost broke Diana's heart over a silly little affair a few years back, but that didn't last long. Things like that never do. And as I said, their relationship is pretty stable. Oh! I haven't upset you by talking about Diana, have I?"

"Not at all. As I said, I'm looking forward to meeting her," Martha said coolly.

"Of course you are. We're rather like an extended family, you know, and it's been hard not seeing her as often as we might like. Of course, her paper should be finished soon. Not that we're unhappy with you, dear. But, well, we've all known each other for so long and . . . "

"I understand completely," Martha said stiffly.

"Oh, good, I had hoped you would. Well, here we are," Helen announced cheerfully.

~~~~~~~~

"I have a great idea," Chris broke the heavy silence on their way home Sunday evening. "Let's go to dinner. Diana's away this week and I hate to cook for just me. What d'ya say, partner?"

"Uh, I need to get some things done at home. Maybe another time," Martha mumbled, staring out the window.

"Okay, that does it!" Chris pulled off the freeway at the next exit, turned onto the first side street and parked. Twisting past the steering wheel, she got right into Martha's face. "What gives? You've been distant the whole weekend. Surely that kiss didn't upset you this much? Why are you so far away?"

Martha sat silent for a long time. She hadn't intended to say anything about her conversation with Helen, but Chris's warm hand on hers and the sad confusion on Chris's face was too much to bear on top of her own feelings. Words began to tumble out, her own fears and confusion along with everything else.

"Helen is a jerk," Chris stated flatly, settling back against the seat more comfortably. "She's my friend and I love her dearly, but sometimes . . . she is such a pain in the ass.

"For one thing, I don't have 'affairs!' Affairs are sordid afternoon encounters filled with lies and sneaking around. Yuck! And the one she speaks so knowingly of occurred very early in my relationship with Diana, when we both still felt insecure and unsure of ourselves in relationship to each other. So it was difficult. And I didn't break her heart, I pissed her off." She stared off into the night.

"But we have always been committed to non-monogamy, even when it wasn't easy. There's been a lot of work, a lot of growth in our relationship that Helen knows nothing about. We don't share that part of ourselves with her because it's just too much hassle. She wants to see us as a monogamous, married couple. So we let her." She looked back over at Martha.

"And, by the way, that 'affair' ended because the woman went to Oregon to live on women's land, not because of any problem between Diana and me.

"It's actually kind of funny Helen chose this weekend to bring this up. At this very moment, Diana is staying with a lover of hers in San Francisco."

"I thought she was doing research for her thesis?"

"She is. Last winter she drove up for a couple of weeks and while she was there, she went to a women's dance. And met Cassie. So, now she stays with Cassie while she's working in San Francisco."

"You're not jealous?"

"Not of Cassie. But that's hardly a fair test of my politics. I mean, hey, she lives in San Francisco, just how often can Diana see her? But Cassie is good for Diana. Diana was slowing up on her dissertation, finding more and more excuses until Cassie gave her a good swift kick. That's just what she needed, someone besides me telling her how important her work is, how important she is."

"And that doesn't bother you?"

"Diana and I bring out the best in each other on a daily basis. We are each other's best friends. But that doesn't mean we don't want any other friends or that we can't use all the support we can get.

"Jealousy has been a problem, especially early on when we doubted our own self-worth and our importance to each other. And yes, I still get twinges now and again when I feel she's spending more time with someone else than with me; usually it's when I'm feeling down about myself, when I feel particularly needy. I try not to put that out on her. And if I really do need something from her, I can always ask. She is my sweetie, after all, and wants to give me what I need."

"So, if your relationship is so good, why do you want other lovers?" Martha thought uncomfortably of Karen.

"We have plenty to share." Chris smiled. "Look, non-monogamy is an important element of all my relationships, but I don't want to dwell on it. You want to go to dinner or what?"

Martha smiled. "Well, I would need to shower first."

"Okay. We'll drop you off to shower and change, I'll go home and do the same, and I'll be back to pick you up in a flash."

As they drove away to dinner an hour later, Martha's eyes twinkled.

"So, Diana's away for the week, huh?"

"Yep. I'm all alone in that big house."

"Maybe you should have someone stay with you."

"Perhaps you should have brought your toothbrush."

"I did."

~~~~~~~~

Martha lay watching the gradual rise and fall of Chris's chest. Rainbows played around the room, early morning sun transformed by crystals hanging in the window. To Martha, the colors seemed a visual manifestation of her feelings. Rainbows were wonderful. Everything was wonderful . . . Chris had made love to her and she had felt only good feelings, powerful, fine feelings, no trace of unpleasantness to mar the sweetness.

142

Chris sighed in her sleep and rolled over. Martha smiled the tender smile of a new lover and took fresh delight in the sensuous curves of Chris's hips, so round and smooth. She sighed, too, and snuggled closer, breathing deeply the musky woman smells until she fell back asleep.

~~~~~~~~~

"I have a great idea," Karen said. "Let's move in together. My apartment—it's big enough for both of us. Or another one if you'd prefer. We'll do it this weekend. We'll have a big party, invite all our friends to help. What d'ya say?"

"You know I go diving on the weekends."

"Okay, let's do it today then, what the heck."

"No."

"C'mon. I love you, you love me, I want to live with you. It's simple. It'll be fun. You'll like it."

"No."

"Why not? Is it because of Chris?"

"Partly. But mostly it's because I'm not ready for that kind of commitment. I'm not ready to live with anyone yet."

"I understand about Chris. I admit it's hard for me, I'm strictly the monogamous type, but I came into this relationship knowing how you felt about her. So, that's okay. I want to live with you, Martha, I'm willing to compromise."

"I appreciate your understanding. But really, that's not the problem. I'll let you know when I'm ready."

"Yeah, okay. But, I want you to know I'm ready whenever you are."

~~~~~~~~~

"Hello?"

"Martha, I'm down at Diablos. You'd better get down here, quick."

"Karen, what's wrong? Are you okay?"

"Yeah, I just came to shoot some pool. I'm fine. But your friend Andy isn't. He's drunk and he's hitting on all the heavy-duty guys around. He won't listen to me, and I think you'd better come get him out of here before he finds someone to take him up on his offer and he gets hurt."

"Be right there."

Martha arrived a little later to find Andy leaning against the corner of the bar, myopically leering at every man in his limited range of vision.

"C'mon, Andy, it's time to go home."

"But I haven't scored yet, Martha. Can't go yet. These boys don't want me to go yet."

Martha glanced around at half a dozen well-muscled men dressed in black leather and shiny metal, all grinning broadly. She turned to Karen for support.

"It's time to go, Andy," Karen agreed. "Say good-bye to the boys."

"'Bye boys," he obediently repeated. "Gotta go now. Can't play any more today. Hey, wait a minute! I don't wanta go, Martha. I don't have to go, an' you can't make me."

"Andy, come with us now or I'll tell 'em you're only nineteen."

"If you tell 'em that, they won't let me come here anymore."

"That's right. So, let's go."

They poured him into the front seat between them. Martha scooted close to the door and rolled down the window.

"Dragon breath," Karen laughed.

"Nobody light a match," Martha agreed. "What the hell were you doing in there, Andy?"

"Tryin' to score. Man has a right to, y'know. Man has a right to drown a broken heart." He patted his shirt pocket. "A broken heart. Right here. Man's gotta . . . " He passed out.

Martha reached into his pocket. She knew what it was the minute she took out the folded up piece of paper.

"Listen to this: 'Dear Andy, well, this is it! They are finally shipping us out! Man, are we ready! We are lean, mean, fighting machines! Here is a picture of me and Lisa on my last leave. You probably already heard, but we're getting married when I come back. Yep, I'm taking the old plunge. Congratulations, huh? Well, take care and please don't write me anymore. It upsets Lisa. Sincerely, Steve.'"

"Shit. No wonder he got drunk."

Martha refolded the letter and tucked it gently back into his pocket, saying nothing. She leaned out the window and let the wind blow hard into her face.

~~~~~~~~

"Just a minute!" Martha put the plate in the drainer and dried her hands. She hurried to answer the bell, but no one was there. Annoyed, she began to turn away when she glanced down and saw a single yellow rose lying cradled in a bed of green fern. She picked it up. The attached card read, "Thanks," in Andy's handwriting. Smiling, she closed the door and went to find a vase.

~~~~~~~~

Karen sat on the sofa with Martha's head in her lap. She peeled an orange and separated it into sections, one by one, squeezing the sweet juice into Martha's mouth before popping the pulp into her own.

"So tell me about yourself, Martha Jean Henderson. I want to know all the details, all the teeny, tiny parts that make up you."

"Oh, you know all the important parts already." She stuck out her tongue and watched Karen drip orange juice onto it.

"No, I mean it. Tell me about your childhood. What's the South really like?"

"Come on, Karen, I've told you before I don't want to talk about it."

"I didn't know you meant *ever*. Look, I gather it was rough, but no matter how rough it was, you still have to deal with it sooner or later. What better time and place than with me? I'll be here for you, Martha. I love you."

She knocked Karen's hand away and sat up. "Rough? What the hell do you know about rough? Just leave me alone about this, okay?"

"No, it's not okay. I care about you, Martha. While you push the past away, you also push everything else away, too, including me. Make peace with the past, Martha. Let me in; let me get close to you."

"I don't know what the hell you're talking about. I am close with you! I sleep with you, don't I?"

"That's not what I mean and you know it. It's like you're always behind a wall or something. I can see you but I can't touch you; it keeps you safe and it keeps everyone else out. Let it go, Martha."

Martha jumped up. "I am not going to live in the past, for you or for anyone." She ran from the room.

"It's living *with* the past I'm asking you to do," Karen called after her.

~~~~~~~~

"I.D.'s, please."

Karen fumbled through her pockets and finally found her driver's license. The woman with the flashlight glanced at the card and then at Karen.

She held out her hand to Martha.

Martha tried to be as casual as Karen had been, hoping the woman couldn't hear her heart pounding. She seemed to be taking an awfully long time with Martha's card. She clicked off the flashlight and handed the card back without comment. Martha took a deep breath and hurried to catch up with Karen.

The room was dark and crowded. Lining the bar, the regulars cruised everyone who came in, their desperation as tangible as the smoke. Martha followed closely behind Karen as they wound their way to the edge of the dance floor.

"Wanta dance?" Karen shouted into her ear.

Shaking her head, Martha shouted back, "Let's wait for a slow one."

Karen nodded. Grinning, she pointed to a woman dressed in red and black satin, pants tight, blouse cut low. She danced, unaware of the stir she caused, in perfect harmony with the music, energy igniting energy. The intensity reminded Martha of the dolphin.

"I'll be right back." Karen pointed the sign on the back wall that said "rest rooms."

Martha nodded and went back to watching the dancer.

"Well, hello sweetheart," a strange voice breathed in her ear. "You must be new in town. I've never seen you before and I keep close tabs on beauties like you."

"Uh, I'm waiting for someone."

"Well, wait no longer—here I am, the woman of your dreams."

"Look, I said..." Martha turned around too quickly and knocked the other woman's elbow with her shoulder, spilling the woman's drink all over both of them.

"Goddammit, look what you've done! This is my best shirt!"

"Sorry."

"How sorry?" the woman purred.

"Not that sorry. I'm with someone. But even if I weren't, I don't accept offers from strangers."

The woman shook her head. "Your loss, sweetheart."

Karen walked up. "Better luck next time, Betty." Turning to Martha she said, "She's annoying, but harmless."

Betty snorted and stomped away.

"Can we go, Karen?"

"Just one dance?"

Martha shook her head. "I don't feel so well. The smoke, the smell..." She indicated her wet clothes.

"Okay. We can always dance at my place."

~~~~~~~~

Martha opened the door, then turned around and stood in front of it. "Okay, you can come in on one condition: We don't discuss politics, religion, work, or any serious subject. This is a very important holiday. Today is Ida Mae Schumacher's birthday! And Ida Mae doesn't hold with seriousness on her birthday."

Karen looked confused. "Who is Ida Mae Schumacher?"

"I have no idea. But today is her... let's see..." She did some mental arithmetic. "One hundred and seven, I think. It's her one hundred seventh birthday."

"Who is she?" Karen asked again.

"Ten years ago—I was nine—right on the back page of the local newspaper they announced Ida Mae Schumacher's 97th birthday. Well, there was a picture of old Ida Mae and she looked so stern and solemn that we, my brothers and sisters and I, decided we had to do something to cheer her up, it being her birthday and all. So, we had a party for her where only unserious things could be done."

"Did she have fun?"

"Oh, she wasn't there—the paper didn't give her address or phone number. I guess we could have looked it up, but that didn't occur to us at the time. The party was in her honor, you see. We taped her picture on the wall and sang silly songs to her and blew out a candle—one was all we could find—and we had a grand old time. I haven't thought of old Ida Mae in a very long time."

Karen grinned. "And today's the big day, huh? So, how shall we celebrate?"

Martha hugged her from behind. "I know just the way." She slid her hands down and slowly unbuttoned Karen's jeans. She pushed them down, out of the way.

"You're not wearing any underwear." She turned Karen around and dropped to her knees, burying her face into Karen's soft curls, pulling Karen closer, harder onto her mouth. Karen moaned and swayed.

"I can't stand up," she breathed. "I have to sit down. Or lay down. Or something."

Martha helped her step out of her jeans and led her to the bed.

Two hours later Martha rolled over and sat up. "I know what let's do."

"Oh, no, my dearest," Karen groaned. "Not again! I can't. I'm exhausted!"

Martha giggled. "I was thinking about food."

"Ah, yes. But, I'll bet you gave the cook the day off in old Ida Mae's honor, didn't you?"

"Ah, yes, so I did. We'll just have to dine out this evening."

"A capital idea. However, in that case, I must first refresh myself in your water closet as I'm sure my fragrance is a bit less sweet than a rose." She leered. "Let's be honest, I smell like a woman who's been making love all day."

"Oh, I like how you smell."

"Me, too. But I'm not willing to share it with the general public. Care to join me in the bath?"

"Splendid idea, my dear."

In the shower, all wet and slippery, Martha dropped the soap. When she bent over to retrieve it, Karen, making sounds like a motor began to vigorously rub Martha's rear end.

"What are you doing?"

"I'm playing car wash. I'm washing the back seat."

"The back seat is clean now, thank you," Martha chuckled.

"Okay, turn around."

"What are you doing now?"

"Brrr . . . brrr . . . brrr . . . I'm washing your headlights!"

Martha leaned against the tile, laughing. "Well, you be careful, my headlights are a little sensitive this evening. Perhaps you polished them too much already."

"Oh, I don't think so—they seem to like it, see?"

Martha playfully slapped her hand away. "I'm getting out now. I can see where this game is headed and it is not towards food! Now, you hurry up!" Laughing, she ducked out of the shower and had just began to dry off when she heard someone pounding on the front door.

"Martha? Martha! Are you all right? Are you okay, Martha? Martha!"

As soon as the door opened slightly, a frantic-looking Ellen rushed in to confront dripping, towel-clad Martha.

"My god, Martha, I was worried sick! I've been trying to call for hours! Hours! And when you didn't answer the door—I've been knocking for the longest time—well, I was just worried sick! I couldn't imagine what was wrong! Are you okay? What happened to your phone?" She sank onto the sofa.

"Just now," Martha pointed out the obvious, "I was in the shower. The phone must have been knocked off the hook. Calm down, Ellen. What did you want? When you called, I mean."

"What did I want? It's Monday. Don't we always do our laundry together on Monday nights? I had wanted to get an early start today is all."

"Oh, shit. I forgot."

From the bathroom, a voice could be heard singing "I Love You Truly," and then a very naked Karen walked out toweling her hair.

"So, my little petunia blossom, have you decided where . . . " Her leer suddenly dropped into one of those frozen little smiles reserved for such awkward social situations. "I'll just bet you're Ellen," she said, hastily wrapping the towel around her.

"Uh, yes," Ellen said slowly, confused.

"Hello. I'm Karen." Looking at Martha, she pointed rather lamely off towards the bedroom. "I'll just uh, go and uh, get dressed now. See ya."

Not knowing quite how to handle this, Martha glanced towards Karen's retreating figure and back to Ellen. "Uh, I'd better get dressed, too. And get the clothes together. Be right back."

Ellen nodded slowly, still confused.

"Chicken!" Martha whispered as she closed the door.

"What did you want me to do?" Karen snorted. "That woman has incredible timing!"

"It's my fault. I forgot all about the stupid laundry. She counts on it every Monday. I think it's the high point of her week."

"But is it the high point of your week?"

"Huh?"

"It seems like you feel that you owe people whatever they want from you. I'm just asking what you get out of this."

"Ellen is having a hard time, she needs someone to talk to and I'm her best friend. And I do have to do my laundry. What's the big deal?"

"It's not. No problem here. Well, I guess I'll be heading out now so you two can go enjoy your laundry."

Martha stroked Karen's arm. "Come with us. I'll bet you have wash that needs doing, too."

"Huh, uh, not a chance. But I'll tell you what—in a couple of hours I'll bring back some pizza and we'll have a picnic in your living room. I'll even round up some ants if you want."

"Leave out the ants and you have a deal." Martha kissed her. "You still taste like me," she smiled, remembering.

"I like tasting like you." She stood. "Walk me to the door?"

"It's not exactly what I had in mind."

Martha closed the front door behind Karen and Ellen asked, "Why was she taking a shower here?"

Martha winked. "I've decided to rent out my bathroom to needy but deserving students."

Ellen didn't even smile.

Martha sighed and picked up her basket of clothes. "Her shower's busted. Ready?"

Andy tossed her a paint brush. "Gaff what we're gonna do today?" he grinned.

Martha looked up in surprise—Andy hadn't done puns with her for a very long time. Not since Steve's last letter . . .

"Whatever it is, I'd rudder be sailing."

"Well, you can't just sail through with the easy jobs."

She shook her head and picked up the paint.

"Gotcha!" he laughed. But Martha thought he still sounded a little hollow.

~~~~~~~~

"Stop complaining about being lonely and go meet people!" Martha threw down the towel she'd just folded and grabbed another.

"It's not so easy to meet people when you're married and eight months pregnant!" Ellen protested.

"Yeah, well, you know my answer to that."

"Yeah, I know. Go back to school! But I hate school!"

"So do something else, just shut up about it! God, I'm sick to death of your constant whining and complaining!"

"You know what I'm sick of, Martha? I'm sick of your judgments, your 'Holier-than-thou' attitude! You have all the answers and you magnanimously bestow them upon us lesser beings out of pity for our struggles. Just shut up and leave me alone!"

"Leave you alone? You call me at least every other day, you practically beg me to do laundry with you every damn week—on your schedule, not mine—and then you go on and on and on about how depressed you are, how ha-a-a-ard your life is, how no one understands or cares, how your life is ruined . . . shit, it never stops! You never stop! You're worse than my sister Carol Ann! Being around you is exhausting, Ellen!"

"I didn't know you had a sister."

"There's a lot about me you don't know. And that's another thing—how come you never ask how things are going for me? How come I always feel like I'm letting you down when I don't have any horrible, depressing, awful things to tell you about? How come I feel like I have to pretend to be as miserable as you are? Well, I'm tired of pretending, Ellen! My life is good! I'm happy! I may not have all the answers, but I obviously have some!" She began stuffing all her clothes, folded and unfolded, into her basket.

"Well, you can take those answers and shove 'em! I don't need your stupid answers or your stupid advice! And as for calling you so much, well, it'll be a cold day in a very warm place before I do it again!"

"Great! And don't hold your breath until next Monday 'cause I'm not doing your goddamn laundry with you anymore!" Martha yanked up her basket and walked out the door.

~~~~~~~~

"What are you doing?" Martha complained. "I liked that station."

"I want to listen to this for a while," Karen answered, turning the knob.

"I hate country western music!"

"Oh, that's right, they play country in the South a lot, don't they?" Karen replied cheerfully.

"Look, I really don't like it. It's sexist, degrading bullshit—'kick me, beat me, stomp on me and I'll love you for it.' It's disgusting!"

"Get off it. It's not any more sexist or disgusting than the crap on your favorite station. You just trash everything that reminds you of the South. How about we listen to it for ten minutes, just ten minutes, then you can change it back. Deal?"

"No! Turn it back."

"Look, I promise you won't turn into a raving right-wing political conservative in just ten minutes. I'll protect you. Just ten minutes."

Martha gave her a sour look. "But I might throw up on you."

Karen laughed and turned the music louder. "I'll take my chances."

Martha stared out the window and counted street signs and stop lights. And tried not to listen.

Chapter Seven

Martha groggily answered the phone. "Yeah?"

"Martha, I had her."

"What? Who is this?" She reached up and switched on the lamp.

"It's Ellen, Martha. I had the baby. It's a girl. I know we had a fight and everything, but you're still my best friend and I wanted you to be the first to know."

"Oh, Ellen, that's great. Congratulations." Martha struggled to wake up. "It's a little girl? What's her name?"

"Tiffany Dawn. And she's beautiful, Martha. Seven pounds five ounces. I'm sorry to wake you, but I wanted you to be the first to know. Well, Mom wants to make a few more calls so I better let you go. But come see us real soon, okay?"

"So your parents are there? And Mark. That's good."

"Well, just Mom. Dad's at home and Mark is . . . well, he'll be in later. And you will come see us, won't you?"

"Of course I will. Now you get some rest."

Martha hung up the receiver and turned off the light. Ellen was a mother. Ellen wasn't even nineteen yet. Well, she had been born when her mother was just nineteen, and Bobby was already two years old. Martha sighed and rolled over. Bobby. Carol Ann. The kids. She hadn't talked to any of them in forever. Carol Ann still wrote letters regularly, but Martha could never even bring herself to open them. And she'd never written back . . .

A dog barked in the distance. She focused on that: one bark, two barks, three . . .

~~~~~~~

Martha helped herself to Andy's potato chips. "Well, hell. I don't want you to go."

"Yeah, I'm going to miss you, too. But this is such an opportunity, Martha. As long as I can remember, Dad's talked about retiring to Hawaii and now that his twenty years are up, the Navy will move him there for free. It's our chance—we're going into business together, boats in a big way! Not just cleaning and repairing anymore, no sir!

Building and designing! Maybe we'll design the next America's Cup winner. And besides, I hear the surfing is great!"

"Not to mention the surfers."

Andy just grinned.

"You'll be staying with your folks?"

"Just until I find my own place. And we can still be friends, Martha. We can write and you can visit . . . "

"Uh huh." She studied her shoes. "So when's the big day?"

"Two weeks." He cleared his throat and made a big deal of rolling down the top of the potato chip bag. "Uh, I wanted to say thanks . . . for everything, y'know?"

She hit his arm companionably.

"Know what I'm going to miss most?" he continued. "The Pun-ick Wars."

She looked at him in surprise. "The Pun-ick Wars? What the hell is . . . ?"

He smiled that lopsided grin of his. "Gotcha!"

She laughed, finally getting the joke. "Okay, you win." But her throat was tight; never before had he looked so much like Bobby.

~~~~~~~~

"Earth to Karen, come in Karen!"

"Huh? Oh, sorry. I guess I'm not being very good company, am I?"

"As a matter of fact, no. Wanta talk about it?"

"I'd rather not. I'd like to forget it."

"Let me guess, the Women's Center, right?"

"What else?" Karen rubbed her eyes. "I've gotten used to endless staff meetings where nothing gets decided or acted on. I've gotten used to women not following through with their commitments because they're 'burned out.' I've even gotten used to the straight women who hang around all starry-eyed, holding hands and kissing on as many dykes as they can. What I can't get used to is the divisive 'I'm more politically correct than you, nanny, nanny' bullshit."

"Cowshit."

Karen gave her a look. "Ha ha. Today, Phyllis had an absolute shit-fit because I got to be on TV and she didn't. The Battered

154

Women's Shelter was my idea. I did all the research, made all the contacts. I drew up the grant. It exists because I worked my ass off for it. At the staff meeting today, Phyllis flounced in and accused me of 'hogging' all the media coverage. She called me 'elitist.' She claims I'm on an ego trip and that I'm trying to take over the Shelter the same way I've taken over the Center. I'm a collaborator with the male media."

"She's a flake. Don't let her get to you."

"For an hour and a half the whole staff discussed it. They decided she was a flake, too, but it took an hour and a half. Meanwhile, our agenda went down the toilet. We didn't get to discuss daycare at off-campus women's events or how to provide Signing at all women's conferences and concerts. These less-important issues will have to wait until a more appropriate time.

"Hell, the FBI doesn't need to waste agents infiltrating the Center, we have our own obstructionist extraordinaire." She smiled faintly. "Sorry you asked, aren't you?"

Martha took her hand and kissed it. "Not if it helps you be here with me."

~~~~~~~

Chris handed the menu to the waitress and smiled. The waitress winked and went to place their orders.

"Do you know her?" Martha asked, surprised.

"No," Chris grinned. "But I think I should. She's cute, isn't she?"

"I can't take you anywhere," Martha laughed.

"Just being friendly. Every person I meet is a potential friend."

"Or lover. I know you, Chris Palmer. Friendly indeed! You and Maureen are probably the two 'friendliest' women I know!"

"That's true. And I taught her everything she knows."

"I'm sure."

"Look, sweetie, just because you're too busy these days to think about such things . . . "

Martha glanced at her watch. "Busy isn't the word for it. In fact, if they don't hurry with our lunch, I'll have to eat mine on the way to class. I never have any time anymore. I'm either going to class, in class, or studying for class. Oh, and then there's work. Whoever designed the quarter system must have been a puritan sadist who hated the idea that somewhere a student might be resting. Heaven forbid they should be playing!"

"It must be challenging. But then, you knew it would be when you transferred from a laid-back community college." Chris leaned forward. "Well, enough of this idle chit-chat. You must be wondering why I asked you here."

"Silly of me, but I assumed we were having lunch. You're not about to hand me a roll of stolen microfilm and spirit me away to Istanbul, are you?"

"Oh, you guessed! Actually, it's even better than that. I have some secret information that must be acted upon quickly—but, you must swear not to reveal your source."

"You're kidding, right?"

"Only partly. There is an opening for a lab assistant in the Oceanography department at the university. It has something to do with dolphin but I don't know the specifics because it is rather hush-hush. Here is the address. You'll be talking with Dr. Rice or Dr. Curell. I hear they're pretty hard-core conservatives so tone down what you say to them."

"Oh, Chris, this couldn't have come at a better time. Andy's leaving and I do not want to take over the business—I've begun to hate cleaning boats. Thank you, thank you!"

She winked. "My pleasure. Literally. If you're not working so late, I might get to see you more often." She nodded towards the waitress coming their direction with a plate in each hand. "Meanwhile, think I should ask her out?"

Martha laughed.

~~~~~~~~

"Briefly, what we're working on Miss Henderson, is interspecies communication. Combining new data from several scientific fields, Dr. Curell and I are attempting to teach a few basic words to the dolphin in those tanks in an effort to determine whether actual airborne communication between dolphin and Man is possible. Such efforts have proven successful in other experiments and we hope . . . "

156

"Thank you, Dr. Rice," Dr. Curell interrupted. "I think Miss Henderson has enough of the picture now. What we need, Miss Henderson, is someone to record and correlate data. Occasionally, you might be asked to graph results from certain experiments and even perhaps to prepare a presentation on some aspect of our research. I understand you're majoring in marine biology—with an emphasis on cetaceans. We cannot offer much in the way of hands-on experience, but you could witness some important breakthroughs in this area of cetacean research. Does it sound interesting?"

"Oh, yes! The chance to be even a small part of your team is very exciting, Dr. Curell."

"Good. We'll give it a green light, then. Tomorrow afternoon, at three. Sharp."

He showed her to the door. "Just one more thing."

"Yes, sir?"

His smile was still in place but his eyes glittered coldly. Martha sensed tension just beneath his casualness.

"As our findings are still in the formative stage, we'd appreciate our work held in the strictest confidence. I'm sure you understand."

"Yes, sir."

"Very good."

~~~~~~~~

The beach was packed—blanket to blanket people. But Martha had no difficulty finding the right crowd since someone had thoughtfully marked a trail with lavender balloons and signs proclaiming: Women's Summer Solstice Beach Bash. She threaded her way among the sunbathers trying not to kick sand on oiled bodies and came to stand in front of Karen.

"So, how do you like my new bathing suit?" she asked.

Karen looked up and grinned. "Magnificent! The suit's not too bad, either—what little of it there is!"

"I bought it with you in mind."

"You sure did! Want something to drink?"

"Good idea." Martha pushed the hair out of her face. "I forgot to bring anything."

"Well, we have plenty. Beer, cola, and apple juice, courtesy of the WSSBB Committee, of which I am a major contributing member."

"Hey," someone yelled from across the fire ring. "Toss me a beer!"

"Sure thing!" Karen took the request literally and tossed the can, ice sprinkling those underneath its path.

"Hey!" several women complained.

"If you can't stand the cold, stay away from the cooler!" Karen laughed, flinging the ice chips on her hands at the protesters.

It began as easily as that. Soon, ice was flying everywhere. Handfuls were being stuck into bathing suits and shorts, stuffed into shoes. Women tripped over each other, drinks were overturned onto the sand in zealous pursuit of the last bits of frozen fun.

"Well, now someone needs to make an ice run."

"How about you and me?" someone laughed in her ear.

Martha turned around to see Chris and Diana, both of them grinning ear to ear.

"I don't know, I understand that's usually Diana's job."

"Wouldn't that be a great title for my autobiography?" Diana laughed. "'The Icewoman Cometh.' And here you are again, Martha, trying to take my place."

Martha smiled weakly.

Chris leaned close. "Relax. She's teasing."

Karen came up suddenly and slid her arm around Martha's waist. She stuck out her other hand to Diana. "Hi. I'm Karen, Martha's other lover."

Martha shifted uncomfortably.

Karen went on cheerfully, "If you wouldn't mind doing the ice run, we'd all really appreciate it." Turning to Martha she said, "While they're gone, I could really use your help with something. C'mon." She practically dragged Martha away.

Yanking her arm back, Martha stopped and glared at Karen. "That was so incredibly rude! I can't begin to tell you how angry that you ..."

"I just asked them if they wouldn't mind getting ice."

"Don't start that innocent routine, you know what I'm talking about! I can't believe it! 'I'm Martha's other lover!' Like staking out property rights! You have no business ..."

158

"Look, I'm sorry, okay? I just thought we were gonna spend some time together today. I didn't know you planned on being with Ms. Wonderful and Company."

"I didn't know she was going to be here. But even if I had known, you have no right to tell me who I can talk to . . ."

"Sure! Of course! Don't I know I don't have any rights in this relationship! I get to hang around, waiting for handouts, waiting for you to be ready to be lovers with me! Forgive me; I apologize for overstepping my bounds!"

"I thought non-monogamy was politically correct these days."

"Don't look now, but only one of us is non-monogamous, sweetheart."

"That's no one's fault but your own, sweetheart!"

"Right."

~~~~~~~~

Dr. Rice stuck his head in the door of the glass-enclosed cubicle that was designated as her office. "Dr. Curell and I are leaving now, Miss Henderson. Just put the notes in my box when you've finished typing them."

She nodded and waved.

"And remember to close the door firmly. We wouldn't want just anyone to have access, now would we?"

Obediently she shook her head, and breathed a sigh of relief when she heard the outer door close. She leaned back in her chair and stretched. She had at least another hour's work, not just notes, but charts, graphs of the dear doctors' progress in teaching the dolphin to say the word "ball," in attempting to make them understand the meaning of "square" and "triangle." Martha sighed.

She got up and went out to the main lab area, to the dolphin tanks. There were three of them, one for each dolphin, connected by short water-filled tunnels but firmly closed off with solid metal gates so that there was no possibility of the dolphin even seeing each other. They were isolated, for a control, it had been repeatedly explained to her, so that they could not teach each other what one had learned.

Now, they all swam to the sides of the tanks closest to her and waited.

"Sorry you volunteered for this, aren't you?" She smiled at them and stuck her hand in the water of one tank, but the dolphin did not move closer. She waited. They all began to circle the tanks, but the one never did come back to her. In fact, they seemed to stop only at the gates, almost pointedly ignoring her. She shrugged and went back to work.

~~~~~~~~

"You promised to go to the next women's dance with me," Karen reminded.

"I hate dances," Martha groaned.

"You'll like this one, I promise."

"I'll hold you to that."

Karen snickered. "You can hold me anytime. C'mon, it'll be fun. If you don't want to dance, we can watch all the other dykes, meet people . . . "

"Okay, okay."

"Great! Just one more thing. I agreed to put up these flyers for the dance—would you help me out?"

"Ya want me to check coats at the door, too?"

"Naw, we have a coat rack for that."

~~~~~~~~

Martha had another lunch date with Chris, so she decided to hang the last few flyers around the community college campus.

"Why, hello!" said a familiar voice behind her as she thumbtacked the last one.

She turned around. "Ellen!" Martha realized guiltily that she'd only been over once since the baby had been born and she hadn't even called since then. And Ellen hadn't called her at all.

Ellen smiled. "Well, I guess we've both been pretty busy. Me with the baby and all and you with . . . Well, anyway, I finally took your advice." She indicated her arm load of books. "It's been so hard finding childcare for Tiffany, I've decided to open a nursery school, so I'm taking some child development and some business courses."

"That's great, Ellen. I'm glad. How're things going?"

"Pretty good. So far. You were right, it is different than high school."

"How's the kid?"

"She's fine, growing like a weed. Looks just like her dad—his eyes, his smile . . . " Her smile faded. "Mark and I split up a couple of months ago. Oh, I know you never liked him and I know he had his faults, still . . . " She sighed and nodded to herself. "But it was right, his leaving. We weren't good for each other. It wasn't working out."

"How's it working out now?"

"Emotionally . . . " she shrugged. "Financially, okay. I get welfare and Mark pays child support. My parents help out when they can and Mom watches Tiffany for me."

"So, they came around after all."

"Well, Dad and I still aren't on good terms, but Mom . . . Tiffany helped out there. One look at her and Mom just melted."

"Sounds like things are coming together for you at last. I'm glad, Ellen."

"Well, things are on the upswing, at least. So, what've you been up to lately?" Ellen tried to peer around Martha to see the flyer.

"I'm still in school, out at the University of California. Not much time for anything else, the quarter system pretty much keeps me hopping."

"You're still diving, I guess."

"As often as I can."

"And your parents?"

"Same as always. I don't get to see much of them, though. Between school and work . . . "

"Where you working these days?"

"The marine biology department at the university. I'm a lab assistant."

"Oh. So, are you seeing anybody?"

"Well, yes."

"Andy, by any chance?"

"Andy moved to Hawaii with his folks. And besides, you know it wasn't like that between Andy and me."

Ellen shook her head. "That's too bad, I always thought you made such a cute couple. Well, we ought to get together sometime, Martha, have dinner. Oh, you know what? We should have an old-fashioned slumber party. That's it! We can look through our old pictures, talk about the good old days, catch up on current events. Maybe play some records and dance a little. It'd be a blast! Oh, let's do it!"

"We should do that sometime," Martha agreed.

"So, what's the flyer about?" Ellen craned to read it.

"Flyer?"

"Yeah, flyer. You know, the one you just put up?" Ellen firmly pushed Martha aside.

"What does that mean—women only? How can you have a dance ... " Suddenly, her face flushed and she stared at Martha. "Oh. I see."

"Ellen, I hadn't exactly meant for you to find out like this."

"It's okay," she said, but her face had lost all expression. "It's okay."

"I'd like to talk with you about it, but not here, not right now. I'm supposed to meet someone for lunch in a few minutes."

Ellen's mouth dropped open. "That woman, what's-her-name, Kathy, who showered at your apartment! She was a ... she was your ... "

"Karen—her name is Karen. Ellen, don't get weird about this. When we get together ... "

Ellen's face changed radically as she realized she'd just invited a lesbian to a slumber party.

" . . . for dinner," Martha finished, all too aware of Ellen's thoughts.

"For dinner," Ellen echoed distantly. "Yes, we'll get together for dinner."

"Ellen, I've really got to go now. We'll talk."

Ellen nodded. Martha waved and dashed off.

~~~~~~~~

"So, you had a good time, didn't you?" Karen teased. "Tell me you're glad I talked you into going."

"Okay smart-ass, yes, I had a good time." Martha yawned. "But I wish we hadn't stayed so late."

"We'd be home by now if you lived with me." Karen couldn't keep the edge out of her voice.

"Oh, Karen, don't start that now," Martha said wearily.

162

"You never want to talk about it. Why won't you move in with me? I'm healthy, I have all my own teeth. My apartment is perfect for both of us."

Martha sighed. "Don't I have enough shit to deal with? Let's not go through all this again. For the last time, I am not ready for that kind of commitment! Now drop it!"

"We've been lovers over a year and a half! What kind of commitment are you ready for?" Karen shouted.

Martha stared out the window.

~~~~~~~~

"Okay, that's it—I can't stand this, Ellen." Martha pounded the chair arm. "It's as if we're total strangers. We've now talked about every meaningless thing under the sun. Let's get to the real issue between us: the fact that I'm a lesbian."

Ellen said nothing, so Martha continued with the speech she'd carefully rehearsed the night before. Finished, she noticed Ellen's smile seemed a bit thin and her eyes seemed unable to focus anywhere near the couch where Martha sat.

"Yoohoo, Ellen! It's your turn, say something."

Gazing out the window, absently nodding while she spoke, Ellen finally said, "Well, I can't say I'm too surprised. I always did think there was something . . . different . . . about you. You always were so . . . hard, so . . . aggressive. And you never did date. But I didn't think you hated men . . . "

"Did you hear anything I said? My loving women has nothing whatsoever to do with men, positively or negatively. I love women— how we think, how we move, who we are. If it matters, which I don't believe it does, I think men are just fine. But emotionally, sexually, I prefer women."

"Well, I guess what you do in private is your own business, just so long as you don't try to push it off on other people. And just so you know I'm not like that—I like men way too much to give them up. But, we can still be friends. And, of course, I won't tell anybody."

Martha didn't know whether to be angry or amused by such a stereotypical response. Knowing Ellen, she'd expected it. But that didn't make it easier. She stood up.

"I gotta go. Early class in the morning. Listen, don't try so hard to figure it all out. 'Why' doesn't matter much anyway. I am a lesbian, that's all."

Ellen looked at her for the first time. "Doesn't it just gross you out?"

"No, Ellen, it makes me very happy." Martha smiled and walked out.

~~~~~~~~~

"Hey, pass the marshmallows will ya, Karen?"

"Patience is a virtue, Lori. Want any more, Martha? I doubt we'll get 'em back this direction for a while, seeing as how Lori thinks I've been hogging them all." She made a face at her friend across the fire pit.

"Now, children," Martha admonished, "there's plenty of marshmallows to go around."

"Yeah," someone else added, "if you two don't share well, you're gonna have to go to your rooms. I wanta hear Debbie's guitar, not your bickering."

Everyone laughed and Karen threw the half full package to Lori, then leaned over to Martha. "Having a good time?"

"Reminds me a lot of summer camp."

"I never went to camp. Well, sixth grade camp, but that's not the same. So, I guess these weekend outings are to make up for my deprived childhood."

"Sure you don't mean depraved?"

The sound of another car pulling off the road onto the barren patch designated as the parking lot drew everyone's attention. They all strained to see through the twilight until finally, the woman came close enough to recognize.

"Hey, Karen, look who's here," Mary teased.

"Yeah, Karen, if you hurry, she might let you carry her sleeping bag."

"That's not what Karen wants to do with Carmela's sleeping bag," someone else laughed.

"You're just jealous," Karen retorted. "You'd trip over each other trying to move fast enough if she asked you for help. But she won't," she ended smugly.

"Who is Carmela?" Martha felt a little out of it.

Karen answered without taking her eyes from the advancing figure. "She's what you might call a political activist. She sings and writes poetry, the radical dyke kind. She left half of this city brokenhearted when she moved back East to build a women's community on land. We went out a couple of times—I had a pretty big thing for her. And no one will let me forget it. She comes to town occasionally and pops in to say hi."

Carmela was stunning, Martha had to admit, the kind of woman who made heads turn and hearts pound. Something about her reminded Martha of Chris.

"Hi, Carmela," several woman called.

"Howdy!" She sat down near the fire. "Hello, Karen."

Martha had never seen Karen blush before, but now her face was scarlet. "It's good to see you, Carmela."

"It's good to be back. So, what are you crazy ladies up to these days? C'mon, now, I want all the juicy details."

After a while, when all the stories were recounted and the fire had mostly died down to glowing coals, Debbie once again brought out her guitar and the mood slowed and mellowed.

"I'll be back in a little while," Karen whispered in Martha's ear.

Martha closed her eyes and nodded, content to listen to the music as it flowed into and became part of the evening breeze that played in her hair and tickled her skin. And underneath the music, she could hear crickets and the soft crackles of the last pieces of wood succumbing to the energy of the flames.

All too soon, the circle was empty. One by one, everyone had wandered off to their tents. Debbie had stayed, strumming soft chords, until the fire was nothing but pale specks in the dark ashes, but now she, too, had retired to the comfort of her lover and their sleeping bag.

Karen still had not returned. Neither had Carmela. Neither had Carmela's sleeping bag.

Martha went to bed.

The chill of early morning settled in before Karen quietly crawled into their tent.

"I'm going home as soon as the sun's up," Martha said stiffly.

"How come? What's up?"

"What do you mean, how come? It's only obvious."

"I don't get it."

"Do you have any idea what time it is?"

"You can't possibly be upset about my spending some time with Carmela."

"I can't?"

"No, you can't. You're the one who's pushed non-monogamy down my throat for two years. My being with Carmela doesn't effect our relationship any more than you being with Chris."

"Did you make love?"

"Do you make love with Chris?"

"So, you did it just to spite me."

"I don't believe this! What an ego you have! I did IT, as you say, because Carmela and I are old friends and I enjoy being with her."

"Good. Because I'm going home."

"Is this crazy, or what? Fine. Don't let me stop you."

"I won't."

They both lay rigidly awake until dawn.

~~~~~~~~

She stuffed the roll of neatly typed notes into Dr. Rice's mailbox and walked out to the main lab. She reached for the light switch. Suddenly, the dolphin began racing around their tanks, leaping and splashing, whistling in ways she'd never heard them. She ran over to the tanks and just as suddenly they stopped. Water lapped over the pool edges and fell to the cement floor, splashing loudly in the sudden silence. She looked in each tank but could see nothing out of the ordinary, and now the dolphin were just floating around the gates. Maybe they had been bored. She turned to leave. They began to whistle again. She turned back and they stopped. But they weren't facing her direction at all, they were at the gates again. She felt a strong urge to go over and flip the switch that would raise those barriers. She even walked back and put her hand on it. But she had been warned again and again that that was not to be done. If she were caught... She shook her head as if to clear it and turned out the lights, and firmly shut the door behind her.

~~~~~~~~

"Martha, I just can't do this anymore. I love you more than I ever thought I could love anyone and I want more than just seeing you whenever you can squeeze me into your busy schedule. I want to share my life with you—all the days and nights, all the little things. I want to be your partner in life, not just your lover."

"Sounds like heterosexual marriage to me."

"If it does, you're hearing my words but not listening to their meanings. I'm not interested in being tied to each other, I want us to be bonded with each other—to love and support and nourish ourselves as well as each other. Goddammit, Martha! I want more of what's good between us, not less!"

Martha remained silent and Karen sighed.

"Look," Martha said finally, "I love you, too. I don't understand what's keeping me from saying, 'Yes, okay, we'll live together,' but I just can't! I can't make that kind of commitment right now. Please understand and give me the time and space I need!"

"This is ripping me apart! It's hard enough for me that you see Chris—but that you won't make any kind of permanent commitment to our relationship is driving me crazy. It seems like you want to make me jealous. Chris is a wonderful woman, but what about me? She doesn't have to ask anything of you because she has a primary relationship that meets her needs. You are my love, the only relationship I have, the only one I want! She lives with her partner—I get to see you whenever you have time. I can't seem to get through to you! Why don't you stop telling me to understand your needs and try just once to understand mine! It takes two people to make a relationship, baby, and I'm getting damn tired of carrying it for both of us!"

"I don't know what to do. You are trying to force me into something I just can't agree to. It wouldn't work out, I know it. I'm not ready! Besides, why don't you talk to Carmela? I'm sure she'd jump at the chance."

Karen stood up. "This doesn't have anything to do with Carmela, goddammit! In case you're interested, I haven't seen her since the camp-out."

She grabbed her jacket and rammed her arms into the sleeves.

"I think maybe I need to take a little time and space myself, get my perspective back. I want what I want and I'm obviously going to have to deal with not getting it. Well, sweetheart, I survived quite nicely before I met you, and I can make it just as well now without you. I just need to get my perspective back." She headed for the door. "See you around."

"Karen, I really do love you," Martha called after her.

"And I love you. I just can't live this way anymore!" She closed the door behind her.

Staring out the window, Martha watched numbly as Karen got in her car and drove away.

"One times one is one, one times two is two, one times three is three . . . "

~~~~~~~~

They'd been calling her for quite a while but she didn't realize it. All she felt was a kind of vague restlessness that increased with each passing day until, finally, she could ignore it no longer.

One warm Monday afternoon she packed up the graphs she'd been working on for Dr. Curell and decided to follow her inner voices wherever they lead.

They lead her right to Ocean Park.

Changes had taken place in her long absence. The pool had been enlarged and Pacific Whiteside and Atlantic dolphin now swam alongside many other unfamiliar ones. Apollo was gone, shipped to another park somewhere, quite probably because he tried to tickle someone else's hand with his tongue. There were only a few left that she knew.

And she hadn't even really said goodbye.

Today, no one lingered by the pool. Not even an attendant was in sight. Taking her usual position, Martha leaned far out over the edge, hands thrust underwater, and waited. After half an hour or so passed with no dolphin even looking in her direction, she began to feel as if

168

she had made a mistake in coming. Her ribs hurt, her shoulders felt stiff, and the glare from the water was awful. She decided to go home. She stood and stretched and turned away.

But now, the dolphin seemed to take an interest. They formed a circle directly in front of her, just out of reach, and began clicking and whistling. As if choreographed, the bunched up group began an intricate dance, swimming over, under, and around each other as if weaving a blanket of movement and sound but at same time, watching her, coming close and breathing on her only to move away again. It was pretty, and it teased something at the back of her mind.

Hugging the inside edge, one of the Whiteside swam close and stopped beside her. Yet every time she reached out, the dolphin moved a little farther to the right, just out of reach. Looking up, Martha noticed that all the others had gone to the far side of the pool, floating just below the newly built raised observation platform. Unthinkingly, Martha followed the Whiteside, and found herself standing on that platform. At once, all the dolphin, strangers and old friends alike, crowded close. She had to lean over a waist-high railing as far as she could, making her feel a little light-headed, but the dolphin were so eager, straining up to touch her fingers as she reached down. Holding on to the rail with one hand, she stretched to stroke as many of the dolphin as she could.

She stretched too far, or perhaps her grip loosened for an instant—she felt herself falling and splash! She was in the water.

Her mind ripped open. Impossible swirls of color, wondrous shapes and images danced behind her closed eyes. Clicks and whistles, music of incredible complexity that she not only heard but physically felt created a kaleidoscope of sensations in her body. She went crazy. Sensory overload. She felt pulled, pushed in and out of her body, other bodies differently shaped. She was one, she was many. She was in the dolphin petting pool and she wasn't suppose to be and they were going to take away her annual pass . . .

From far away she heard human voices, felt hands lifting her out of the water.

"Are you all right? Do you need some help? Are you okay?" Someone shoved a towel at her.

She dropped the towel and pushed the hands away. She turned back to the dolphin. They were all bunched up in the center pool watching her. Humming . . . She gulped air.

An attendant appeared with two security guards and kindly but firmly escorted her to the first-aid station. She didn't wait for the nurse. As soon as the guards left, so did Martha. Blindly, head aching, she stumbled out of the park and by some grace found her car. Clutching the wheel, her body wracked by sobs, she shook uncontrollably. Her breath came in ragged gasps.

How long she sat there perched on the edge of madness she never knew, but slowly, minutes stretching out like hours, she regained some measure of control. Concentrating on breathing deeply and evenly, she tried to forget what had just happened. But she couldn't. She wanted to go back, she needed to go back. She needed to understand. How could something like that happen and then just be over, forever closed to her. There was something more . . . something just out of reach . . .

She started the car and slowly drove away. She rode around for a while, unable to clear her head, and finally found herself at the lab, without having made any conscious decision to go there.

She smoothed out her now-dry clothes and ran a comb through her hair.

"Hello, Martha," the security guard smiled in surprise. "What brings you here so late? Dr. Rice and Dr. Curell have both gone home already."

"Hi, Frank. I've been worrying all day that I made a mistake on one of the graphs I did this morning for Dr. Curell," she lied. "I just have to go check."

He smiled again and nodded. "I guess that'd be all right. Just remember to lock everything back up when you leave." He pressed a little button on his desk and waved her through the now unlocked door that separated the labs from the entrance.

She closed the lab door and looked around, bewildered. She had no idea why she lied to Frank, but then, she could hardly have told him the truth—she didn't know herself why she was there. She switched on the overhead lights. Everything was as usual. The filters hummed, the dolphin swam calmly in their separate little pools.

But now they stopped swimming and stared at her. As one, they swam over and faced the gates. She walked slowly, unthinkingly, to the control panel on the far wall and flipped a switch. The gates groaned open. She slowly and deliberately removed her clothes, neatly folding and laying them carefully aside. She dove into the warm water.

Immediately, all three dolphin were beside her. And just as immediately, her senses were assaulted with a repeat of the afternoon's encounter. She cried out, but the dolphin were right there, touching and supporting her as her mind stretched wider and wider.

Sometime later, time having ceased to matter, she became aware they were guiding her to the pool's edge. Exhausted, she pulled herself out. Drying off the best she could with paper towels, she dressed and even remembered to lock the door on her way out.

"Did you find it?" Frank asked.

"Find it?" Martha repeated.

"The mistake." Frank eyed her suspiciously.

"Oh. Yes, I did, thanks. G'night."

~~~~~~~~~

Martha sat in her living room in the dark. Swimming through seas rich in life, tickled by undulating forests of kelp, she tasted colors her eyes had never seen. Filled with joy that bordered on pain, she heard music sweeter than any ever played, songs that told a history far older than the world she knew. As intense as her first dive had been, it had not prepared her for this. She ignored the phone, the doorbell, everything except her most basic needs, anything that pulled her attention.

After three intoxicating days she came to four sobering conclusions: She hadn't fallen into the pool at Ocean Park—she'd been pulled. Dolphin communicate by three-dimensional visualizations that include all the five senses, and probably more. And not only are they really people, but they are quite possibly the most intelligent life form on the planet.

On the fourth day she dressed and went to work.

"Sorry," the new guard at the door shook his head, "I can't let you in. This paper lists all authorized personnel and you're not on it."

"For chrissake, I work in lab forty-two with Dr. Rice and Dr. Curell! I have for over a year now! Call 'em!"

The guard continued to shake his head but he picked up the phone. He quickly turned back to face her. "They say you no longer work here. Sorry."

"What do you mean? Wait! Did they say why? Call them back and ask them why! I've been sick for three days, too sick even to call in, but I'm okay now. I have something important to discuss with them! Please call them back!"

The guard was adamant. "You'll have to leave now."

"But I need this job . . . "

"Goodbye." He showed her the door.

She drove straight home and called the lab.

"Who is calling, please?" asked an impersonal voice.

"Uh, Martha Henderson. It's important."

After a longish pause the voice returned. "I'm sorry, neither Dr. Curell nor Dr. Rice can speak to you at this time. Thank you for calling." The voice hung up before Martha could say anything.

She put the receiver down and then immediately picked it up again. She dialed Karen's number. She hung up again before it had a chance to ring.

~~~~~~~

Rummaging through the closet, Martha found Karen's green wool pullover. Tenderly rubbing its softness against her cheek, she breathed deeply—it still smelled like Karen. Tears burned behind her eyes. Abruptly, she threw it down and kicked it as far back into the closet as she could. She slammed the door. With a sigh, she reopened it slowly and, putting the sweater neatly on a hanger, hung it on the rod beside her things. This time she closed the door more gently.

~~~~~~~

It was clear Ellen had been drinking.

"Maybe I should come back some other night," Martha suggested.

"No, no, it's okay. I just got a little carried away with the cooking sherry is all. But I want you to have dinner with me."

172

"Where's Tiffany?"

"She's in bed already. I wanted some time to talk, y'know, woman-to-woman. It's hard to talk with a little one around. Have a seat." Ellen was looking at her funny. Something was up.

Martha followed her into the kitchen. "So, what can I do to help?"

"Just sit down and relax, I'm making you dinner tonight."

Martha smiled tightly and nodded, but she didn't sit down. "How's school?"

"Good," Ellen said, opening the oven. "You were right about meeting people. I met this really nice guy the other day . . . "

"This isn't going to be another 'Aren't men wonderful and isn't heterosexuality grand?' number, is it?"

"Martha!"

"Well, you've gotta admit you've been leaning very heavily in that direction since our Big Talk."

"I was going to say," Ellen went on primly, "I met this really nice guy who is gay and we had a long talk. He helped me understand some things and I want to apologize for being so, well . . . difficult. Friends?"

"Sure, friends." Martha stuck out her hand for the handshake that had been their custom since their very first fight back in junior high. But instead of taking her hand, Ellen moved in close and hugged her, planting a sloppy, alcoholic kiss on her cheek.

"That's good. Old friends are the best y'know. Best friends. 'The twins,' that's what they used to call us. We gotta stick together, you and me. Best friends forever."

During dinner, out of the blue, Ellen asked, "So, how come you never made a pass at me?"

Martha choked and stared at her.

"No, I'm serious," Ellen continued in what she seemed to believe was a seductive voice. "I really want to know. You don't find me attractive, or what?" She rose and moved to stand behind Martha, leaning over just enough that her breasts brushed against Martha's back. She whispered into Martha's ear, "How come you found all those other girls so hot but not your closest friend? Don't you love me?"

Martha slid out of her chair and walked over to the sink. "Ellen! You never gave the slightest indication . . . "

"You're the lesbian, you're the one who's supposed to make the first move—and now I wanta know why you haven't."

"Ellen, we've been friends a long time. You're like my sister!"

"So, you don't find me attractive!" Ellen pouted cutely.

"I don't know what to say, Ellen. What is it you want? Are you trying to tell me you're a lesbian?"

"I'm trying to tell you I think best friends should be close with one another. Don't you love me enough to be close with me?" She slowly began to unbutton her shirt.

"I think I'd better go now." Martha walked out to the living room.

Ellen stomped after her, the simpy act over.

"So! Lesbians are just like men—they lead you on and then dump you! You're all a bunch of animals! You don't know anything about loving someone, just using them! Well, I wouldn't sleep with you, anyway! Who'd want to? It's unnatural! Ugly, nasty!"

"Good-bye, Ellen. Thanks for supper." She opened the door.

"Goddamn queer! Get outta here!"

Martha closed the door behind her just as something smashed against it from the inside.

~~~~~~~~

The phone woke her out of a sound sleep. "Hello?" she mumbled.

"I'm sorry! I'm so sorry for everything! I don't know why I did it! I was drunk! Oh, I feel so bad!"

"It's okay, Ellen, calm down. I know you were drunk. It's okay. We'll talk about it all later."

"Oh, you don't understand! Your mom . . . I'm so ashamed. Tell her I'm sorry. I didn't mean it! I'd call back, tell her myself, only I'm scared. She'll hate me. You already hate me, don't you? Oh, I'm so sorry!"

"Ellen, what about my mom?"

Feeling sick, she listened as Ellen blubbered about calling Jean and telling her that her daughter was a "goddamn queer."

"Oh, shit! How could you . . . how dare you . . . " She heard a click and the receiver went dead in her hand. She sank back onto her pillow. "Oh, shit!"

~~~~~~~~~

Lunch was a little strained, as the whole morning had been, neither of them wanting to bring up the subject they both knew had to be discussed. Jean fussed with the centerpiece, arranging and rearranging the flowers. Martha folded and unfolded her napkin. She took a deep breath.

"Ellen told me about the call the other night. She wants you to know she's sorry."

Jean didn't look up from the flowers. "It was a little upsetting, to get a call like that. And so late at night. She sounded drunk. I didn't know Ellen drank."

"She was. She was drunk. Nevertheless, she was right. Sort of." Martha shrugged. "I don't think of myself as a goddamn queer, I think of myself as a lesbian. I am a lesbian, Mom. I've been trying to find the right way and the right time to tell you for a long time. I wanted something subtle, but I could never think of any subtle way to say it. I'm sorry you had to find out like this. I should have told you."

Jean smoothed the tablecloth. She stirred her iced tea. She did not look at Martha.

"Please say something, Mom."

"I don't know what to say, Martha Jean. Of course, I don't want it to be true. It's against everything I was raised to believe in. I guess it makes me wonder where I went wrong, how I failed you."

"Mom, don't be absurd. You didn't fail me! What does that mean, anyway?"

"It means you weren't raised like this. Who lead you into this? It couldn't have been Ellen. Was it somebody at that college? That diving instructor you used to go on about . . . did she . . . ?"

"Mom, no one lead me into anything. It's who I am, who I've always been. I had gay friends in high school . . . "

"Who?"

" . . . but they didn't make me a lesbian."

"Oh, Martha! Have you talked to anyone about this? A counselor, a psychologist?"

"Mom, this is not a problem. This is my life, how I'm choosing to live it!"

"But Martha, what kind of life . . . "

"You've probably heard a lot of stories about what lesbians are like, but Mom, they're mostly untrue. I'm still the same me I've always been, only I'm no longer hiding and pretending not to be something that I am."

Her mother looked away.

"Mom, I want you to be happy for me."

"You're my daughter and I love you—but *happy*?" She shook her head. "I don't think *happy* is a word that applies."

~~~~~~~~

She automatically reached over to shut off the alarm. But no matter how many times she hit the button, the damn alarm wouldn't stop. She opened her eyes a crack and peered blearily at the clock. Darkness. It wasn't morning. The phone. The phone was ringing.

"Hello?"

"Kincaid? This here is Carol Ann, your sister."

"I know you're my sister, Carol Ann," she grumped. "I hope you didn't call me at . . . three twenty-five in the morning just to share this insight with me."

"Kincaid, are you sittin' down?"

"Carol Ann, I'm lying down. What do you want?"

"Kincaid, there's been an accident. Bobby's dead, Kincaid, our big brother is dead. Kincaid?"

"Yeah, I'm here."

"The funeral is Wednesday. Kincaid, did you hear me?"

"Uh huh."

"You are comin', aren't you?"

"Yeah, Carol Ann, I'll come." What else could she do?

"Well, better bring some summer clothes. It's unseasonably warm this year. And you know you don't have to worry about a motel, you can always stay here with me an' Donnie."

"Thanks, Carol Ann."

"Travel safely, now."

She lay in the darkness staring at the ceiling like she used to do as a kid. Maybe Karen was right. There seemed no way to just leave the past behind. Sitting up and turning on the light, she reached for the phone. Might as well get started.

Chapter Eight

Twenty-one years old and her first flight—it should have been fun and exciting. Instead, a phrase Karen had once used kept running through her mind, something about "living with the past." She absently rubbed her burning eyes. Living with the past was something Bobby hadn't been able to do, either. She shivered.

~~~~~~~~

What she noticed first was the green grass—with no sprinklers or water hoses in sight. It rained here! She'd lived long enough with avocado green and eucalyptus grey-green that true green was a feast. And the pines—acres and acres, tall and straight, and nobody had planted them, they just grew, generation after generation springing up in the same soil, roots deep and intermingled. The warm spring air heavy with their perfume stirred long buried memories of her childhood.

"Been a long time, huh?" Donnie glanced at her as he drove.

"Quite a while."

"Well, I'm sure things haven't changed all that much."

"But I have."

"Huh? Oh, yeah, sure. Well, they say you can't come home again, but I don't believe that. Born a Southerner, die a Southerner. Ain't that right?"

She didn't answer.

"I never been to California. Always wanted to, though. Wanted to take Carol Ann to Disneyland for our honeymoon, but... you know how that goes. You seen Disneyland?"

"Yes."

"Is it as grand as they let on?"

She smiled. "It's pretty grand, all right."

Donnie nodded but didn't answer and she couldn't think of anything else to say, so they drove on in silence. The silence became uncomfortable. Donnie turned the radio on. He fiddled with the knobs. He turned the radio off. Abruptly, he signaled a lane change and pulled over to the curb.

"I'm not much for small talk, 'specially when there's somethin' on my mind. I know we don't know each other, an' you might think I'm buttin' in, but I am part of the family now, an' I want to talk to you 'bout Bobby 'fore we get home. Carol Ann's pretty broke up an' I'm tryin' to spare her all I can. Now, I don't know how you an' Bobby got on . . . "

She stared at her hands, folded neatly in her lap. "We weren't close."

He nodded. "Meanin' no disrespect to the family, I never thought much of him, myself. He ran with a rough crowd an' he treated Carol Ann like dirt. Always in an' out of trouble . . . I bailed him outta jail more times than I care to count—for Carol Ann's sake—an' never so much as a thank you from him. We all hoped the Army would turn him aroun', make a man outta him," he shook his head, "but he came back from 'Nam worse than ever—always drinkin' an' actin' a fool.

"That's how it happened . . . he was drunk an' drag racin' up aroun' Twin Oaks Ridge. On a Sunday evenin'. Y'know how the road sorta curves aroun' an' drops off sheer on one side? He was in the wrong lane goin' up when he met a car comin' down. They swerved into the hillside, he went down the cliff. The hospital did all they could, but . . . I'm sorry to be so blunt, Kincaid, I just thought you oughta know, an' I didn't want you to ask Carol Ann."

She nodded. "I'd like to make arrangements to go to the funeral home early tomorrow. I'll go again with you and Carol Ann during the family time, but I'd like some time alone there first."

Donnie glanced at her. "You sure you want to do that? Even if you weren't close, losin' kin ain't easy."

She stared straight ahead. "It's important to me, Donnie, I have some things to sort out. I'll be okay."

He nodded and started the car.

~~~~~~~~

"Oh, Kincaid, I am so glad to see you! I wanted to come to the airport, but the baby had just dropped off . . . an' I try to get in a nap when he does, I'm that tired lately. But I'm so glad you're here!"

"Carol Ann, a baby?"

"James Allen, four months old day after tomorrow. But you knew that. You got my letters, didn't you? I wrote right straight away when I found out, an' again after he was born. I even sent pictures."

Martha shifted uncomfortably. "No, I didn't get them."

"Well, isn't that the oddest thing?"

"What is, Sugarbabe?" Donnie came in with Martha's luggage.

"Kincaid didn't get my letters about Jamie."

"Well, I 'spect she knows 'bout our little wonder by now. You've had a whole two minutes with her. Showed her all the pictures yet?" He winked.

"Donald James, this is hardly the time for jokes. Now, you make yourself scarce. Jamie's still sleepin' an' we got us some sisterly catchin' up to do. Let's go sit in the kitchen, Kincaid, I got some gumbo on the stove. I expect you're hungry, such a long trip an' all, an' I hear they don't give you enough on those old airplanes to keep body an' soul together."

Martha followed, wondering if there was meat in the gumbo. Had Carol Ann remembered that she was a vegetarian?

"Kincaid, I declare you are so brown you look just like Grandma Kincaid! Speakin' of Grandma, there's a box of her things up in the attic I want to go through with you 'fore you leave. Don't let me forget, now. Her cedar chest is up there, too. It's yours, you remember. Her old quilt is in there, the special one. That's yours, too, bein' the oldest girl. You knew her last words were of you? You an' her mama. She sure thought a lot of you."

"She thought a lot of all of us kids, Carol Ann."

"But, you were somethin' special to her, Kincaid, an' you know it. It's okay, that's all past now, I ain't jealous anymore. So, tell me 'bout California. Is it as crazy as they say?"

~~~~~~~~

The silence in the room hung heavy, thick. Even the door closed quietly behind her. She walked resolutely toward the shiny metalic-blue coffin, the top raised as she'd requested. They had tried to talk her out of that, gently at first, finally saying they hadn't been able to repair all the damage to his face, but she'd persisted, needing to see the reality of death to believe in it.

It was Bobby. Older, taller, a little more filled out than the skinny, lanky adolescent she'd left—nevertheless, it was Bobby. His body. What was left of it. She reached out and touched his hand. Cold. Hard. She shivered and drew her hand back, rubbing it quickly with her other one. Dead. No energy, no life-force. Empty. Like Hermes— only Bobby's eyes were closed.

She briefly wondered where the energy went. Was there a heaven, a hell? Or did life simply turn off, like the light when you flipped the switch? She knew the rhetoric, the proper Southern Baptist response, but she didn't know the answer. And she found no comfort in "the faith of our fathers." Where was Bobby?

She pulled a chair close and tried to think about him, about the brother she had grown up with, but her thoughts refused to focus, her brain felt as heavy as the air. The cloying sweetness of the flowers grew overwhelming in the closeness. Or perhaps it wasn't the flowers at all. Still, the longer she sat, the more uncomfortable she became. She rose to leave. The chair slid soundlessly over the carpet. The door closed noiselessly behind her, making the silence complete once more.

~~~~~~~~~

Carol Ann returned to the table and sat down stiffly. "The phone's for you. She asked for Martha. You still goin' by Martha these days?"

"Hello, Martha."

"Hello, Karen."

"I got your sister's number from your Mom. She told me about your brother. How are you doing?"

"I'm okay, I'm hanging in. It's nice of you to call."

"Could you come pick me up at the airport? It's too late for me to rent a car tonight and besides, I don't know my way around here."

"What are you talking about?"

"I need you to pick me up and help me find a room somewhere. Will you do that?"

"Where are you? Aren't you in California?"

"No, I'm here, at the airport."

"Here? What are you doing here?"

"Where else would I be when you need support? I love you, Martha."

~~~~~~~~

"It's nice of Carol Ann to let me stay here. Southern hospitality, I assume."

"She wouldn't be so hospitable if she could see us now," Martha noted dryly. They were lying naked, cuddled close on the bed. "But she'd be oh, so polite. Yes, it's only good manners for her to ask you to stay. And good manners for you to accept—but only for a short time. Personally, I would have preferred a hotel, but I caught myself just in time and remembered my own manners." She rested her head against the softness of Karen's breast.

"Donnie seems nice."

"Donnie is easily impressed. He thinks I'm holding up admirably. But then, he only has Carol Ann to judge by—and she bawls at the merest mention . . . "

"Why do you say it like that? Crying is an important part of the healing process."

"Yeah, but I can't tell if she's crying for Bobby or for some fantasy brother she made him up to be. He never was anyone's ideal of a brother and the last few years he was a real jerk-off. Carol Ann has always had a difficult time with reality."

"I take it you don't ever cry—even when you're sad, or scared, or lonely?"

Martha shrugged. "What good would it do?"

"It usually makes people feel better. You know, better out than in."

Martha traced the bumpy pattern of the chenille bedspread.

"When Carol Ann called, I tried to think of a way to get out of coming here. I didn't want to deal with it—not Bobby, not any of it. He'd made it quite clear long ago that he didn't have any use for any of us. I mean, why come now? What did it matter if I came two thousand miles to his funeral? Hell, he'd been dead to us for years, anyway."

"So, why did you come?"

181

Martha shrugged. "I don't know. Maybe some of the things you used to talk about began to make some sense. Maybe I'm ready to clean up the past and move on.

"I went to see Bobby today and tried to think back to when we were just kids, before the meanness and the nastiness he used as a wall to separate himself from us. I couldn't remember a thing. It was like I was numb. I looked at my brother's dead body and not only did I not cry, I didn't feel anything at all. I don't know if I ever will."

Karen's arm tightened around her.

~~~~~~~~

"I just sorta thought they might come." Martha's toe pushed hard against the blue-grey boards to keep the swing moving. "He was their son, after all, their first child."

"What would you have said to them?" Karen asked.

"I would have asked her why. After she left, I decided it was one of the great cosmic questions of life. Why did my mother leave me? Right up there next to why was I born? I figured to ask God when I died. It would be much simpler just to ask Mama." She shrugged. "But I really no longer need to ask, I guess I know why."

"Why?"

"Stuck in a dead-end life, she saw her escape and grabbed it with both hands."

"Loving you is not part of a dead-end life."

Martha looked away. "We never talked about it, you know. I found the note when I got home from school. Bobby, Carol Ann, and Jimmy all read the note. They left it to me to explain to Patty and Billy Ray. And then, nothing. It was as if we'd never had a mother. Like she'd died and we'd never known her. Sometimes, late at night when I couldn't sleep, I pretended she really had died. I made up great, elaborate stories about it. But we never talked about her. Once I did, to Bobby. Just that once."

She stood and went to lean against the porch rail. "And I want to ask him why he did that to Carol Ann. He never laid a hand on me. Not like that, anyway. Why did he pick on her? She never stuck up for herself. I could've handled it better if it'd been me—I'd've fought back."

182

"It wasn't your fault, Martha. You were a child, too."

"But I was oldest. Well, next to Bobby." She plopped back down on the swing. "Boy, Patty sure has grown up. And wearing lipstick! God, Mammaw Wilson would pitch a hissy fit if she were alive to see that! You know, I didn't even recognize Jimmy. He used to be so skinny . . . And, that Billy Ray, I bet he's a heartbreaker. They're all strangers to me, Karen. It's like they're all a family and I'm a distant relative."

"If you lived here it would be different, Martha."

"I don't know. Maybe."

~~~~~~~~

"It's all here, I saved ever'thing—all of Grandma's things, all of Mammaw's, as much as I could from our old house on Van Buren. You bein' the oldest now," Carol Ann's voice caught and she dabbed at her eyes. "It's right you should take what you want. I offered Bobby, but he wasn't interested. Right under here is Grandma's cedar chest. I 'spect you'll want that."

Martha nodded. She lifted the lid slowly and breathed in the rich scent.

"That's Grandma's weddin' dress there on top." Carol Ann gingerly picked up the folds of yellowed lace and held it close. "She must've been such a beautiful bride!"

"Would you like to keep the gown?"

"Oh, Kincaid! I couldn't ask that of you. Her weddin' dress!"

"I think she would have wanted you to have it, Carol Ann."

"You think so?" She danced in the cramped space, taking great care that the dress touched nothing.

Gently moving the quilts and doilies and embroidered pillowcases, Martha saw something small and round drop to the bottom. She reached down. A small beaded bag—Grandma's medicine bag. Memory stirred. A dream. Grandma had wanted her to have it. Grandma had tried to give her the bag, but she couldn't hold on to it. And then, Grandma sang to her.

"Oh, my goodness," Carol Ann exclaimed. "I haven't seen that for years. She used to wear it 'round her neck, on a braided thong— you 'member? She wore it ever' time she went out."

"I remember. And you were always telling her it looked tacky."

"Why, I did no such thing!"

"You did. You used to pout until she tucked it into her dress so no one would see."

"Why, I never did! I can't imagine why you would say such a thing!"

Martha changed the subject. "You said my tan made me look like Grandma, but I always thought I looked like Mama."

Carol Ann shook her head. "No, you've always taken after Grandma. An' she sure favored you, that's for sure. Ever'one always said you seemed more like her daughter than her granddaughter."

Martha pressed the bag to her cheek and breathed deeply of the warm, leathery scent. Scenes from childhood flooded her mind. Long, hot days in the garden with her grandmother, learning just when to pick the okra, the squash, thanking them for becoming supper. Learning to fashion gourds into dippers and planters and squirrel feeders. Long whispered talks while the little ones napped about how animals talked to one another. Singing the sun up. Telling stories to the corn to make it grow taller. "A spark from a old fire," Grandma had called her. Singing the sun up!

"Carol Ann, I'm not crazy! I didn't make these things up! She taught me. She passed it on to me, all the old ways. I remember. I know real things. Oh, Carol Ann! She taught me to hear and to see."

"What are you goin' on about, Kincaid?"

But Martha was running downstairs and didn't hear. "Karen! Karen, get your shoes on. I want to go to my grandmother's house. I want to see where her garden used to be."

~~~~~~~~

"A parking lot. They turned my grandma's beautiful garden into a parking lot for a shopping mall! That's disgusting."

"Yes, it is."

"I didn't expect the garden to be here, but a parking lot ... Let's go see what they did to the house I grew up in, it isn't far."

"Now, this is where we lived after Carol Ann was born." She pointed to an ancient white clapboard house, paint peeling, the screen door hanging by one hinge.

184

"Hasn't changed much. Screen's still broken." She opened the car door and got out. "Come on around back, I'll show you my tree. For a long time, she was my best friend. She hid me from my father and kept me safe, she sang songs to me, she listened to all my stories."

Turning the corner of the house, Martha ran forward. "She's here, she's still here! I was afraid . . . " She ran her hands over the rough, uneven bark. "Listen. If you listen real hard, you can hear her singing to you . . . " Her voice caught, her breathing deepened into sobbing. She hid her face from Karen and leaned against the tree.

"This is so dumb! I don't even know why I'm crying!" Her tears still fell, unchecked by her embarrassment.

Karen moved in close and stroked Martha's hair. "It doesn't matter why. It doesn't matter. Just do it, let it come."

Martha looked up and saw the tender smile on Karen's face and cried all the harder.

~~~~~~~~

Martha rolled over in the darkness. Karen's hand found hers under the covers.

"You awake?" Martha was surprised.

"Uh huh."

"Can we talk, then? So much is coming back . . . "

Karen squeezed her hand in reply and rolled over to face her.

"God, it's no wonder I forgot so much. I was just a child, and it was so confusing . . . On one hand, Grandma taught me how to hear underneath and see beyond the normal. She used to call it "feeling the power." When she talked to me, I knew she was telling me the truth. I really did feel the power, deep inside and all around." She sat up. "Like diving, Karen! Like you've seen the light swim, I heard the light sing! I heard the plants sing. I knew Grandma's stories made the corn grow taller and straighter; I saw it happen. I knew we were all part of the dance of the universe, each with our own steps and our own rhythm. I felt connected with the Earth and everything on her."

She laid back down.

"But, on the other hand, I lived with people who said my grandma was crazy. They didn't seem to be able to hear or see, or even care that they couldn't. They hunted and fished and laughed at me when I cried for the animals. They made fun of me. Stories were told at every family gathering about my active imagination. It wasn't safe to know what I knew, so I pretended that I was pretending. Does that make sense? When I talked to animals, or sang with trees, I let on I was just play-acting. But after a while, I began to believe that I really was making it all up. I felt as if I were just pretending that animals talked or that trees sang. As I got older, I tried to stop the game and when I couldn't, then I began to feel crazy. I was crazy if I believed that it all really happened, and I was crazy because I couldn't stop pretending that it did.

"When I got outta here, when I was adopted by Walter and Jean, I made sure to put it all behind me. I forgot to even pretend. The game stopped all by itself. Except for one time at summer camp . . . And of course, the dolphin . . . "

Her breath caught. She turned and buried her face into Karen's breast.

"Oh, Karen, I lost so much! I want it back. I want it back!"

~~~~~~~~

"Here you go," Martha handed Karen a frosty glass of iced tea.

"Fancy," Karen smiled, removing the slice of lemon and dunking it in her glass in true Southern fashion.

Martha settled down beside her on the swing.

"So, what do you want to do today?" Karen asked, gently pushing the swing with her toes.

"Well, I'd sorta like to go to Sherman's Park," Martha said. "It was one of my favorite places when I was a kid. Used to have pony rides and sometimes old man Bowers would bring his wagon and give us hay rides around the park for a quarter. And there's this pretty little creek . . . "

"I still have a hard time believing fresh water flows anywhere but from a faucet."

Martha chuckled and sipped her tea.

Karen cleared her throat. "I think your sister has caught on to our relationship."

"Oh, I don't think so. I'm sure I'd have heard about it if she had."

186

"She glares at me every time I talk to you. She acts like I farted or something."

"Oh, that's just because you're calling me Martha."

"That is your name, isn't it? I mean, I've noticed everyone here calls you Kincaid, but I assumed it was a nickname like Slim or Shorty."

"It was our last name and it's also what people called our father. And when I was little, it's what people called me . . . "

The clatter of a busy diner greeted them as her daddy held the door open and motioned her in ahead of him.

"Hey, Kincaid! Who's that gorgeous blonde you got with you?" a man in khaki work clothes and a broad grin called loudly from the counter.

Her daddy lifted her way up in the air and sat her down on top of that counter so she was as tall as the man with the big smile.

"She's my girl!" her daddy said proudly.

The lady behind the counter came over. "Why, she's the spittin'-image of you, Carl!"

"Naw—she's a whole lot cuter," the man beside them teased.

Everybody laughed, especially her daddy.

"Say, sweetheart," her daddy asked the lady who was pouring his coffee, "you got any of that scrumptious apple pie left?"

"Sure do, handsome."

"Well, bring me a slice of that, will ya?" He grinned up at his daughter. "Better make that two."

"What's your name, darlin'?" the man with the big smile asked. At her shy silence, he smiled even more. "Let me guess—your name is . . . Snow White?"

She shook her head.

"Cinderella?"

She giggled and shook her head again.

"You're not Minnie Mouse, are ya? Oh, I got it now, you're Daffy Duck!"

She giggled. "You're silly! I'm Kincaid—just like my daddy!"

Everybody laughed again and her daddy ruffled her hair. "That's right, you're Daddy's little girl, aren't you?"

She nodded emphatically.

Karen was looking at her intently. "You okay?"

Martha sighed and nodded. "Just remembering. Since the funeral, scenes from my childhood just seem to pop up. Whole scenes—as if I were watching a movie, seeing myself from the outside, somehow. It's weird.

"Anyway, everyone called me Kincaid, everyone but my mother and my sixth grade teacher. Somewhere along the line, it stopped being about identifying with my father and became a statement about who I was. As I got older, he drank more and did such awful things. Then, I'd hear the name "Kincaid" and I'd associate it with him again. When Walter and Jean adopted me, it seemed like an easy way to make a complete break with the past. It's funny though, even after all these years, whenever anybody calls me Martha, it takes a second to realize they're talking to me."

"You've never looked like a Martha to me, either. I think Kincaid suits you much better."

"You know, I just remembered something my grandmother said to me the last time I saw her. She said, 'I understand their taking you to California, a man's gotta go where there's work. But taking my name away from you, now that's hard.' Kincaid was her last name, too, and it was a connection between us." She shook her head. "If only I could get past all the ugliness associated with it."

She leaned back and closed her eyes. She could hear children playing down the street and closer, the swing creaking as they rocked.

She sat on the steps watching her daddy fix the porch swing.

"Hand me that screwdriver, will ya?" He pointed in the general direction of a pile of tools.

She didn't exactly know what a screwdriver looked like, so she studied them all for a while, wanting to choose the right one.

"That one," he coached patiently. "The one with the red handle."

She knew red. She handed him the thing with the red handle. Looking at it carefully as he took it from her, she nodded her head wisely—the thing with the red handle was a screwdriver.

"Thanks, Kincaid," he smiled at her, "you're a big help to your daddy."

She ran into the house, the screen door banging behind her. "Mama! Mama! I'm helping Daddy fix the swing! I'm a big help!"

Her mama was in the bedroom, changing the baby's clothes. "That's fine, Martha. Give me that towel, please. Carol Ann just spit up all over herself again an' I had just gotten her dressed, too. I don't know what I am goin' to do with this child!"

"Marie!" her daddy called. "Marie, I got the swing all fixed. Come try it out with me!"

Her mama didn't get up. She was still fussing with the baby.

"Mama! Daddy wants you to try the swing!"

"I'm a little busy right now."

"But Daddy wants . . ."

"Martha Jean, I told you I am busy! Now run along!"

She hurried back to the porch. "Mama says she's busy right now, Daddy."

"Yeah, she's always too busy for somethin'!" He jerked his toolbox open and began to throw his tools inside.

"Daddy, I'll sit on the swing with you."

He didn't even look at her. "That's okay, Kincaid, you go ahead. I got to go out for awhile."

"Can I go with you, Daddy?"

"Not this time." He left without even waving good-bye.

Martha stood up abruptly and strode purposefully down the steps. "Let's go, Karen. I need to get out of here for a while. Let's go show you what a creek looks like."

~~~~~~~~

She woke up crying. Rolling away from Karen, she pushed her face into the softness of the pillow.

"Martha?"

"It's okay, go on back to sleep." But her voice sounded shaky even to her.

"Come here, let me hold you." Karen's voice was thick, sleepy. She moved close and Karen's arms encircled her, a hand stroked her arm. Soon her sobs eased and she lay still, quiet in the comfort of her lover's warmth. The silence became deep. Karen's breathing slowed and became soft snores, but Martha lay awake in the darkness, staring at the shadows on the ceiling . . .

It was late. She was supposed to be asleep but she was thirsty. She was supposed to get drinks from the upstairs bathroom, but bathroom water tasted funny. So, mindful of the third step, she crept down to the kitchen because her mama and daddy were still in the living room.

"Well, Carl, we got to do somethin'. The landlord came by again today."

"Marie, I go out lookin' for work ever' day." He sighed. "An' ever' day it's the same: They take one look at my limp, read my application, an' it's 'Sorry, fella, can't help you.'" His voice sounded bitter.

"Oh, they glad-handed us when we came home, all right! Then it was 'Great job, boys, welcome home!' But that was politics. Money, now that's another matter altogether! It was a fine, patriotic thing to get our asses shot off in Korea fightin' their war for 'em, but when it comes to hirin', it's 'No thank you, son, we need whole men, men with all their parts still attached!'" He pounded the chair arm. "I tell 'em I can outwork any man they got an' they just look at my leg an' say they'll keep my application on file. Bullshit! The same old bullshit ever' time!"

"I know all that, Carl. An' it just ain't right. But we still got to pay the rent, feed the children . . . we got to do somethin' mighty quick."

"What the hell you want me to do, woman? Kill myself? We sure as hell got no insurance for you to collect!"

"I need to get a job, Carl."

"Like hell!"

"Carl, there ain't no other way as I can see. We need the money real bad. There's an openin' down to Miller's Market . . ."

"No! No wife of mine is gonna . . ."

"I already told' em I'd take it. I start Monday."

The front door slammed.

"Don't you go drinkin' up what money we got left!"

"Fuck you!" her daddy yelled from the front yard. "Fuck all of you!"

Her mama cried a long time.

Kincaid went back to her room, careful not to wake the baby. But she still couldn't sleep.

Nor could she tonight. Her body ached with memories.

~~~~~~~~

Karen stood up, yawning, and switched off the TV. "Come on, honey, let's go to bed."

"Oh, not yet. Let's do something. I know—let's go for a walk."

"Martha, it's two o'clock in the morning. Donnie and Carol Ann went to bed hours ago. Everyone else in the world is asleep. I'm asleep, only my eyes are too tired to know it. Let's go to bed."

Martha didn't move.

"Is it the dreams?"

"They're not dreams, exactly. And no, it's not that. Well, not entirely. It's the weather. Don't you feel it?" Just then a gust of wind rattled the front windows and door. "It's going to storm!"

"Yeah, just the right time to snuggle deep into soft, dark covers and . . . "

Martha chuckled. "Okay, okay, we'll go to bed."

Karen was asleep even before Martha turned off the light, leaving Martha wide awake, restless, beside her.

A blue-white flash lit the room and thunder shook the bed. Martha got up quietly and tiptoed downstairs. She opened the front door and breathed deeply of the damp air, heavy with rain-smell. The wind called her and she slipped out to the porch, in the dark, in her nightgown, to the swing. Her bare legs stuck out, she waited for the cool rain to blow in on her. She had missed this!

Thunder rolled across the darkened sky heralding the warm, sweet-smelling rain. Three-year-old Billy Ray danced delightedly while big heavy drops plastered his hair and clothes. Patty, having been intent on pouring sand from her bucket, just as happily poured rainwater. Jimmy stomped and splashed in every puddle he could find, a big grin lighting up his face. Kincaid watched from the swing, enjoying the sudden shower as much as the others.

"Martha Jean!"

"Yes, Mama?"

"I thought I told you to watch those children! You get' em in here an' clean' em up right this minute!"

"I am watchin'' em, Mama. We're just playin' awhile in the rain."

"Well, I got too much to do to worry with wet, muddy young' uns runnin' through the house. You bring' em in an' clean' em up!"

Reluctantly, she rounded up the openly rebellious crew.

Sitting on the bathroom floor, drying hair and washing off mud, she stared out the window at the grey clouds, wishing she was anyone else.

Now, flashes froze the raindrops in mid-air. Thunder shook the house and rumbled away across the sky. Martha sighed.

The screen door creaked. "Martha?"

"Karen, I'm sorry, I tried not to wake you when I got up."

"Are you kidding? Who could sleep? I thought that last one landed in the backyard. Now I know why scary movies always include dark and stormy nights. I kept waiting for you to come back to bed and then I decided to come looking for you."

"Aw, don't tell me you're scared?"

"Hey, not me. But, if you are, I could keep you company . . . "

"Oh, I love it! It's so . . . exciting!"

"Now that's an interesting thought."

"Come sit beside me and enjoy this." Martha held out her arm and Karen snuggled close. It wasn't long before Karen was snoring loudly despite the thunder. Martha held her close and smoothed her hair. Bobby had been afraid of thunder, too. He pretended he wasn't, even

192

came out and sat with her on the porch sometimes. She'd never let on, but she'd known. He'd always held in so much . . .

"*Bobby, will you say the blessing?*"

He looked up at his mama in surprise. The blessing for Sunday dinner was his daddy's place. But his daddy was not home. And now, the potatoes were cold, the roast dry, and the little ones were nodding off. He straightened his shoulders.

"*We just thank You, Lord, for all You have done for us and we just pray that You will continue to bless us and hold us close to Your Heart as we honor You on this Holy Day. In Jesus's Name, Amen.*"

"*Where's Daddy?*"

"*Hush, Billy Ray.*" *Ten-year-old Bobby was taking his new responsibility seriously. "Should I carve the roast, Mama?*"

She smiled warmly. "Yes, Bobby, thank you."

They all watched quietly as he stood and solemnly walked around to the end of the table to take up the big carving knife with great care and deliberation. No one so much as smiled when the knife slipped and clattered to the plate.

"*Oh, ho!*" *Their daddy staggered in the door. "The little chick thinks he's a rooster! Get outta my place, boy.*"

Bobby's face reddened. He started to move, but not quite fast enough to suit his daddy. With a shove, he pushed Bobby aside.

"*Go sit down, boy!*" *He grabbed the knife and hacked off a huge slab of roast beef for himself.*

"*Ugh! Dry!*" *He threw his fork down and shoved his plate away. "Good God, Marie, when you gonna learn to cook? I get better'n this at the diner!*"

"*I expect you get lots of things better at the diner,*" *their mama said quietly.*

"*Damn right!*"

Looking him straight in the eye, she folded her napkin and left the table.

Bobby rose to follow her.

"*Sit down, boy!*"

"I wanta go talk to Mama."

"I said sit down, goddamnit! You best listen to your daddy!"

Bobby had the same cold look their mama just had. "You're not my daddy," he said evenly, "you're just an old drunk!"

His father crossed the distance between them in just two steps. He back-handed Bobby hard enough to knock him off his feet, then picked him up and hit him again. And again, and again, until Bobby's nose began to bleed and Carol Ann screamed.

"Carl!" Their mama came running in. "Carl, stop it! Leave him alone! Carl! He's just a boy!"

His hand paused in mid-air. He looked at his wife. He looked at his son. He looked at the blood on his hand. He shoved the bruised and bloodied child to his mother.

"Go on," he roared, "get outta here. But that chick better learn his place mighty quick! There's only one rooster 'round here!" He sat down heavily in his chair. "Well, what are y'all starin' at?"

Nobody was staring.

"Stop that bawlin'!" He reached out and slapped Carol Ann.

That started Patty and Billy Ray in to wailing.

"Shut up, goddamnit! SHUT UP!"

They just cried harder.

"Aw, shit! To hell with you!" He stood and slammed his chair into the table so hard Patty's glass of milk turned over. Still roaring and swearing, he knocked all the food crashing to the floor. "To hell with all of you!" The front door slammed behind him.

Released from his presence, the little ones ran crying from the room. Kincaid and Carol Ann silently cleaned up the mess.

Rain rolled down Martha's legs and speckled her nightgown. But it wasn't rain that trickled down her cheeks. Oh, Bobby ... Martha rocked the swing and pulled Karen closer.

~~~~~~~

"Looks like your friend is sleepin' late this mornin'," Carol Ann observed as she tested the baby's bottle.

"The thunderstorm kept her awake last night."

"She ain't afraid of a little thunder is she, a grown woman like her?"

"Doesn't thunder and lightning much in California. She's just not used to it."

"So, tell me Kincaid, you got a beau out there in California yet?"

Martha took a sip of coffee and shook her head. "Not looking for one, either. Know what I remembered last night? Remember Bobby's favorite saying?"

Carol Ann grinned and nodded. "Eat matches . . . "

"And shit fire!" they laughed in unison.

"Yeah, he got that from Grandpa. Grandpa was all the time saying that when they couldn't hush him up." Carol Ann laughed again.

"I don't remember Grandpa much."

"I 'member he had a scratchy beard an' used to like to blow on my belly."

"I hated that."

"Me, too."

"Carol Ann, do you ever think about how it used to be? You know, when we were kids?"

"Oh, yeah . . . " Carol Ann's eyes were dreamy. "I 'member holidays at Mammaw's an' family picnics an' catchin' hoptoads an' lightning bugs an' makin' apple jelly with Grandma . . . "

"But, what about the times that weren't so good? What about the beatings, the drinking, the fighting? What about when Mama left? Do you ever think about those things?"

"No, I don't."

"I haven't much either, but I think it's time we did, Carol Ann."

"Well, I prefer to look for the silver linin' myself."

"A silver lining can't change the awful things that happened to us. They did happen and we have to deal with them one way or another."

"Why are you bringin' up all this hateful old stuff, anyway? Just to hurt my feelin's an' make me sad?"

"Of course not, Carol Ann. I'm trying to make sense of everything, trying to put it to rest so I can get on with my life. Doesn't the past ever interfere with your life? Doesn't what Daddy did to you ever get in the way when you're with Donnie?"

"I don't know what you're talkin' about. An' I can't see how wallowin' in unpleasantness does anyone any good!"

"Carol Ann, we're adults now. It's time to face reality, to deal with things how they were, not how we wanted them to be. It's time to move on."

"You got no call to go stirrin' all this up! I got more important things to think about now. I got a husband an' a little baby to take care of."

"Pushing it all down doesn't work, Carol Ann, believe me—I've tried it for years."

"When you have a family of your own, you'll think differently, Kincaid, wait an' see."

"Jesus H. Christ, Carol Ann! Are you really this shallow or is this just an act for my benefit?"

"Kincaid!" Her face crumpled. She grabbed the baby and ran from the room.

"Damn!" Martha pounded the sofa in helpless frustration.

~~~~~~~~

"What did you expect?" Karen asked.

"I expected her to be real with me. I expected to have an honest conversation that consisted of more than empty platitudes and cliches."

"Come on, give her a chance. You can't blame her for not being ready when you are."

"God, you sound like her. And where do you get off defending her? You're the person who pushed me to deal with all this shit when I thought I wasn't ready to deal with it."

"And now you are. You're being an excellent example for her to follow. And she will, when she's ready. Meanwhile, you don't need her to change for you, you know. You can live your own life even if Carol Ann stays exactly the same and never grows an inch."

Martha looked disgusted. "I'm going to make a sandwich."

~~~~~~~~

196

With a flick of her wrist, Martha released her stone. She counted seven skips.

Karen's stone fell two feet away with a wet plop.

Martha tossed another, counted five skips.

Karen tried again. Another plop.

Martha laughed and sat down on the grassy bank. She patted the ground beside her. "Maybe you should take a break. Don't want to throw your arm out before you even get the knack."

"Good idea."

Martha lay back, her arm shading her eyes. "Bobby taught me how to skip stones. I've been able to think about Bobby the last few days, since the funeral. How he never seemed to care about anyone or anything. How he built a wall of indifference around himself," she smiled wryly, "and never let anyone in. He was pretty much alone, didn't even have the trees or animals like I did. Although, they couldn't save me completely either . . .

"And, yes, I put up a wall, too. I kept everyone at a manageable distance, never letting anyone get close enough to hurt me. My relationship with Chris has a lot of distance in it. I can love her, care about her, but I know there's a limit to what she will give me, what she wants from me. The limits, the boundaries, have made it safe.

"But you challenged the distance and it scared me. So, I kept pulling back." She shook her head. "I don't want a wall around me. It didn't work for Bobby . . . " She shuddered. "I love you, Karen. I want to let you in. I just don't know how."

"We'll find a way, I promise."

~~~~~~~~

Sunday morning Carol Ann, Donnie, and James Allen went to have their eternal souls saved.

The house was quiet as Martha ate her breakfast alone in the dining room, while Karen was still asleep upstairs. She padded out to the living room with her orange juice, and, yawning, turned on the tv.

"JESUS! Yes, I say JE-SUS died for YOU! HE died and took your SINS away! Yes, HE did! And what, I say WHAT have you done for HIM today? Corinthians tells us . . . "

Martha turned off the TV. She stood up and stretched. She wandered awhile, finally ending up in the attic. Fumbling in the darkness, unable to find the light switch, she made her way cautiously through the clutter to the dimly outlined window and raised the yellowed, brittle shade. The window stuck, but she grunted and strained and at last managed to push it up half-way. Turning around, she sat down beside the pile Carol Ann had indicated as her grandma's things.

Not looking for anything in particular, she reached for the closest box. Pictures. There she was, frozen in time at age 9, all knees and arms—"gawky," Mammaw Wilson had called her. Grandma had told her she was beautiful. She'd believed Mammaw Wilson.

Her father in his uniform. Her mother. Her father and mother together in front of an old car. A baby picture, a baby she'd never seen before. She turned the picture over—on the back, in her grandmother's handwriting, were the words: "Jeanine's baby," and a date: "1936." Who the hell was Jeanine? Martha shrugged and grabbed another handful of pictures.

Baby Bobby in a washtub in the yard. Jimmy's first birthday. Their trip with Grandma to the Grand Canyon. Carol Ann, at three or four, in her pajamas unwrapping a present in front of the Christmas tree. Grandpa washing an old car. Grandma and Grandpa, the year before he died, sitting on their porch. Who took that?

She picked up a hard, thick, sepia-colored print. Grandma and Grandpa's wedding picture: Grandpa standing all stiff and somber in a dark suit with a high starched collar, and Grandma, standing tall and straight beside him in her high-necked, long sleeved white lace gown. The inscription on the back read: "Bessie Mae and John Jacob Kincaid, August 4, 1919."

Another old picture. Grandpa standing beside a young Indian woman in a beaded buckskin dress. Grandma? Martha turned the picture over. "Proud Wolf Running and John J. Kincaid, August 4, 1919." Grandma! Proud Wolf Running. Her own wolf image flashed in Martha's mind. Proud Wolf Running.

A puff of wind brought the smell of sun-warmed green grass into the still, dusty room. She took a deep breath. The room suddenly felt too close. She gently slid the picture of her grandmother into her pocket and carefully replaced the rest, pushing the box back over to the pile. She closed the attic door softly behind her.

The whole house felt stuffy. She opened the front door but when she pushed on the screen, it caught against the Sunday paper. She bent and picked it up. Going to the porch swing, she rummaged to find the funnies but got only halfway through when the magnolias, just beginning to bloom, called her out to the yard. She tucked the newspaper under her arm and wandered around to where honeysuckle trellised the back fence. Giggling, she pulled a handful of blossoms and carefully nipped off the ends, gently pulling out the tiny drops of sweet nectar and shaking them onto her tongue. They tasted just as good as she remembered. She stuck the flowers in her hair to save them, just as she had as a kid. It hadn't been all bad back then . . .

She sauntered down the sidewalk with honeysuckle flowers in her hair, a rich lady out taking the air, her shorts transformed into swirls of luxurious red velvet that flowed gracefully around her as she walked. On her shoulder, she twirled a beautiful silk parasol—which might have looked like an old branch to the less sophisticated.

"Hey, Kincaid." Her big brother, Bobby, sat in the yard idly tossing maple wings into the air and watching them twirl down. Two-year-old Jimmy was busy with a kitchen spoon, digging holes in the soft dirt. Carol Ann was making little bug villages out of twigs and grass and the dirt that Jimmy scooped up.

"Hey, Bobby."

She plopped down beside him with a big sigh. Out of the corner of her eye she saw her little brother moving toward the flower bed. "Jimmy Joe, don't you go diggin' up your mama's tulips, now."

It was summer. Too hot to sit still and too hot to move.

"I know, let's go to Mammaw's," Carol Ann said, wiping a dirty hand across her face.

"Naw, let's just stay here." Bobby chucked a dirt clod at a bumblebee.

"I bet Mammaw has some watermelon in the 'fridge," Kincaid said slowly. "I bet it's real cold . . ."

Bobby grinned at her and stood up. "Well, now, maybe she does. Bet I can spit seeds further'n you."

She just grinned back and reached for little Jimmy's grubby hand.

Martha finally settled beneath the only pine in Carol Ann's yard, and once again picked up the newspaper. But she couldn't seem to concentrate, beginning an article only to find herself staring up into the branches above.

Suddenly a big silly grin lit her face and she giggled again. Pulling off her shoes and placing them on top so the paper wouldn't blow, she jumped up and grabbed the first branch in easy reach and pulled herself into the tree. Climbing wasn't as easy as it used to be, but it wasn't as difficult as she had feared it might be. She leaned against the rough bark and breathed in deeply, exhaling soul-cleansing sighs. The wind whispered to her. She listened. The wind sang to her, and from far inside, from a place long buried within her, came an answering song. She sang with the wind. She sang as tears traced paths down her now dirty cheeks, she sang as she laughed out loud, she sang as she danced up and down on the branch, unable to sit still any longer.

She had come home.

~~~~~~~~

She got up to go pee without bothering to switch on the lights against the early morning grey. Once up, she realized she was also thirsty. But somehow she could not force herself to turn on the bathroom tap, so she quietly crept downstairs to the kitchen. Replacing her glass on the counter and turning to leave, she glanced out the kitchen window. Out of the corner of her eye, she caught a glimpse of movement, a shadow swaying between the darker shadows of the trees, sharply outlined against the lightening eastern sky. As she watched, the figure stood still and raised its arms. The hair on her neck prickled as she felt, rather than heard, singing. Someone was in Carol Ann's backyard singing the sun up!

The sky became blue and everything under it golden with sunlight. The figure lowered its arms and slowly turned . . .

"Grandma!" Martha flew to the back door and flung it wide.

The old woman looked directly into her eyes and smiled then turned away again and walked back toward the trees.

"Grandma!" Martha ran after her, the screen door banging loudly in the early morning quiet. It was just a few steps away but when she reached the old pine, her grandmother was not there. Of course she was not there.

Martha reached out absently, meaning to pull off a honeysuckle blossom, but instead her fingers brushed against a broad, green leaf. There was a vibration, a humming . . . She laughed delightedly and for the next several minutes grabbed leaf after leaf, checking and rechecking the honeysuckle's morning-song. It was real! It had always been real. She laughed as tears rolled down her cheeks, unnoticed. She reached for more.

~~~~~~~~~

Martha leaned back and let Karen push the swing. The heavy spring air, like warm water trickling over her face and arms, carried the faint scent of magnolias and early jasmine. She closed her eyes. The creak of the swing, the heat, and the breath of wind all blended to create an almost-tangible feeling of time as a single entity—past, present, and future all touching, merging, uniting into a whole. A giant quilt, each life a piece.

An ordinary, Southern spring day. So unlike California. And yet . . .

"The dolphin know. About the dance of the universe, about the song. It's what they were tryin' to tell me. They wanted to remind me. An' to let me know I wasn't alone." She sat up. "It's time to go home, now."

"Home?"

Martha nodded. "This is where I was born, where I'm from, my source. I'll never lose that again. But home is where I live now, the present from which I can grow into whatever the future holds for me."

Karen smiled and squeezed her hand.

~~~~~~~~~

"I just hate y'all rushin' off like this," Carol Ann sniffed.

"Carol Ann, it's been two weeks."

"Well, it ain't been near long enough."

"Flight two seventeen now boarding at gate four."

"That's us," Karen said, grabbing her suitcase. "Thanks for everything. If you're ever in California . . . "

"Well, thank you for bein' such a good friend to our Kincaid. There's not many these days who'd come so far for a friend, I can tell you that." Donnie stuck out his hand.

Martha turned to Carol Ann. "I am sorry 'bout Bobby, but I'm glad I got the chance to come back. It's been really important to me. It's goin' to make a big difference in my life. Well, take care of yourself. An' little Jamie."

"Now you keep in touch, Kincaid. At least answer my letters."

"Carol Ann, you know how I am 'bout writin'." Seeing her sister's face fall, she softened. "I'll try Carol Ann—but I'm not promisin'."

"Oh, Kincaid, I don't want it to be another ten years before I see my sister again!" She threw her free arm around Martha and hugged her tightly.

"Hey, be careful of my nephew!" Martha leaned over and kissed the baby. "Be happy, Jamie, grow up proud an' strong. Be happy, Carol Ann."

"Say bye-bye to your Aunt Kincaid, Jamie. Bye-bye." Carol Ann held him in a sitting position and moved his arm up and down.

Donnie pulled Martha to him in a big bear hug. "You take care of yourself out there," he said gruffly. "There's quite a few folks back here who think a lot of you."

"You take care, too, Donnie. Thanks for ever'thing. Bye!"

"Y'all come back soon, y'hear?"

"Bye!"

Martha took the window seat. "I'm tryin' to soak up all the green I can," she explained. "I wish I could smell the pines."

Somewhere over Texas Karen broke the silence.

"I'm always surprised to look down and not see any little black lines dividing the states. I mean, how are we supposed to know which one we're over?"

Martha laughed and turned away from the window.

"So, Karen, is your apartment still big enough to include me?"

Karen nodded, her eyes shining.

"Good." Martha smiled and drew a deep breath. "There's just one more thing—from now on, my name is Kincaid."

~~~~~~~~

She stood in the pre-dawn chill expectantly facing east. Waves crashed behind her and rushed in, gently tugging the sand from beneath her wiggling toes. She took a deep breath and raised her arms as if embracing the whole world. Music rose within her, but her throat constricted self-consciously. She swallowed hard. Softly, she began again.

The sky lightened. The waves flowed in, ebbed out. Her lungs filled to overflowing and at last, she sang. Down the beach a figure separated from the shadow of the rocks, as if pulled by the magic and the music.

Two voices blended, dancing like the gulls that dipped and soared overhead. Two energies merged into one, separated into many, flowed together in the same rising tide of power. They were singing the sun up. They were giving grace, blessing the new day.

The warmth of the sun on their faces finally stilled their voices, though the music echoed in their hearts. Again they heard the roar of the ocean, felt the bite of the cold water. They turned to each other, hearts pounding, eyes glistening. Karen could only stare in awe, but Kincaid managed a smile and reached out to wipe her lover's cheeks. In silence, arm-in-arm, they walked down the beach and back to their car.

Mother Courage Press

In addition to *Singin' the Sun Up*, Mother Courage publishes the following titles.

Lesbian

NEWS by Heather Conrad is a gripping novel of a women's computer takeover to make the empire builders and the money makers stop destroying the people and the earth. Paper $9.95

Night Lights by Bonnie Shrewsbury Arthur. More than your traditional lesbian romance, this novel tackles various issues—with a light touch that will make you laugh out loud. Paper $8.95

Hodag Winter by Deborah Wiese. A first grade teacher is fired because she is a lesbian. She and her lover and friends fight back. Paper $8.95

Mega by B. L. Holmes. Science fiction lesbian romance set against a future of giant cities and vast pollution of the Earth. Paper $8.95

Rowdy & Laughing by B. L. Holmes. She's not gay, she's rowdy and laughing. Poems encompass the joy of life and being in love. Paper $4.95

Senior Citizen by B. L. Holmes. A musical comedy, this funny and touching play explores the dual themes of rejection of the aged, gays and lesbians. Paper $8.95

Travel Adventure

Women at the Helm by Jeannine Talley. Two women sell everything and begin an adventure-filled cruise around the world in a 34-foot sailboat. Paper $11.95

Biography

Olympia Brown, The Battle for Equality by Charlotte Coté. Biography of an unsung foremother, talented orator and the first ordained woman minister in the US who fought a life-long battle for equal rights for women. Paper $9.95

Self-Help, Sexual Abuse, Prevention

Fear or Freedom, a Woman's Options in Social Survival and Physical Defense by Susan E. Smith. This book realistically offers options to fear of social intimidation and fear of violent crime with an important new approach to self-defense for women. Paper $11.95

Warning! Dating may be hazardous to your health! by Claudette McShane. Date rape and dating abuse study emphasizes that women need not put up with any kind of abuse, are not to blame for being abused and can regain control of their lives. Paper $9.95

The Woman Inside, from Incest Victim to Survivor by Patty Derosier Barnes. This workbook is designed to help an incest victim work through pain, confusion and hurt. Paper $11.95

Why Me? Help for victims of child sexual abuse, even if they are adults now by Lynn B. Daugherty, Ph.D. Important and informative book for beginning the process of healing the psychological wounds of child sexual abuse. Paper $7.95

Something Happened to Me by Phyllis E. Sweet, M.S. Sensitive, straightforward book designed to help children victimized by sexual or other abuse. Paper $4.95

I Couldn't Cry When Daddy Died by Iris Galey. Courageous and sensitive personal account of an incest survivor. Story of inspiration and hope. Paper $9.95

Rebirth of Power, Overcoming the Effects of Sexual Abuse through the Experiences of Others, edited by Pamela Portwood, Michele Gorcey and Peggy Sanders, is a powerful and empowering anthology of poetry and prose by survivors of sexual abuse. Paper $9.95

Humor

Womb with Views, A Contradictionary of the Enguish Language by Kate Musgrave is a delightful, more than occasionally outrageous social commentary, cartoon-illustrated, feminist dictionary. Paper $8.95

New Age

Welcome to the Home of Your Heart by Dorothy "Mike" Brinkman. Messages of universal love, caring and compassion given to Brinkman by an entity named Jenny. Paper $11.95

If you don't find these books in your local book store, you may order them directly from Mother Courage Press at 1533 Illinois Street, Racine, WI 53405. Please add $2 for postage and handling for the first book and 50¢ for each additional book.